IVÁN TURGÉNIEFF

RÚDIN: A ROMANCE
ฆ ฆ A KING LEAR OF
THE STEPPES ฆ ฆ

THE NOVELS AND STORIES OF
IVÁN TURGÉNIEFF

RÚDIN: A ROMANCE ✧ A KING LEAR OF THE STEPPES ✧ ✧

TRANSLATED FROM THE RUSSIAN BY
ISABEL F. HAPGOOD

NEW YORK
CHARLES SCRIBNER'S SONS
1903

THE DE VINNE PRESS

PREFACE

" Rúdin," published in 1857, was Turgénieff's first long story. Those who had studied the author's cast of mind as displayed in his preceding short stories—particularly in " The Diary of a Superfluous Man," " Two Friends," " The Hamlet of Shshtchígry County," and others—were not unprepared to find portrayed in " Rúdin," in fuller form, another type of " the superfluous man."

Not one of Turgénieff's writings of his first period called forth so much bewilderment and so many disputes as " Rúdin." The reason for this lay not only in Rúdin's character, but also in the fact that the author had regarded it as necessary to complete the characterisation directly from himself, as it were, by making several of the acting personages of the tale express their opinions, all in one line, concerning the hero. Moreover, this composite opinion undergoes a radical change in the course of the narrative, passing from severe condemnation to complete justification. But this is sufficiently explained by the different angles from which Rúdin is viewed. Turgénieff never conceals his sympathies and his antipathies

PREFACE

toward his characters; but in " Rúdin " alone does he resort to the expedient of explanatory comments, of warning the reader not to allow himself to be fascinated by the hero's charms, and of initiating him into the man's genuine personality by condemnatory excerpts from his past history.

Rúdin would, in fact, seem to be possessed of two distinct characters; and the author would seem to have changed his mind—say some—about him, as Púshkin changed his about Evgény Onyégin, in the course of composition. It has been asserted, in explanation, that Turgénieff himself said that he had drawn Rúdin from the well-known agitator of that epoch, Mikhaíl Bakúnin; and that the apparent duality of his views concerning his hero arose from his sympathy for the men of the '40s in general, combined with extreme antipathy for Bakúnin in particular. Thus, Rúdin would appear in the double capacity of a portrait and of a representative of an entire and fairly numerous phalanx. Bakúnin's friend, Alexander Hertzen, even considered it necessary to controvert this view, and to deny all resemblance between Rúdin and Bakúnin. Indeed, it seemed self-evident to those who knew Bakúnin well, that all Rúdin had in common with him was his uneasy shifting from place to place, and his foggy loquacity. The truth on this point would seem to be this: If Bakúnin did, in reality, inspire Turgénieff with the idea for Rúdin, yet the author's creative genius promptly generalised and broadened that idea into the portrait of a class and of a transition period in Russian society, whose lifelikeness no one could gainsay.

Some Russian critics of that day maintained that all contemporary Russians had in their souls a certain amount of the Rúdin element; and declared that there had been and still were plenty of genuine Rúdins among them, engaged in doing both good and harm to those about them: fascinating young men, and inciting them to enthusiasm, with varying results; making young girls fall in love with them, and teaching them painful but valuable lessons in life, as Rúdin taught Natálya.

Some of the contemporary critics, however, deny that Rúdin is a true type of the men of the '40s in general, and say that, at most, he represents a comparatively small group, capable of mental impulsiveness though devoid of heart, possessed of oratorical talent without warmth, and of enthusiasm without boldness, and, in particular, without personal dignity.

Again: Rúdin is, in the opinion of some contemporary Russian critics, an extremely complicated character; in the opinion of others, he is perfectly simple. He is, in effect, say the latter, identical with "The Hamlet of Shshtchígry County," with unimportant differences. The education of the two men, at home and abroad, was the same; on neither of them did German philosophy and literature have more than a superficial influence; both had rotated in "circles." But "Hamlet" simply rotated in those "circles" which he so severely condemns, while Rúdin played a prominent part in them. At one time "Hamlet" had even played a part entirely analogous to that of Rúdin. He had enjoyed great success for a season as a talker and poser. But the essential difference in this respect was—that whereas "Hamlet" got tired, and felt ashamed of chattering the same thing over and over again incessantly, and withdrew to the country partly for that reason and partly owing to "unpleasantnesses," Rúdin experienced no shame, and did not retire from the arena, in spite of repeated "unpleasantnesses."

Another curious point about Rúdin is, that he seems to be a composite of the two types into which Turgénieff afterward (in a speech made in 1860) divided all men, namely, Hamlets and Don Quixotes. Rúdin is, in fact, a Hamlet and a Don Quixote, in almost equal proportions.

The remaining characters in the story speak for themselves. They are admitted to be faithful representatives of the society of that epoch.

Turgénieff says of "Rúdin," in his preface to the edition of his romances published in 1880: "I wrote it in the country, in the very midst of the Crimean war. It had a purely-literary success, not so much in the editorial department of the *Contemporary,* where it made its appearance, as outside of it.—I remember that the late Nekrásoff, on hearing me read it, said to me: ' Thou hast devised something new; but between ourselves, in secret, I will say, thy Rúdin is a bore.' —It is true that, several weeks later, that same Nekrásoff, while talking with me about his poem ' Sásha,' which he had just written, remarked: —' Thou wilt see that in it I have, to a certain extent, imitated thy Rúdin—but thou wilt not be angry, I hope?' "

The Russian critics never made any special remarks about " A King Lear of the Steppes." Apparently, they considered it able to interpret itself to readers, by its human interest and the faithfulness of its types.

I. F. H.

CONTENTS

RÚDIN:
A ROMANCE
(1855)

RÚDIN:

A ROMANCE

I

IT was a calm summer morning. The sun already stood quite high in the heavens, but the meadows were still glittering with dew; the recently awakened valleys breathed forth perfumed freshness, and in the forest, still damp and noiseless, the little early birds were singing blithely. On the crest of a sloping hill, covered from top to bottom with rye which had just burst into bloom, a tiny hamlet was visible. Along the narrow country road, in the direction of this hamlet, was walking a young woman, clad in a white cotton gown, a round straw hat, and with a parasol in her hand. A groom followed her at a distance.

She was walking in a leisurely way, and seemed to be enjoying her stroll. Round about, over the tall, waving rye, with a soft rustle, flowed long waves, shifting from a silvery-green to a reddish hue. High aloft, the larks were carolling. The young woman was walking from her own village, large enough to contain a church, which

3

she owned, and which was distant not more than a verst from the hamlet whither she was directing her way; her name was Alexándra Pávlovna Lípin. She was a widow, childless and fairly wealthy, and she lived with her brother, retired captain of cavalry, Sergyéi Pávlitch Volýntzeff. He was not married, and managed her property.

Alexándra Pávlovna reached the hamlet, halted at the outermost cottage, a very aged and lowly hut, and calling up her groom, she ordered him to enter it and inquire after the health of the house-wife. He speedily returned, accompanied by a decrepit peasant with a white beard.

" Well, what news? " inquired Alexándra Pávlovna.

" She is still alive, ... " said the old man.

" May I enter? "

" Why do you ask? Certainly."

Alexándra Pávlovna entered the cottage. It was cramped, and stifling and smoky inside. Some one was tossing about and moaning on the oven-bench. Alexándra Pávlovna gazed about her and descried, in the semi-darkness, the yellow and wrinkled head of an old woman bound up in a checked kerchief. Completely covered, even her chest, by a heavy peasant coat, she breathed with difficulty, feebly throwing apart her scraggy arms.

Alexándra Pávlovna stepped up to the old woman and touched her fingers to the latter's brow . . . . it was fairly blazing with heat.

4

"How dost thou feel, Matryóna?" she inquired, bending over the oven-bench.

"O-okh!" moaned the old woman, as she stared at Alexándra Pávlovna. "Badly, badly, my own! My hour of death has arrived, dear little dove!"

"God is merciful, Matryóna; perhaps thou wilt recover. Hast thou taken the medicine which I sent thee?"

The old woman moaned painfully, but did not reply. She had not fully heard the question.

"She took it," said the old man, who was standing by the door.

Alexándra Pávlovna turned to him: "Is there no one with her except thee?" she asked.

"There is a little girl,—her grandchild,—but she is always going off. She cannot sit still; she's such a fidgety creature. She's too lazy even to give her grandmother a drink of water. And I am old; what can I do!"

"Would it not be well to bring her to me—to my hospital?"

"No! why to a hospital? she will die anyway. She has lived long enough; evidently that is pleasing to God. She will never leave the oven-bench. What's the use of taking her to a hospital? As soon as you try to lift her up she will die."

"Okh!" groaned the sick woman, "beautiful lady, don't desert my orphan; our master and mistress are far away, but thou—"

The old woman fell silent. She had talked beyond her strength.

"Don't worry," said Alexándra Pávlovna; "everything shall be done. Here, I have brought thee some tea and some sugar. Drink some, if thou feelest like it. . . . . Of course, you have a samovár?" she added, glancing at the old man.

"A samovár did you say? We have no samovár, but I can get one."

"Then get it, or I will send my own. And give your granddaughter orders not to absent herself. Tell her that it is a shame."

The old man made no answer, but took the package of tea and sugar in both hands.

"Well, good-bye, Matryóna!" said Alexándra Pávlovna. "I will come again to see thee, but thou must not get despondent, and thou must take thy medicine regularly. . . . ."

The old woman raised her hand and stretched it toward Alexándra Pávlovna.

"Give me thy hand, my lady," she whispered.

Alexándra Pávlovna did not give her her hand, but bent over and kissed her on the brow.

"See to it," she said to the old man as she took her departure, "that you give her the medicine, without fail, as it is prescribed. And give her tea to drink. . . . ."

Again the old man made no reply, and merely bowed.

Alexándra Pávlovna heaved a sigh of relief

when she found herself in the open air. She
opened her parasol and was on the point of setting out homeward, when, all of a sudden, round
the corner of the wretched cottage, seated in a
low-hung racing-drozhky, drove a man of thirty,
clad in an old overcoat of grey variegated woollen
homespun, with a cap of the same. On perceiving Alexándra Pávlovna he immediately drew
up his horse and turned his face toward her.
Broad, devoid of rosiness, with small, pale-grey
eyes and a whitish moustache, it was in harmony
with the hue of his clothing.

"Good morning," he said, with a lazy smile;
" permit me to inquire what you are doing here?"

"I have been visiting a sick woman. . . . .
And whence come you, Mikhaílo Mikhaílitch?"

The man who was named Mikhaílo Mikhaílitch looked her straight in the eye, and laughed
again.

"You do well," he went on, " in visiting the
sick; only would n't it be better to take her to the
hospital?"

"She is too weak; she cannot be touched."

"And you do not intend to abolish your
hospital?"

"Abolish it? Why!"

"Oh, because."

"What a strange idea! What put that into
your head?"

"Well, you are always consorting with Mme.

Lasúnsky, and, apparently, you are under her influence. And, according to her, hospitals, schools—all that sort of thing—are nonsense, useless inventions. Benevolence must be personal, culture ditto; 't is all a matter of soul . . . . that 's the way she expresses herself, it appears. Whose tune is she singing, I 'd like to know? "

Alexándra Pávlovna burst out laughing.

" Dárya Mikhaílovna is a clever woman; I am very fond of her, and I respect her; but she may be mistaken, and I do not believe every word she utters."

" And it 's a splendid thing you don't," retorted Mikhaílo Mikhaílitch, still omitting to descend from his drozhky; " because she has n't much faith in her own words. But I am very glad to have met you."

" Why so? "

" A pretty question! As if it were not always pleasant to meet you! To-day you are just as fresh and charming as this morning itself."

Again Alexándra Pávlovna began to laugh.

" What are you laughing at? "

" How can you ask? If you could only see with what a languid and chilly mien you uttered your compliment! I am surprised that you did not yawn over the last word."

" With a chilly mien! . . . . You always want fire; but fire is of no use. It flares up, creates a smoke, and dies out."

"And it warms," Alexándra Pávlovna caught him up.

" Yes . . . and it burns."

" Well, what if it does! There 's no harm in that. Anything is better than . . . ."

" Well, I 'm going to see whether you will say that after you have once been well burned," Mikhaílo Mikhaílitch interrupted her with vexation, and slapped the reins on his horse's back. " Good-bye! "

" Mikhaílo Mikhaílitch, wait! " cried Alexándra Pávlovna. " When are you coming to see us? "

" To-morrow; remember me to your brother."

And the drozhky rolled off.

Alexándra Pávlovna gazed after Mikhaílo Mikhaílitch.

" What a meal-sack! " she said to herself. And, in fact, bent double, covered with dust, his cap on the nape of his neck, with tufts of yellow hair sticking out from under it, he did resemble a huge flour-sack.

Alexándra Pávlovna quietly wended her way homeward. She walked on with eyes bent on the ground. The trampling of a horse's hoofs close by made her pause and raise her head. Her brother was coming toward her on horseback; alongside him walked a young man of short stature in a lightweight coat thrown open on the breast, a light tie, and a light grey hat, with a

slender cane in his hand. He had already long
been smiling at Alexándra Pávlovna, although
he saw that she was walking along buried in
thought, taking no notice of anything, and as
soon as she halted he went up to her and joyfully,
almost tenderly, exclaimed:

"Good morning, Alexándra Pávlovna, good
morning!"

"Ah! Konstantín Diomíditch, good morning!" she replied. "You are coming from
Dárya Mikhaílovna's?"

"Exactly so, ma'am, exactly so, ma'am," responded the young man, with a beaming countenance; "from Dárya Mikhaílovna's. Dárya
Mikhaílovna has sent me to you, ma'am; I pre-
ferred to go on foot. . . . . It is such a magnificent morning, and the distance is only four versts.
I arrive—you are not at home, ma'am. Your
brother tells me that you have walked to Semyó-
novko, and he was on his way to the fields, so I
walked along with him, ma'am, to meet you.
Yes, ma'am. How pleasant it is!"

The young man spoke Russian with purity and
correctness, but with a foreign accent, although
it was difficult to determine with precisely what
accent. There was something Asiatic about his
features. A long nose with a hump, large motionless, goggle-eyes, thick red lips, a retreating
brow, hair black as pitch,—all these things in him
betokened an Oriental origin; but the young

man's surname was Pandalévsky, and he called Odessa his native place, although he had been reared somewhere in White Russia at the expense of a wealthy and benevolent widow. Another widow had obtained a position for him in the government service. As a rule, middle-aged ladies were very fond of playing the part of protector to Konstantín Diomíditch; he understood how to render himself agreeable to them, to insinuate himself into their favour. He was at present living in the house of the wealthy Dárya Mikhaílovna Lasúnsky, in the capacity of an adopted son, or a visitor. He was very endearing in his manners, very obliging; susceptible and secretly sensual, he possessed an agreeable voice, played quite well on the piano, and had a habit, when he was talking with any one, of fairly riveting his eyes on him. He dressed with great neatness, and wore his clothing an extremely long time, shaved his broad chin with care, and made every hair on his head lie in its appointed place.

Alexándra Pávlovna listened to his speech to the very end, then turned to her brother.

" I keep meeting people to-day: just now I had a chat with Lezhnyóff."

" Ah! with him? Was he on his way somewhere? "

" Yes; and just imagine, in a racing-drozhky, in some sort of a linen bag, all covered with dust. What an eccentric fellow he is! "

"Yes, possibly; only he's a splendid man."

"Who is that—Mr. Lezhnyóff?" inquired Pandalévsky, as though in surprise.

"Yes, Mikhaílo Mikhaílitch Lezhnyóff," replied Volýntzeff. "But farewell, sister; it is time for me to ride to the fields; they are sowing thy buckwheat. Mr. Pandalévsky will escort thee home."

And Volýntzeff started his horse into a trot.

"With the greatest pleasure!" exclaimed Konstantín Diomíditch, and offered Alexándra Pávlovna his arm.

She gave him hers, and both turned into the road which led to her home-farm.

Apparently it afforded Konstantín Diomíditch great satisfaction to walk arm in arm with Alexándra Pávlovna. He stalked along with mincing steps, smiled, and his Oriental eyes even became suffused with moisture, which, however, not infrequently was the case with him; it cost Konstantín Diomíditch no effort whatever to be overcome with emotion and to shed tears. And who would not have found it pleasant to walk arm in arm with a pretty, young, and graceful woman? Of Alexándra Pávlovna the whole of . . . . Government unanimously said that she was charming; and . . . . Government was not mistaken. Her straight little nose alone, with its almost imperceptibly tilted tip, was enough to

12

drive any mortal out of his senses, not to mention her velvety-brown eyes, her ruddy-golden hair, the dimples in her plump cheeks, and other beauties. But the best thing of all about her was the expression of her lovely face: trustful, good-natured, and gentle, it touched and attracted. Alexándra Pávlovna's glance and laugh were those of a child; the ladies thought her rather simple-minded. . . . . Could anything further be desired?

"Dárya Mikhaílovna sent you to me, you said?" she asked Pandalévsky.

"Yes, ma'am, she sent me, ma'am," he replied, pronouncing the letter *s* like an English *th*.[1] "They desired me and commanded me, without fail, urgently to request you to do them the honour to dine with them to-day. . . . They" (when Pandalévsky spoke of a third person, especially of a lady, he strictly kept to the plural number)— "they are expecting a new guest with whom they wish, without fail, to make you acquainted."

"Who is it?"

"A certain Muffel, a baron, a gentleman of the Bedchamber from Petersburg. Dárya Mikhaílovna made his acquaintance not long ago at Prince Gárin's, and expresses herself with re-

---

[1] This *s* is a respectful addition at the end of a word, representing *sudárynya* (Madam), like the abbreviated "ma'am": or, in the case of address to men, of *gosudár*, sir. Pandalévsky also uses the third person plural of the verbs and pronouns, with the same object: that of showing ingratiating respect. —TRANSLATOR.

gard to him in the most laudatory terms, as an
amiable and cultured young man. The Baron
also occupies himself with literature, or, to speak
more accurately . . . . akh, what a charming
butterfly! permit me to call your attention to it
. . . . to speak more accurately, with political
economy. He has written an article about some
very interesting question, and he wishes to submit
it to the judgment of Dárya Mikhaílovna."

" An article on political economy? "

" From the point of view of the language,
ma'am, Alexándra Pávlovna, from the point of
view of the language, ma'am. I think you are
aware that Dárya Mikhaílovna is an expert in
that direction, ma'am. Zhukóvsky was wont to
take counsel with her, and my benefactor who
resides in Odessa, the venerable Roksolán Mediaróvitch Ksandrýka, all-worthy in good deeds
. . . . surely, the name of that person is known
to you? "

" I have never so much as heard it."

" You have not heard of such a man? Amazing! What I set out to say was, that Roksolán
Mediaróvitch has always entertained a very high
opinion of Dárya Mikhaílovna's information
concerning the Russian language."

" But is not that Baron a pedant? " asked
Alexándra Pávlovna.

" Not in the least, ma'am. Dárya Mikhaílovna declares that, on the contrary, the man of

the world is immediately perceptible in him. He talked about Beethoven with such eloquence that even the old Prince experienced raptures. . . . . I should have liked to hear it, I confess; for that is in my line. Permit me to offer you this beautiful wild flower."

Alexándra Pávlovna took the flower, and after proceeding a few paces dropped it in the road. . . . . Her house was distant a couple of hundred paces, not more. Recently erected and whitewashed, it peeped with an air of welcome from amid the dense verdure of ancient lindens and maples with its broad, bright windows.

" And so, ma'am, what do you bid me report to Dárya Mikhaílovna," began Pandalévsky, slightly nettled at the fate meted out to his flower; " will you come to dinner? She invites you and your brother."

" Yes, we will certainly come. And how is Natásha?"

" Natálya Alexyéevna, thank God, is well, ma'am. But we have already passed the turn to Dárya Mikhaílovna's estate. Allow me to make my adieux."

Alexándra Pávlovna stopped.—" And will you not come in?" she asked, in an undecided tone.

" I should be heartily glad, ma'am, to do so, but I am afraid of being late. Dárya Mikhaílovna wishes to hear a new Étude by Thalberg;

so I must prepare myself and practise it. Moreover, I must confess I have some doubts as to
whether my conversation would afford you any
pleasure."

" Yes, indeed . . . . why not? " . . . .

Pandálevsky sighed, and dropped his eyes expressively.

" Farewell for the present, Alexándra Pavlovna! " he said, after a brief pause, bowed, and
retreated a pace.

Alexándra Pavlovna turned and went home.

Konstantín Diomíditch also wended his way
homeward. All sweetness instantly vanished
from his countenance; a self-confident, almost
harsh expression made its appearance thereon.
Even the gait of Konstantín Diomíditch under-
went a change; he now took longer strides, and
trod more heavily. He had traversed a couple of
versts, flourishing his cane in a free-and-easy
manner, when, all of a sudden, he again began
to smirk; he had caught sight, by the roadside, of
a young, tolerably comely peasant lass, who was
driving the calves out of the oats. Konstantín
Diomíditch, as warily as a cat, approached the
girl and entered into conversation with her. At
first she made no answer, then flushed up and
began to laugh, and at last covered her lips with
her sleeve, turned away, and said:

" Go along, master, really . . . ."

Konstantín Diomíditch menaced her with his finger and ordered her to bring him some corn-flowers.

"What dost thou want with corn-flowers? art thou going to weave wreaths?" retorted the girl; "come now, go along, I mean it . . . ."

"Hearken, my amiable little beauty," began Konstantín Diomíditch . . . .

"Come now, be off with you," the girl interrupted him; "yonder come the young gentle-men."

Konstantín Diomíditch glanced round. In fact, Ványa and Pétya, the sons of Dárya Mikhaílovna, were running along the road; they were followed by their teacher, Basístoff, a young man twenty-two years of age, who had only just finished his studies. Basístoff was a well-grown young fellow, with a foolish face, a large nose, huge teeth, and pig's eyes, homely and awkward, but kind, honourable and upright. He was carelessly dressed, wore his hair long,—not out of foppishness, but out of laziness,—was fond of eating, fond of sleeping, but also fond of a good book, a heated argument, and hated Pandalévsky with all his soul.

Dárya Mikhaílovna's children adored Basístoff, and also feared him not a little; he was on intimate terms with all the other members of the household, which did not particularly please the mistress of the house, descant as she might on the theme that no such thing as prejudices existed for her.

"Good morning, my dears!" began Konstantín Diomíditch; "how early you have set out for your walk to-day! But I," he added, addressing Basístoff, "went out long ago; my passion is to enjoy nature."

"We saw how you were enjoying nature," muttered Basístoff.

"You are a materialist; God only knows what you were thinking just now. I know you!"

Pandalévsky, when he conversed with Basístoff or persons like him, became somewhat irritated, and pronounced the letter *s* quite clearly, even with a slight hiss.

"You don't mean to say that you were inquiring your way of that girl, do you?" remarked Basístoff, rolling his eyes to right and left.

He felt that Pandalévsky was staring him straight in the face, and this was extremely disagreeable to him.

"I repeat, you are a materialist, and nothing else. You insist on beholding only the prosaic side in everything. . . ."

"Children!" Basístoff suddenly issued his command, "do you see the silver willow yonder in the meadow; let's see which of you will run to it the more quickly . . . . one, two three!"

And the boys set off, at the top of their speed, for the willow-tree. Basístoff flew after them.

" Peasant! " thought Pandalévsky; " he is spoiling those horrid boys. . . . . A regular peasant! "

And, casting a glance of satisfaction over his own neat and elegant little figure, Konstantín Diomíditch tapped the sleeve of his coat with his wide-spread fingers a couple of times, shook his collar, and went his way. On reaching his own room he donned an old dressing-gown, and with anxious countenance seated himself at the piano.

II

THE house of Dárya Mikhaílovna Lasúnsky was considered to be almost the leading one in the Government of . . . . A vast stone structure, erected after drawings by Rastrelli in the taste of the past century, it rose majestically on the crest of a hill, at whose foot flowed one of the chief rivers of central Russia. Dárya Mikhaílovna herself was a distinguished and wealthy noblewoman, the widow of a privy councillor. Although Pandalévsky was wont to narrate of her that she knew all Europe, and that Europe also knew her, yet Europe knew very little about her. Even in Petersburg she did not play a prominent part; on the other hand, in Moscow every one knew her and frequented her house. She belonged to the highest society, and bore the reputation of being a rather peculiar woman, not particularly amiable, but extremely clever. In her youth she had been very handsome. Poets had written verses to her, the young men had fallen in love with her, men of importance had dangled in her train. But since that time twenty-five or thirty years had elapsed, and not a trace of her former charms remained. " Is it possible," every one who beheld her only for the first time involuntarily asked himself—" is it possible that that gaunt, sallow, sharp-nosed, though not yet elderly woman ever was a beauty? Can she be the one about whom the lyres tinkled? " . . . . And every one was amazed within himself at the mutability of all things earthly. Pandalévsky, it is true, thought that Dárya Mikhaílovna's magnificent eyes had been marvellously well preserved; but then, that same Pandalévsky asserted that all Europe knew her.

Dárya Mikhaílovna came every summer to her country place with her children (she had only three: a daughter, Natálya, aged seventeen, and two sons, respectively ten and nine years of age) and kept open house—that is to say, she received men visitors, especially bachelors; country ladies she could not endure. In consequence, she caught it from those same ladies. Dárya Mikhaílovna, according to them, was both proud and immoral, and a frightful tyrant; but the principal thing was—she permitted herself such freedom of speech that it was downright shocking. As a matter of fact, Dárya Mikháilovna was not fond of putting any restraint on herself in the country, and in the free simplicity of her demeanour there was perceptible a slight tinge of the scorn of the fashionable dame from the capital toward the decidedly uncultured and petty persons who surrounded her. . . . . She behaved to her town acquaintances, also, in a very free-and-easy, even scoffing manner, but there was not a trace of scorn.

By the way, reader, have you noticed that a person who is unusually absent-minded in the society of his inferiors never is absent-minded with persons of a higher standing? Why is this? However, such questions lead to nothing.

When Konstantín Diomíditch, having at last learned the Thalberg Étude by heart, descended from his clean and cheerful little chamber to the drawing-room, he found the entire domestic circle already assembled there. The salon had already begun. The mistress of the house had settled herself on a broad couch, with her feet tucked up under her, and was twirling a new French pamphlet in her hands; by the window, over their embroidery-frames, sat, on one side, the daughter of Dárya Mikhaílovna, and, on the other, Mlle. Boncourt, the governess, a dried-up old spinster, sixty years of age, with scratch-wig of black hair under a motley-hued cap, and cotton-wool in her ears; in the corner near the door Basístoff had taken up his post, and was reading a newspaper; beside him, Ványa and Pétya were playing at draughts; and leaning against the stove, with his arms folded behind his back, stood a gentleman short of stature, with rumpled grey hair, a swarthy face, and shifty little black eyes —a certain Afrikán Semyónitch Pigásoff.

A strange man was this Mr. Pigásoff. Embittered toward everything and everybody, especially toward women, he scolded from morning until night, sometimes very pertinently, sometimes quite stupidly, but always with enjoyment. His irritation went to the point of childishness; his laugh, the sound of his voice, his whole being, seemed permeated with gall. Dárya Mikháilovna gladly welcomed Pigásoff; he diverted her with his sallies. They really were rather amusing. It was a passion with him to exaggerate everything. For example: no matter what calamity was mentioned in his presence, —whether he was told that a village had been set on fire by the lightning, or that a peasant had chopped his hand off with an axe,—on each occasion he inquired with concentrated exasperation, " And what is her name? "—that is to say, what was the name of the woman who was the origin of the catastrophe; because, according to his conviction, a woman is the cause of every misfortune, and all that is necessary is to investigate the matter thoroughly. One day he flung himself on his knees before a lady with whom he was barely acquainted and who was pressing her hospitality upon him, and began tearfully, but with fury depicted on his countenance, to entreat her to spare him, that he was guilty of no offence toward her, and never would be. On one occasion a horse ran away down hill with one of Dárya Mikháilovna's laundresses, hurled her into a ditch, and came near killing her. From that day forth Pigásoff never mentioned that horse otherwise than as "the good, good little horse," and considered the hill and the ditch as particularly picturesque localities. Pigásoff had not been lucky in life, and he had assumed this whim. He had sprung from poor parents. His father had discharged divers petty duties, hardly knew how to read and write, and took no heed for the education of his son; he fed and clothed him, and that was all. His mother had spoiled him, but had died early. Pigásoff had educated himself, entered himself in the school of the district, then in the gymnasium, had taught himself French, German, and even Latin, and, on leaving the gymnasium with an excellent certificate, had betaken himself to Dorpat, where he had waged an incessant struggle with want, but had gone through the three years' course to the end. Pigásoff's abilities were not above the ordinary; he had distinguished himself by his patience and perseverance, but that which was especially strong in him was his sense of ambition, the desire to get into good society, not to get left behind, in despite of fate. Hence he had studied diligently, and had entered the University of Dorpat out of ambition. His poverty enraged him, and developed in him observation and cunning. He expressed himself in a way peculiar to himself; from his youth up he had made his own a special sort of bitter and irritable eloquence. His thoughts did not rise above the general level; but he spoke in such a way that he might have appeared to be not only a clever, but even a very clever man. On receiving the degree of bachelor of arts Pigásoff decided to devote himself to the profession of teaching; he comprehended that, on any other road, he could not, in any possible manner, overtake his comrades (he had endeavoured to select them from the highest circles, and had understood how to curry favour with them; he even flattered them, though he grumbled all the while). But at this point, to speak plainly, his material gave out. A self-taught man, not out of love for learning, Pigásoff, as a matter of fact, knew too little. He broke down grievously in the disputation, while another student, who lived in the same room with him, and at whom he had constantly jeered, a very shallow-brained man, but one who had received a regular and substantial education, won a complete triumph. This failure drove Pigásoff into a fury; he flung all his text-books and note-books into the fire, and entered the government service. At first matters did not go badly; he was a fairly good official, not very active, but, on the other hand, extremely self-confident and dashing; but he wanted to become a person of importance at one bound. He got entangled, stumbled, and was compelled to resign. For

25

three years he kept quiet in a village which he had acquired, and suddenly married a wealthy, half-educated woman who owned landed property, and whom he had caught with the bait of his free and easy, scoffing manners. But Pigásoff's disposition had become too irritable and acidulated; family life weighed heavily on him. His wife, after living with him for several years, went off in secret to Moscow, and sold her estate to some clever speculator, just as Pigásoff had built a farm-house on it. Shaken to the very foundation by this last blow, Pigásoff entered into a law-suit with his wife, but gained nothing thereby. He was living out his life alone; roamed about among the neighbours, whom he reviled behind their backs and even to their faces, and who received him with a certain constrained half-laugh, although he did not inspire them with any serious alarm; and he never took a book into his hand. He owned about one hundred souls; his peasants were not in distress.

" Ah! *Constantin!* " said Dárya Mikhaílovna, as soon as Pandalévsky entered the drawing-room; " will *Alexandrine* come? "

"Alexándra Pávlovna bade me thank you, and she will deem it a particular pleasure to do so," replied Konstantín Diomíditch, bowing graciously on all sides, and touching his beautifully arranged hair with his plump but white little hand.

" And will Volýntzeff come, too? "

" Yes, ma'am."

" And so, Afrikán Semyónitch," went on Dárya Mikhaílovna, turning to Pigásoff, " in your opinion, all young ladies are unnatural? "

Pigásoff's lips curled on one side, and he nervously twitched his elbow.

" I say," he began in a deliberate voice—he always spoke slowly and distinctly, even in a violent fit of anger—" I say that young ladies in general—as to present company, of course, I hold my peace. . . . "

" But that does not prevent your thinking of them," interrupted Dárya Mikháilovna.

" I hold my peace concerning them," repeated Pigásoff. " All young ladies in general are unnatural in the highest degree—unnatural in the expression of their feelings. If a young lady, for instance, is frightened or delighted or grieved at anything, she will infallibly, in the first place, communicate to her body some sort of elegant curve, like this " (and Pigásoff bent his form and spread out his hands in the most hideous manner), " and then she will shriek, ' Akh! ' or she will fall to laughing or weeping. But I once succeeded " (here Pigásoff smiled in a self-satisfied way) " in getting a genuine, unfeigned expression of sentiment out of one remarkably unnatural young lady."

" How did you do it? "

Pigásoff's eyes flashed.

" I hit her in the side with an aspen stake, from behind. She fairly yelled, and I said: ' Bravo! bravo! There, that was the voice of nature, that was a natural shriek. Do you always act in that way henceforth!' "

Every one in the room burst out laughing.

" What nonsense you do talk, Afrikán Semyónitch!" exclaimed Dárya Mikhaílovna. " As if I would believe that you would strike a girl in the side with a stake!"

" By heaven, it was with a stake—with a very big stake, like those which are used for the defence of a fortress!"

" *Mais c'est une horreur ce que vous dites là monsieur,*" cried Mlle. Boncourt, as she gazed sternly at the children, who were convulsed with laughter.

" But do not believe him," said Dárya Mikhaílovna; " do not you know him? "

But it was a long time before the indignant Frenchwoman could regain her composure, and she kept on muttering something to herself.

" You need not believe me," continued Pigásoff in an indifferent voice; " but I affirm that I have told the actual truth. Who should know it, if not I? After this, I suppose you will not believe, either, that our neighbour, Mme. Tchepúzoff, Eléna Antónovna, herself—observe, herself—told me how she tortured her own nephew?"

"That 's another invention of yours!"

"Permit me, permit me! Listen, and judge for yourselves. Observe that I have no desire to calumniate her; I am even fond of her—as fond as one can be of a woman; in her whole house she has not a single book, except an almanac, and she cannot read in any other way than aloud —she goes into a perspiration with the exertion, and complains afterward that her eyes have swelled out in lumps. . . . . In short, she is a fine woman, and has plump maids. Why should I calumniate her?"

"Well," remarked Dárya Mikhaílovna, "Afrikán Semyónitch has mounted his hobby and he will not dismount from it until evening."

"My hobby! . . . . But women have three hobbies, from which they never dismount—unless they are taken off."

"And what are those three hobbies?"

"Reproaches, hints, and rebukes."

"Do you know, Afrikán Semyónitch," began Dárya Mikhaílovna, "it is not for nothing that you are so embittered against women. Some woman or other must have. . . ."

"Offended me, you mean to say?" Pigásoff interrupted her.

Dárya Mikhaílovna became somewhat confused; she recalled Pigásoff's unhappy marriage, ... and merely nodded her head.

"One woman did, in fact, offend me," remarked Pigásoff; "although she was kind, very kind. . . ."

"Who was she?"

"My mother," ejaculated Pigásoff, dropping his voice.

"Your mother? In what way could she offend you?"

"By giving me birth. . . ."

Dárya Mikhaílovna contracted her brows in a frown.

"It seems to me," she began, "that your conversation is taking a melancholy turn. . . . . *Constantin,* play us Thalberg's new Étude. Perchance the sounds of music will tame Afrikán Semyónitch. . . . . For Orpheus tamed the wild beasts."

Konstantín Diomíditch seated himself at the piano, and played the Étude in a very satisfactory manner. At first Natálya Alexyéevna listened with attention, then betook herself again to her work.

"*Merci, c'est charmant,*" said Dárya Mikhaílovna; "I love Thalberg. *Il est si distingué.* What have you been thinking about, Afrikán Semyónitch?"

"I have been thinking," began Pigásoff slowly, "that there are three classes of egoists: the egoists who enjoy life themselves and let others live also; the egoists who enjoy life themselves and do not let others live also; and, lastly, the egoists who do not live themselves nor let others live. . . . . Women, for the most part, belong to the third class."

"How amiable of you! There is only one thing which surprises me, Afrikán Semyónitch, and that is the self-confidence of your verdicts; just as though you could never make a mistake."

"Who says so! I make mistakes also; a man, also, may err. But do you know what the difference is between an error on the part of one of us men and the error of a woman? You do not know? It is this: a man may, for instance, say that twice two does not make four, but five or three and a half; but a woman will say that twice two makes a stearine candle."

"It strikes me that I have already heard that remark from you. . . . . But allow me to inquire what connection has your thought about the three sorts of egoists with the music which you have just been listening to?"

"None whatever, and I was not listening to the music."

"Well, thou, my good fellow, art incorrigible. I see, one may as well drop it," retorted Dárya Mikhaílovna, slightly distorting Griboyedoff's verse. "And what do you love, if music does not please you? Literature, pray?"

"I love literature, only not that of the present day."

" Why not? "

" This is why. Not long ago I was crossing the Oká on a ferry-boat with some gentleman or other. The ferry-boat made a landing at a steep place: the carriage had to be dragged up by hand. The gentleman had a very heavy calash. While the ferrymen were straining themselves and dragging the carriage ashore, the gentleman grunted so, as he stood on the boat, that one even felt sorry for him. . . . . Here, I said to myself, is a new application of the system of the division of labour! And that's the way with the literature of the present day: others drag, do the work, and it grunts."

Dárya Mikhaílovna smiled. "And that is called the reproduction of contemporary existence," went on the irrepressible Pigásoff; "and a profound sympathy with social problems, and something else besides. . . . . Okh, I have no patience with those big words! "

" But the women, whom you assail so,—they, at least, do not use big words."

Pigásoff shrugged his shoulders.

" They don't use them, because they don't know any."

Dárya Mikhaílovna blushed slightly.

"You are beginning to utter impertinences, Afrikán Semyónitch! " she remarked, with a constrained smile.

Complete silence reigned in the room.

" Where is Zolotonósha? " one of the little boys suddenly inquired of Basístoff.

" In the Government of Poltáva, my dearest," put in Pigásoff; " in the very heart of Khokhlándia." [1] (He was delighted at the opportunity to change the subject.) " We were speaking of literature just now," he went on; " if I had any spare money, I would immediately become a Little Russian poet."

" What do you mean by that, too? A fine poet you would make! " retorted Dárya Mikhaílovna; " do you mean to say that you understand Little Russian? "

" Not in the least; and it 's not necessary."

" Why not? "

" Because it is n't. All one has to do is to take a sheet of paper and write at the top, ' Meditation ' ; then begin thus, ' Hey, thou my fate, fate! ' or, ' The little kazák Naliváiko is sitting on the mound! ' And then, ' Under the mountain, under the greenwood, grae, grae, voropae, hop! hop! ' or something in that style. And there you have it. Print it and publish it. The Little Russian will read it, will prop his cheek on his hand, and will infallibly fall a-weeping,—such a sentimental soul is he! "

" Good gracious ! " exclaimed Basístoff. " What 's that you are saying? There 's no sense

---

[1] " Khokhól " (topknot) is an ironical nickname for Little Russians. Hence Khokhlándia, Little Russia.—TRANSLATOR.

to it. I have lived in Little Russia, I love it, and
I know its language. . . . . 'Grae, grae, voropae' is perfect nonsense."

"Possibly, but the Topknot will fall a-weeping, all the same. You say, 'language.' . . . .
But does such a thing as a Little Russian language exist? I once asked a Little Russian to
translate the following phrase—the first one that
came into my head: 'Grammar is the art of reading and writing correctly.' Do you know how he
translated it? ' Khrammyr ais the aiert of ryead-
ing ynd wryaiting corrayctly.' . . . . Is that a
language, in your opinion,—an independent language? Why, sooner than agree to that, I'm
ready to let my best friend pound me up in a
mortar. . . . ."

Basístoff was on the point of retorting.

"Let him alone," said Dárya Mikhaílovna.
"Surely you know that you will hear nothing
but paradoxes from him."

Pigásoff smiled sarcastically. A lackey entered and announced the arrival of Alexándra
Pávlovna and her brother.

Dárya Mikhaílovna rose to welcome her
guests.

"How do you do, *Alexandrine!*" she said, as
she advanced to meet her. "How clever of
you to come! . . . . How do you do, Sergyéi
Pávlitch!"

Volýntzeff shook Dárya Mikhaílovna's hand, and went up to Natálya Alexyéevna.

"And how about that Baron, your new acquaintance—is he coming to-day ? " inquired Pigásoff.

" Yes, he is coming."

" He 's a great philosopher; they say he fairly squirts Hegel."

Dárya Mikhaílovna made no answer, seated Alexándra Pávlovna on the couch, and placed herself beside her.

" Philosophy," went on Pigásoff, " is the highest point of view. That will be the death of me also; those highest points of view. And what can be seen above them? If you want to buy a horse, you would n't inspect it from a watch-tower, would you? "

" That Baron was to bring you some article or other, was he not ? " asked Alexándra Pávlovna.

" Yes," replied Dárya Mikhaílovna, with exaggerated carelessness; " an article about the relations between trade and industry in Russia. . . . But have no fears; we will not read it here. . . . . I did not invite you for that. *Le baron est aussi aimable que savant.* And he talks Russian so well! *C'est un vrai torrent . . . . il vous entraîne.*"

" He talks Russian so well," remarked Pigásoff, " that he deserves to be praised in French."

" Grumble on, Afrikán Semyónitch, grumble

on. It suits your dishevelled hair admirably. But why does not he come? Do you know, messieurs et mesdames?" added Dárya Mikhaílovna, glancing around her. "Let us go into the garden. . . . There is still an hour before dinner, and the weather is splendid. . . ."

The whole company rose and went into the garden.

Dárya Mikhaílovna's garden extended clear to the river. It contained many ancient linden avenues, with golden shadows and fragrant with emerald openings at the ends, many arbours of acacias and lilacs.

Volýntzeff, with Natálya and Mlle. Boncourt, betook themselves to the densest thickets of the garden. Volýntzeff walked by the side of Natálya and maintained silence. Mlle. Boncourt followed at a little distance.

"What have you been doing to-day?" inquired Volýntzeff at last, twisting the tips of his very handsome, dark chestnut moustache.

His features greatly resembled those of his sister; but their expression had less vivacity and life, and his handsome, caressing eyes had a somewhat melancholy look.

"Why, nothing," replied Natálya. "I have been listening to Pigásoff scold, embroidering on canvas, and reading."

"And what have you been reading?"

" I was reading . . . . the ' History of the Cru-
sades,' " said Natálya, with some hesitation.

Volýntzeff looked at her.

" Ah! " he ejaculated at last; " that must be
interesting."

He broke off a branch and began to twirl it
in the air. They walked on another twenty paces.

" Who 's that Baron with whom your mama
has become acquainted? " Volýntzeff put another
question.

" A gentleman of the Imperial Bedchamber, a
newcomer; *maman* praises him highly."

" Your mama is capable of being carried away
by her feelings."

" That proves that she is still very young in
heart," remarked Natálya.

" Yes. I shall soon send you your horse. It
is almost trained. I want to have it set out on a
gallop on the instant, and I shall accomplish
that."

" *Merci!* . . . . But I feel ashamed. You are
training it yourself . . . . they say that is very difficult."

" In order to afford you the slightest gratifi-
cation, you know, Natálya Alexyéevna, I am
ready . . . . I . . . . to do more than such trifles."

Volýntzeff stopped short.

Natálya cast a friendly glance at him, and
again said, " *Merci!* "

" You know," went on Sergyéi Pávlitch after
a prolonged pause, " that there is nothing.... But
why do I say this? Surely you know it all! "

At that moment a bell rang in the house.

"*Ah! la cloche du dîner!* " cried Mlle. Boncourt; " *rentrons.*"

" *Quel dommage!* " said the old Frenchwoman
to herself, as she mounted the steps of the balcony behind Volýntzeff and Natálya; " *quel
dommage que ce charmant garçon ait si peu de
ressources dans la conversation. . . . .*" Which
may be translated into Russian thus: " Thou art
very nice, my dear fellow, but rather a sorry
figure."

The Baron did not arrive for dinner. They
waited half an hour for him. The conversation
at table flagged. Sergyéi Pávlitch did nothing
but gaze at Natálya, beside whom he sat, and
diligently pour water into her glass. Pandalévsky vainly endeavoured to interest his neighbour, Alexándra Pávlovna; he was all bubbling
with sweetness, but she almost yawned in his
face.

Basístoff rolled little balls of bread and
thought nothing; even Pigásoff held his peace,
and when Dárya Mikhaílovna observed to him
that he was very far from amiable to-day, he
replied crustily: " When am I ever amiable?
That 's not my business. . . . And, with a bitter
laugh, he added: " Wait a bit. You see, I 'm kvas,

du prostói[1] Russian kvas; but there's your Gentleman of the Bedchamber. . . ."

"Bravo!" exclaimed Dárya Mikhaílovna. "Pigásoff is jealous—jealous in anticipation!"

But Pigásoff made her no reply, and only cast sidelong glances.

Seven o'clock struck, and all again assembled in the drawing-room.

"Evidently he is not coming," said Dárya Mikhaílovna.

But lo! the rumble of an equipage resounded, a small tarantás[2] drove up to the door, and a few moments later a footman entered the drawing-room and presented a letter on a silver salver to Dárya Mikhaílovna. She ran her eye over it to the end, and, turning to the lackey, inquired:

"And where is the gentleman who brought this letter?"

"He is sitting in his carriage, madam. Do you command that he shall be received, madam?"

"Ask him in."

The footman left the room.

"Just imagine—how vexatious!" went on Dárya Mikhaílovna; "the Baron has received orders to return at once to Petersburg. He has

[1] Plain kvas is a sort of small beer, made by pouring water on sour, black rye bread, or the rye meal, letting it ferment, and flavouring with raisins, straw, watermelon-juice, etc. — TRANSLATOR.

[2] The Russian posting carriage; springless, shaped like a barrel split lengthwise, filled with straw or hay. Sometimes there is a seat, sometimes not. — TRANSLATOR.

sent me his article by a certain Mr. Rúdin, his
friend. The Baron wished to introduce him to
me—he praised him highly. But how annoy-
ing this is! I was in hopes that the Baron would
spend some time here."

"Dmítry Nikoláevitch Rúdin," announced
the footman.

III

THERE entered a man of thirty-five, tall, somewhat round-shouldered, curly-haired, swarthy of complexion, with an irregular but expressive and clever face, with a faint gleam in the quick, dark blue eyes, a straight, broad nose, and finely chiselled lips. His garments were not new, and were too tight for him, as though he had outgrown them.

He walked briskly up to Dárya Mikhaílovna, made her a brief inclination, told her that he had long wished to have the honour of being presented to her, and that his friend the Baron greatly regretted that he was unable to take leave of her in person.

The shrill tone of Rúdin's voice did not correspond to his stature and his broad chest.

" Be seated. . . I am very glad," said Dárya Mikhaílovna, and, after introducing him to the entire company, she inquired whether he belonged in the neighbourhood or had just arrived.

" My estate is in the T . . . Government," replied Rúdin, holding his hat on his knees. " I have not been here long. I came hither on business, and have settled down, for the time being, in your county town."

41

" At whose house? "

" The doctor's. He was an old comrade of mine in the university."

" Ah! at the doctor's. . . People speak highly of him. They say he understands his business. And have you known the Baron long? "

" I met him last winter in Moscow, and now I have just been spending about a week with him."

" He is a very clever man—the Baron."

" Yes, madam."

Dárya Mikhaílovna sniffed at a knot in her pocket-handkerchief which was saturated with eau de Cologne.

" Are you in the service? " she inquired.

" Who? I, madam? "

" Yes."

" No. . . I am on the retired list."

A brief pause ensued. The general conversation was resumed.

" Permit me to be so curious as to inquire," began Pigásoff, addressing Rúdin, " are you acquainted with the contents of the article which the Baron has sent? "

" I am."

" That article deals with the relations of trade . . . . or no, what's its name?—of industry to trade in our fatherland. . . I believe that was the way you were pleased to express it, Dárya Mikhaílovna? "

" Yes, it does deal with that . . ." said Dárya Mikhaílovna, and laid her hand on her brow.

" I am, of course, a poor judge of such matters," went on Pigásoff; " but I must confess that the very title of the article strikes me as extremely . . . . how can I say it most delicately? . . . extremely obscure and confused."

" Why does it seem so to you? "

Pigásoff grinned, and cast a fleeting glance at Dárya Mikhaílovna.

" And is it clear to you? " he said, again turning his foxy little face toward Rúdin.

" To me? Yes."

" H'm! . . . Of course you must know best about that."

" Have you a headache? " Alexándra Pávlovna inquired of Dárya Mikhaílovna.

" No. It's a way I have . . . *c'est nerveux.*"

" Permit me to inquire," began Pigásoff again, in his thin, nasal voice—" your acquaintance, Mr. Baron Muffel . . . I believe that is his name? "

" Yes, exactly."

" Does Mr. Baron Muffel make political economy his special study, or does he merely devote to that interesting science the hours of leisure which are left in the midst of worldly amusements and the duties of the service? "

Rúdin stared intently at Pigásoff.

" The Baron is a dilettante in this matter,"

43

he replied, flushing slightly; "but his article contains much that is both just and original."

"I cannot dispute your statement, as I know nothing of the article. . . But I will venture to inquire whether the composition of your friend Baron Muffel does not, in all probability, stick more closely to general arguments than to facts?"

"It contains both facts and arguments founded on facts."

"Just so, sir; just so, sir. I must inform you that, in my opinion . . . . and I may be allowed, on occasion, to say a word of my own: I spent three years in Dorpat . . . . all these so-called general arguments, hypotheses, systems . . . . excuse me, I am a rustic, I blurt the truth straight out . . . are of no earthly use. The whole thing is mere reasoning, and serves only to mystify people. Hand over your facts, gentlemen, and that's all we ask of you."

"Really!" retorted Rúdin. "Well, but the meaning of the facts should be set forth?"

"General arguments," pursued Pigásoff; "those general arguments, surveys, deductions, will be the death of me. That whole business is founded on so-called convictions; everybody prates about his convictions and demands respect for them to boot."

And Pigásoff brandished his clenched fist in the air. Pandálevsky smiled.

" Very fine, indeed! " remarked Rúdin; " so, according to you, there are no such things as convictions? "

" No—and they don't exist."

" That is your conviction? "

" Yes."

" How can you say that there are none? There's one for you, the very first thing."

All the persons in the room smiled and exchanged glances.

" But permit me, permit me," Pigásoff was beginning. . . .

But Dárya Mikhaílovna clapped her hands, cried, " Bravo, bravo, Pigásoff is vanquished! " and quietly took Rúdin's hat from his hands.

" Wait a bit before you rejoice, madam; you'll have plenty of time," put in Pigásoff, with vexation. " It is not enough to utter a keen word, with an air of superiority; one must prove, refute. . . . We have digressed from the subject under discussion."

" Very well," remarked Rúdin, coldly; " it is a very simple matter. You do not believe in the advantage of general arguments, you do not believe in convictions. . . . "

" I do not believe in them. I do not. I do not believe in anything! "

" Very good. You are a sceptic."

" I see no necessity for using so learned a word. However . . . . "

"Do not keep interrupting continually!" interposed Dárya Mikhaílovna.

"Bite him, Towser, bite him!" said Pandalévsky to himself, at that moment, and grinned to the full extent of his mouth.

"That word expresses my thought," continued Rúdin. "You understand it; then why not use it? You do not believe in anything. . . . Then why believe in facts?"

"Why? that's excellent! Facts are definite things; everybody knows what facts are. . . I judge them by experience, by my own instinct."

"But may not your instinct be deceiving you? Your instinct tells you that the sun goes round the earth . . . . or, perhaps, you do not agree with Copernicus? You do not believe him, either?"

Again a smile flitted across all faces, and the eyes of all present were riveted on Rúdin. "Come, he's not a stupid man," thought each one.

"You are pleased to do nothing but jest," began Pigásoff. "Of course it is very original, but it does not suit the subject."

"In what I have said so far," retorted Rúdin, "there has been, unfortunately, but too little that is original. All that has been known for a very long time, and has been said a thousand times. The question is. . . ."

"What?" inquired Pigásoff, not without impertinence.

In a dispute he was wont first to jeer at his opponent, then he became rude, and, finally, sulked and retreated into silence.

" This," went on Rúdin. " I must confess that I cannot help feeling sincere pity when clever people attack, in my presence. . . "

" Systems? " interrupted Pigásoff.

" Yes, if you like, call it systems. Why does that word alarm you so? Every system is founded upon knowledge of the fundamental laws—the principles of life. . . "

" But it is impossible to know them, to discover them . . . good gracious! "

" Pardon me. Of course they are not accessible to every one, and it is natural to man to err. But you will, in all probability, agree with me that, for example, Newton discovered at least a few of those fundamental laws. He was a genius, let us admit that; but the discoveries of geniuses are great precisely because they become the property of all men. The effort to discover general principles in partial phenomena is one of the radical properties of the human mind, and the whole of our civilisation. . . . . . "

" So that 's what you 're after! " interrupted Pigásoff, in a drawling tone. " I am a practical man, and I do not enter into, and have no wish to enter into, all those metaphysical subtleties. . . "

" Very good! That depends on your will.

47

But observe that your very desire to be a practical man is, in its way, a system, a theory. . . . "

"Civilisation, you say!" put in Pigásoff; "a pretty thing you 've taken it into your head to surprise us with! Who cares for it, that much-lauded civilisation! I would n't give a copper farthing for your civilisation!"

"But how improperly you are arguing, Afrikán Semyónitch!" remarked Dárya Mikhaílovna, inwardly delighted to the last degree with the composure and elegant courtesy of her new acquaintance. "*C'est un homme comme il faut,*" she thought, casting a glance of approving attention at Rúdin's face. "I must attract him by friendly treatment." She mentally uttered these last words in Russian.

"I will not undertake to defend civilisation," went on Rúdin, after a brief pause; "it does not stand in need of my protection. You do not love it . . . every one has his own taste. Moreover, that would lead us too far. Permit me merely to remind you of an ancient adage: ' Jupiter, thou waxest wroth; therefore, thou art in the wrong.' What I wished to say was that all these attacks upon systems, upon general arguments, and so forth, are particularly vexatious because, together with the systems, people reject knowledge in general, science and faith therein, consequently, also, faith in themselves, in their powers. But people need that faith; they cannot live on impressions alone, it is a sin for them to fear thought and not to believe it. Scepticism has always been distinguished by sterility and impotence. . . . "

" All that is mere words! " muttered Pigásoff.

" Possibly. But permit me to call your attention to the fact that by saying, ' All that is mere words! ' we frequently desire to rid ourselves of the necessity of saying anything more pertinent than mere words."

" What do you mean, sir? " asked Pigásoff, and screwed up his eyes.

" You have understood what I meant to say to you," retorted Rúdin, with involuntary but instantaneously repressed impatience. " I repeat, if a man has no strong principle in which he believes, no ground whereon he stands firmly, how can he understand the details, the significance, the future of his nation? How can he know what he ought to do himself if . . . . "

" Honour to whom honour is due! " said Pigásoff abruptly, bowed, and retired to one side, without looking at any one.

Rúdin looked at him, laughed slightly, and fell silent.

" Aha! he has beaten a retreat! " said Dárya Mikhaílovna. " Do not disturb yourself, Dmítry. . . . Excuse me," she added, with an affable smile, " what is your patronymic? "

" Nikoláitch."

"Do not disturb yourself, my dear Dmítry Nikoláitch. He has not deceived any of us. He wants to pretend that he does not *wish* to argue any more. . . . . . He is conscious that he *cannot* argue with you. But you had better take a seat nearer to us and we will have a chat."

Rúdin moved his chair closer.

"How is it that we have not made acquaintance before?" went on Dárya Mikhaílovna. "I am amazed! . . . Have you read this book? *C'est de Tocqueville, vous savez.*"

And Dárya Mikhaílovna handed Rúdin the French pamphlet.

Rúdin took the thin little book in his hand, turned over a few pages, and, laying it on the table again, replied that he had not read that particular work of M. Tocqueville, but had often meditated on the subject which the latter dealt with therein.

A conversation arose. At first Rúdin seemed to waver, seemed unable to make up his mind to speak out, could not hit upon words, but at last he warmed up and began to talk. At the end of a quarter of an hour his voice alone resounded in the room. All present clustered in a circle around him.

Pigásoff alone remained at a distance in the corner near the fireplace. Rúdin talked cleverly, fervently, judiciously; he displayed much learning, much reading. No one had expected to find in him a man of great parts. . . He was so ordinarily dressed, so few rumours about him had been in circulation. It struck them all as strange and incomprehensible that such a clever person could suddenly make his appearance in country parts. All the more did he surprise and, we may say, enchant them all, beginning with Dárya Mikhaílovna. . . . She was proud of her discovery, and began to plan ahead how she would introduce Rúdin to society. In her first impressions there was much that was childish, despite her years. Alexándra Pávlovna, to tell the truth, understood very little of all that Rúdin said, but she was greatly amazed and delighted; her brother, also, was astonished. Pandalévsky watched Dárya Mikhaílovna and waxed envious. Pigásoff said to himself, ' I 'll give five hundred rubles, and I 'll get a still better nightingale! ' . . . But Basístoff and Natálya were the most dumfounded of all. Basístoff was almost deprived of breath; he sat the whole time with gaping mouth and eyes protruding from their sockets, and listened, listened as he had never listened to any one since he was born, while Natálya's face became overspread with a brilliant crimson hue, and her gaze, immovably riveted upon Rúdin, both darkened and shone radiantly. . .

" What magnificent eyes he has! " Volýntzeff whispered to her.

" Yes, they are nice."

"Only it's a pity that his hands are large and red."

Natálya made no reply.

Tea was served. The conversation became more general, but from the mere suddenness with which all fell silent the moment Rúdin opened his mouth, one could judge of the strength of the impression he had produced. All of a sudden Dárya Mikhaílovna was seized with a whim to tease Pigásoff. She approached him, and said in an undertone, "Why do you remain silent, and merely smile maliciously? Just make an effort, grapple with him again," and, without awaiting his reply, she beckoned Rúdin up with her hand.

"There is still one thing which you do not know about him," she said to him, pointing at Pigásoff; "he is a terrible woman-hater, he is incessantly attacking women; please turn him into the paths of truth."

Rúdin looked at Pigásoff . . . . involuntarily looked down on him: he was the taller by two heads. Pigásoff almost curled up with wrath, and his sallow face became pallid.

"Dárya Mikhaílovna is mistaken," he began in an unsteady voice. "I do not attack women alone. I am not very fond of the human race as a whole."

"What can have given you such a poor opinion of it?" asked Rúdin.

Pigásoff looked him straight in the eye.

"Probably the study of my own heart, in which I discover, day by day, more trash. I judge of others by myself. Perhaps that is unjust, and I am a great deal worse than other men; but what am I to do? 'T is a habit!'"

"I understand you and sympathise with you," returned Rúdin. "What noble soul has not experienced the thirst for self-depreciation? But one must not remain in that helpless position."

"I humbly thank you for issuing a certificate of nobility to my soul," retorted Pigásoff; "but my position is all right, it is n't a bad one, so that even if there is any issue from it—why, I don't care! I shall not seek it."

"But that means—pardon the expression—that you give the preference to the satisfaction of your self-love over your desire to be and to live in the truth. . . ."

"Most certainly!" exclaimed Pigásoff; "self-love I can understand, and you, I hope, understand it, and every one understands it; but the truth—what is truth? Where is it, that truth?"

"You are repeating yourself, I warn you," remarked Dárya Mikhaílovna.

Pigásoff hunched his shoulders.

"Where 's the harm in that? I ask; where is truth? Even the philosophers do not know what it is. Kant says, 'This is it'; but Hegel says, 'No, you are mistaken; this is it.'"

"But do you know what Hegel says about it?" asked Rúdin, without raising his voice.

"I repeat," went on Pigásoff, who was now in a rage, "that I cannot understand what is truth. In my opinion, it does not exist in the world at all—that is to say, the word exists, but the thing itself does not."

"Fie! Fie!" cried Dárya Mikhaílovna. "Aren't you ashamed to say that, you old sinner! There is no truth? After that, what is there in the world to live for?"

"Why, I think, Dárya Mikhaílovna," retorted Pigásoff, with irritation, "that, in any case, you would find it easier to live in the world without truth than without your cook, Stepán, who is such a master-hand at making beef broth! And tell me, for mercy's sake, what do you want of truth? Why, you cannot make a mob-cap out of it!"

"A jest is not an answer," remarked Dárya Mikhaílovna; "especially when it runs into aspersion." . . .

"I do not know what the truth is like, but, as a matter of fact, evidently it puts your eyes out," muttered Pigásoff, and stepped aside in wrath.

But Rúdin began to talk about self-love, and talked very sensibly. He demonstrated that man without self-love is a cipher, that self-love is the lever of Archimedes, wherewith the earth may be moved from its place, but that, at the same time, only he deserves the appellation of man who understands how to control his self-love as a rider controls his horse, who sacrifices his personality to the general welfare. . . . .

" Selfishness," he wound up, " is suicide. The selfish man withers up like an isolated, sterile tree; but self-love, in its quality of an effective effort toward perfection, is the origin of everything great. . . Yes! a man must break the obstinate egoism of his individuality in order to give it a right to announce its meaning! "

" Cannot you lend me a pencil? " Pigásoff asked Basístoff.

Basístoff did not immediately understand what Pigásoff had asked him.

" What do you want of a pencil? " he said at last.

" I want to write down, at least, that last phrase of Mr. Rúdin's. If I don't write it down, I shall certainly forget it! And you must admit that such a phrase is equivalent to taking all the tricks in the game."

" There are things at which it is a sin to laugh and sneer, Afrikán Semyónitch! " said Basístoff, with heat, and turned his back on Pigásoff.

In the meanwhile, Rúdin had stepped up to Natálya. She rose; her face expressed perplexity.

Volýntzeff, who was sitting beside her, rose also.

" I see a pianoforte," said Rúdin, softly and

RÚDIN

affably, like a prince on his travels. "Do not you play on it?"

"Yes, I play," said Natálya; "but not very well. Konstantín Diomíditch, yonder, plays much better than I do."

Pandalévsky thrust forward his face and showed his teeth.

"You have no reason to say that, Natálya Alexyéevna; you play quite as well as I do."

"Do you know Schubert's 'Erlkönig'?" inquired Rúdin.

"He does, he does!" interposed Dárya Mikhaílovna. "Sit down, *Constantin.* . . And you love music, Dmítry Nikoláitch?"

Rúdin merely bent his head slightly, and passed his hand over his hair, as though preparing to listen. . . . Pandalévsky began to play.

Natálya stood by the piano, directly opposite Rúdin. At the first sound his face assumed a very beautiful expression. His dark blue eyes slowly roved about, now and then halting on Natálya. Pandalévsky finished.

Rúdin said nothing, and walked to the open window. A fragrant mist lay in a soft veil over the park; the near-by trees breathed forth a slumberous coolness. The stars glowed softly. The summer night lulled itself and soothed. Rúdin gazed out into the obscure park and turned round.

"This music and this night," he said, "have

56

reminded me of my student days in Germany
—our reunions, our serenades. . . ”

"And have you been in Germany?" asked
Dárya Mikhaílovna.

"I spent a year at Heidelberg and about a
year in Berlin."

"And did you dress in student fashion? I
am told that they dress rather peculiarly there."

"In Heidelberg I wore big boots with spurs,
and a braided hussar jacket, and my hair grew
down to my shoulders. . . . In Berlin the students
dress like everybody else."

"Do tell us something about your student
life?" said Alexándra Pávlovna.

Rúdin began to narrate. He was not quite
successful in his narration. His descriptions
lacked colour. He did not understand how
to excite laughter. However, Rúdin speedily
passed from stories of his foreign adventures to
general reflections upon the significance of
learning and science, upon the universities and
university life in general. In broad, bold out-
lines, he sketched a vast picture. All listened to
him with profound attention. He talked in
a masterly manner, fascinatingly, not quite
clearly . . . but this very lack of clearness imparted a certain charm to his speech.

The abundance of his thoughts prevented Rúdin from expressing himself definitely and accurately. Images followed images; compari-

sons, now unexpectedly daring, again strikingly faithful, succeeded each other. His impatient improvisation breathed forth not the conceited refinement of an experienced chatterer, but inspiration. He did not seek his words; they came obediently and freely of their own accord to his lips, and every word seemed to pour forth straight from his soul, glowing with all the fire of conviction. Rúdin possessed what is almost the highest mystery—the music of eloquence. He understood how, by thrumming upon one of the heart's chords, to make it emit a troubled sound and set all the others to quivering. Any given hearer might not be able to understand precisely what the speech was about; but his breast heaved high, some curtains or other parted before his eyes, something radiant blazed up in front of him.

All of Rúdin's thoughts seemed to be directed toward the future; this imparted to them an impetuous, youthful character. . . . . . Standing at the window, looking at no one in particular, he talked on; and, inspired by the universal sympathy and attention, by the proximity of young women, by the beauty of the night, carried away by the flood of his own sensations, he rose to eloquence, to poetry. . . The very sound of his voice, concentrated and quiet, heightened the spell; it seemed as though something lofty, unexpected by himself, were being uttered by his mouth. . . Rúdin spoke about that which gives eternal significance to the temporal life of man.

"I remember a Scandinavian legend," he said in conclusion; "a king is sitting with his warriors in a long, dark shed, around the fire. It is night—winter. All at once a tiny bird flies in through one open door and flies out through another. The king remarks that the bird is like man in the world: he has flown in from the darkness, and he flies forth into the darkness, and has not remained long in the warmth and the light. . . . 'King,' returns the oldest of his warriors, 'the bird will not get lost in the darkness, and will find its nest.' . . . Exactly so, our life is swift and trivial; but everything great is effected through the agency of men. The consciousness that one is the tool of those higher powers ought to requite a man for all other joys; in death itself he will find his life, his nest. . . ."

Rúdin paused, and lowered his eyes with a smile of involuntary confusion.

"*Vous êtes un poète*," said Dárya Mikhaílovna, in a low voice.

And they all inwardly agreed with her,—all, with the exception of Pigásoff. Without waiting for the end of Rúdin's speech, he had quietly taken his hat, and as he departed he had remarked in a wrathful whisper to Pandalévsky, who stood near the door:

"No! I'm going to the fools."

RÚDIN

But no one detained him or noticed his absence.

The servants brought in the supper, and half an hour later all had driven or walked away. Dárya Mikhaílovna requested Rúdin to stay overnight. Alexándra Pávlovna, as she was returning home in the carriage with her brother, several times began to exclaim and to admire Rúdin's remarkable mind. Volýntzeff agreed with her, but remarked that he had sometimes expressed himself rather obscurely . . . that is to say, not quite intelligibly, he added, being desirous, probably, of making his own thought clear; but his face clouded over, and his gaze, riveted upon one corner of the carriage, seemed to have become more melancholy than ever.

Pandalévsky, as he prepared himself for bed and took off his silk-embroidered suspenders, said aloud, " A very adroit man! " and all of a sudden, with a stern glance at his youthful valet, ordered him to leave the room. Basístoff did not sleep all night long, and did not undress until morning dawned; he wrote at a letter to a comrade of his in Moscow, while Natálya, although she undressed and got into bed, did not sleep for a single minute, and did not even close her eyes. With her head resting on her hand, she stared intently into darkness; her pulse beat feverishly, and her breast heaved, from time to time, with a heavy sigh.

IV

THE next morning, Rúdin had just finished dressing when a man-servant presented himself from Dárya Mikhaílovna, with an invitation to be so good as to come to her boudoir and drink tea with her. Rúdin found her alone. She bade him good morning in a very amiable manner, inquired whether he had passed a good night, poured him out a cup of tea with her own hands, even asked whether there was enough sugar, offered him a cigarette, and twice repeated that she was surprised that she had not made his acquaintance long before. Rúdin made a movement to seat himself at some distance; but Dárya Mikhaílovna pointed to a softly stuffed *pâté* which stood beside her arm-chair, and, bending slightly in his direction, began to question him concerning his family, his plans and projects. Dárya Mikhaílovna talked carelessly, listened abstractedly; but Rúdin understood quite well that she was paying court to him, almost cajoling him. Not for nothing had she arranged this matutinal meeting, not for nothing had she gowned herself simply but elegantly, à la Madame Récamier! However, Dárya Mikhaílovna soon ceased to question him; she began to tell him about herself, about her youth, about the people with whom she was acquainted. Rúdin listened with sympathy to her idle prattle, although, strange to say, no matter what person Dárya Mikhaílovna talked about, she still remained constantly in the foreground,—she alone,—and the other individual somehow crept away and vanished. On the other hand, Rúdin learned in detail precisely what Dárya Mikhaílovna had said to such and such a noted dignitary, what influence she had exerted upon such and such a famous poet. Judging from Dárya Mikhaílovna's stories, one might have thought that all the celebrated people of the last quarter of a century had dreamed of nothing else but how to try and see her, how to gain her favour. She talked about them simply, without especial raptures and praises, as of members of her own family, calling some of them eccentrics. She talked about them, and, like a costly setting round a jewel, their names were ranged in a brilliant border around the chief name—around Dárya Mikhaílovna. . . .

But Rúdin listened as he smoked his cigarette, and maintained silence, only now and then interjecting small remarks into the discourse of the loquacious lady. He knew how to talk and was fond of talking himself; he was not only strong at conducting a conversation, but he knew how to listen also. Every one whom he did not alarm at the start unbosomed himself confidentially in his presence, so readily and approvingly did he follow the thread of the other person's narrative. There was much good nature in him,—that special sort of good nature wherewith people who are accustomed to feel themselves superior to others are filled. In argument he rarely gave his adversary a chance to have his say, and overwhelmed him with his impetuous and passionate dialectics.

Dárya Mikhaílovna explained herself in Russian. She liked to show off her proficiency in her native language, although Gallicisms and small French words often occurred in her speech. She deliberately employed ordinary, vernacular terms, but not always with success. Rúdin's ear was not offended by the strange medley of language on the lips of Dárya Mikhaílovna, and the probability is that he lacked the ear for that.

Dárya Mikhaílovna became fatigued at last, and, leaning her head against the cushion at the back of her chair, she fixed her eyes on Rúdin and relapsed into silence.

" I understand now," began Rúdin in a deliberate tone— " I understand why you come to the country every summer. This repose is indispensable for you; the rustic tranquillity, after the life of the capital, refreshes and strengthens you. I am convinced that you must be profoundly sensitive to the beauties of nature."

Dárya Mikhaílovna cast a sidelong glance at Rúdin.

" Nature . . . yes . . . yes, of course. . . . I am awfully fond of it; but you know, Dmítry Nikoláitch, that one cannot get along in the country without people. And there is hardly any one here. Pigásoff is the cleverest man in these parts."

" The choleric old fellow of last evening? " inquired Rúdin.

" Yes, that man. . . . However, in the country, even he is useful—if only to raise a laugh now and then."

" He is far from a stupid man," returned Rúdin; " but he is on the wrong road. I do not know whether you agree with me, Dárya Mikhaílovna, but in negation—in complete and universal negation—there is no blessing. Deny everything, and you may easily pass for a clever person; that is a familiar bait. Good-natured people are ready to conclude on the spot that you stand higher than the thing you deny. And this is frequently untrue. In the first place, a flaw may be discovered in everything; and, in the second place, even if you are stating a fact, you are only the worse off; your mind, directed only toward negation, becomes poverty-stricken, withers away. By satisfying your self-love you deprive yourself of the true joys of contemplation; life—the essence of life—escapes from your petty and splenetic observation, and you will end by snarling and exciting laughter. Only he who loves has a right to censure, to chide."

"Voilà M—r. Pigásoff enterré!" remarked Dárya Mikhaílovna. "What a master-hand you are at defining a man! However, Pigásoff, in all probability, did not understand you. He loves only his own person."

"And reviles it, with the object of having a right to revile others," chimed in Rúdin.

Dárya Mikhaílovna laughed.

"'He judges the sound'—how is it the proverb runs .... 'he judges the sound by the sick.' By the way, what do you think of the Baron?"

"Of the Baron? He is a nice man, with a kind heart, and well informed .... but he lacks force of character ... and all his life long he will remain half a learned man, half a man of the world—that is to say, a dilettante; that is to say, to express it point-blank—nothing. ... But 't is a pity!"

"I am of that opinion myself," replied Dárya Mikhaílovna. "I have read his article... *Entre nous ... cela a assez peu de fond. ....*"

"Whom else have you in the neighbourhood?" inquired Rúdin, after a pause.

Dárya Mikhaílovna flicked the ashes from her tiny, straw-covered cigarette with her little finger.

" Why, there is hardly any one else. Mme.
Lípin, Aléxándra Pávlovna, whom you saw
yesterday; she is very charming—but that is all.
Her brother is also a very fine man—*un parfait
honnête homme.* Prince Gárin you know. That
is all. There are two or three other neighbours,
but they count for absolutely nothing. Either
they are capricious—their airs are dreadful—or
they are shy, or else they are unduly free and
easy. I do not receive ladies, as you know. There
is still one other neighbour, a very cultured, even
a learned man, they say, but a frightfully eccentric person—fantastic. *Alexandrine* knows
him, and, apparently, is not indifferent to him. . .
There, now, you ought to study her, Dmítry
Nikoláitch; she is a lovely creature; all she needs
is to be developed a little. She must be developed, without fail! "

" She is very sympathetic," remarked Rúdin.

" A perfect child, Dmítry Nikoláitch, a real
child. She was married—*mais c'est tout comme.*
. . . If I had been a man I would have fallen in
love with no other sort of women."

" Really? "

" Absolutely. Such women, at all events,
are fresh, and freshness cannot be counter-
feited."

" And everything else can? " inquired Rúdin,
and laughed, which very rarely happened with
him. When he laughed his face assumed a

strange, almost senile, expression, his eyes grew small, his nose wrinkled up. . .

" And who is the man whom you called an eccentric, and to whom Mme. Lípin is not indifferent? " he asked.

" A certain Lezhnyóff, Mikhaílo Mikhaílitch, a landed proprietor of this neighbourhood."

Rúdin was surprised, and raised his head.

" Lezhnyóff, Mikhaílo Mikhaílitch? " he asked; " is he a neighbour of yours? "

" Yes. And do you know him? "

Rúdin did not reply for a space.

" I used to know him before . . . . long ago. He is a wealthy man, I believe? " he added, plucking at the fringe of the arm-chair with his hand.

" Yes, he is wealthy, although he dresses horribly, and drives about in a racing-gig, like a clerk. I would have liked to attract him to my house; he is clever, they say, and I have a matter of business to settle with him. . . . . You are aware, of course, that I manage my own estate."

Rúdin inclined his head.

" Yes, I do it myself," went on Dárya Mikhaílovna. " I do not introduce any foreign nonsense; I hold to my own way,—the Russian way, —and matters, as you see, appear to proceed not altogether badly," she added, with a circular movement of her hand.

" I have always been convinced," remarked

67

Rúdin, courteously, " of the extreme injustice of those people who deny that women have practical sense."

Dárya Mikhaílovna smiled pleasantly.

" You are very condescending," she said; " but what in the world was it that I wanted to say? What were we talking about? Yes! About Lezhnyóff. I have business with him in regard to our boundary lines. I have invited him to my house several times, and I am even expecting him to-day; but he does not come, God knows why . . . he is such a queer fellow!"

The portière was gently parted, and the butler entered, a man of lofty stature, grey-haired and bald, clad in a black dress-suit, a white necktie, and a white waistcoat.

" What dost thou want? " inquired Dárya Mikhaílovna, and, turning slightly toward Rúdin, she added in an undertone, " *n'est ce pas, comme il ressemble à Canning?* "

" Mikhaílo Mikhaílitch Lezhnyóff has arrived," announced the butler. " Do you command that he be received? "

" Akh, good heavens! " cried Dárya Mikhaílovna; " speak of the devil! Ask him in."

The butler withdrew.

" He's such a queer fellow; he has come at last, but inopportunely. He has interrupted our chat."

Rúdin rose from his seat, but Dárya Mikhaílovna stopped him.

" Where are you going? We can talk in your presence. And I wish to have you define him, as you did Pigásoff. When you speak—*vous gravez comme avec un burin*. Stay."

Rúdin was about to say something, but changed his mind and remained.

Mikhaílo Mikhaílitch, with whom the reader is already acquainted, entered the boudoir. He wore the same grey surtout, in his hands he held the same old cap. He bowed with composure to Dárya Mikhaílovna, and approached the tea-table.

" At last you have done us the honour to come to us, Monsieur Lezhnyóff!" said Dárya Mikhaílovna. " Pray take a seat. You are acquainted, I hear," she continued, pointing to Rúdin.

Lezhnyóff glanced at Rúdin, and smiled in a rather singular manner.

" I do know Mr. Rúdin," he said, with a slight inclination.

" We were at the university together," remarked Rúdin, in a low tone, and dropped his eyes.

" And we met afterward," said Lezhnyóff, coldly.

Dárya Mikhaílovna stared at both of them in considerable surprise, and invited Lezhnyóff to be seated.

"You wished to see me," he began, "about the survey?"

"Yes, about the survey; but I wanted to see you anyway. For we are near neighbours, and almost related to each other."

"I am very much obliged to you," returned Lezhnyóff; "but, so far as the boundary-line is concerned, your manager and I have settled that matter definitely; I agree to all his propositions."

"I knew that."

"Only he told me that, without a personal interview with you, the papers could not be signed."

"Yes; I have established that rule. By the way, permit me to ask,—I believe all your peasants are on quit-rent, are they not?"

"Just so."

"And you are taking charge of the boundary-line matter yourself? That is praiseworthy."

Lezhnyóff made no reply for a moment.

"So I have presented myself for the personal interview," he said.

Dárya Mikhaílovna laughed.

"I see that you have presented yourself. You say that in a tone as though. . . You must have been extremely unwilling to come to me."

"I go nowhere," returned Lezhnyóff, phlegmatically.

"Nowhere? But you go to Alexandra Pávlovna's?"

" I have known her brother for a long time."

" Her brother! However, I force no one. . . .
But, pardon me, Mikhaílo Mikhaílitch, I am
older than you and may lecture you a little; what
makes you avoid society like a solitary wolf? Or
is it my house, in particular, that does not please
you? Am I displeasing to you?"

" I do not know you, Dárya Mikhaílovna, and
therefore you cannot be displeasing to me. Your
house is very fine; but I will confess to you
frankly that I do not like to stand on ceremony,
and I do not possess a decent dress-suit; I have
no gloves; and, moreover, I do not belong to
your circle in society."

" By birth, by education, you do belong to it,
Mikhaílo Mikhaílitch!—*vous êtes des nôtres.*"

" Set birth and education aside, Dárya Mikhaílovna! That is not the point. . ."

" A man should live with men, Mikhaílo
Mikhaílitch! What pleasure do you find in sitting, like Diogenes, in a cask?"

" In the first place, he was very comfortable
there; and, in the second place, how do you know
that I do not live with men?"

Dárya Mikhaílovna bit her lip.

" That is another matter. All that is left for
me to do is to regret that I was not considered
worthy to fall into the number of people with
whom you consort."

" Monsieur Lezhnyóff," interposed Rúdin,

"appears to exaggerate a very laudable sentiment—love of liberty."

Lezhnyóff made no reply, and merely glanced
at Rúdin. A brief pause ensued.

"So then, madam," began Lezhnyóff, rising,
"I may regard our affair as completed, and tell
your manager to send me the documents."

"You may . . . although, I must confess, you
are so unamiable . . . that I ought to refuse."

"But, you see, this survey is far more advantageous for you than for me."

Dárya Mikhaílovna shrugged her shoulders.

"You are not willing even to breakfast with
me?" she asked.

"I thank you sincerely. I never breakfast, and
I am in haste to get home."

Dárya Mikhaílovna rose.

"I will not detain you," she said, as she
walked to the window. "I dare not detain you."

Lezhnyóff began to take leave.

"Good-bye, Monsieur Lezhnyóff! Pardon
me for having disturbed you."

"Not at all, I assure you," returned Lezhnyóff, and withdrew.

"What do you think of that?" inquired Dárya Mikhaílovna of Rúdin. "I had heard that
he was an eccentric person, but this passes all
bounds."

"He is suffering from the same malady as
Pigásoff," said Rúdin— "from a desire to be

original. Pigásoff feigns to be a Mephisto-
pheles, this one a cynic. In all this there is
much egotism, much self-conceit, and little truth,
little love. You see, there is a calculation, of a
sort, in this also; a man has donned a mask of indifference and laziness, saying to himself: 'Perchance, some one will think, "There's that man
—how many talents he has wasted!"' But when
you come to look more closely, he possesses no
talents at all!"

"*Et de deux!*" said Dárya Mikhaílovna.
"You are a terrible man at definitions. One cannot hide from you."

"Do you think so?" ... said Rúdin. "However," he went on, "to tell the truth, I ought not
to talk about Lezhnyóff; I loved him,—loved
him as a friend,—but later on, in consequence of
various misunderstandings. . ."

"You quarrelled?"

"No. But we parted—and parted, apparently, forever."

"Exactly so. I noticed that during the whole
of his visit you did not seem to be quite yourself. . . But I am very grateful to you for this
morning. I have passed the time in an extremely
agreeable manner. But I must not abuse your
kindness. I will release you until breakfast, and
will go and attend to business myself. My secretary—you have seen him—*Constantin, c'est lui
qui est mon secrétaire*—must be already waiting

for me. I recommend him to your favour; he
is a very fine, very obliging young man, and is
in perfect raptures over you. Farewell for a
while, *cher* Dmítry Nikoláitch! How grateful
I am to the Baron for having introduced you to
me!" And Dárya Mikhaílovna offered her hand
to Rúdin. He first pressed it, then raised it to
his lips, and went out into the music-room, and
from the music-room to the verandah. On the
verandah he encountered Natálya.

V

DÁRYA MIKHAÍLOVNA's daughter, Natálya
Alexyéevna, might not strike one as pleasing at
first sight. She had not yet completed her
growth, was thin and swarthy, and held herself
in rather a stooping attitude. But her features
were beautiful and regular, although too large
for a girl of seventeen. Especially fine was her
pure and smooth forehead above slender brows
which seemed to have been broken apart in the
middle. She spoke little, but listened and looked
attentively, almost insistently, as though she
wished to account to herself for everything.
She often remained motionless, with drooping
hands, and meditated; on her countenance, at
such times, the inward travail of thought was
expressed. A barely perceptible smile made its
appearance of a sudden on her lips and vanished; her large, dark eyes were slowly raised. . . .
" *Qu'avez-vous?* " Mlle. Boncourt would ask
her, and would begin to chide her, saying that
it was not proper for a young girl to meditate
and assume an air of abstraction. But Natálya was not abstracted; on the contrary, she
studied diligently; she read and worked will-

75

ingly. She felt deeply and strongly, but secretly; even in her childhood she had rarely cried, and now she rarely even sighed, and only turned slightly pale when anything annoyed her. Her mother considered her a good-tempered, sensible young girl, called her, jestingly, "*Mon honnête homme de fille,*" but entertained none too high an opinion as to her mental abilities. "My Natásha, fortunately, is cold," she was wont to say; "she does not take after me . . so much the better. She will be happy." Dárya Mikhaílovna was in error. However, very few mothers understand their daughters. Natálya loved Dárya Mikhaílovna, and did not entirely trust her.

"Thou hast nothing to hide from me," Dárya Mikhaílovna once said to her, "otherwise thou wouldst hide it; apparently, thou thinkest for thyself. . . ."

Natálya looked her mother in the eye, and said to herself: "Why should n't one think for herself?"

When Rúdin met her on the verandah she had gone into the house, in company with Mlle. Boncourt, to put on her hat and go into the garden. Her morning occupations were already finished. They had ceased to treat Natálya like a little girl; for a long time past Mlle. Boncourt had not given her any lessons in mythology and geography, but Natálya was bound to read his-

torical books and other edifying works every
morning in her presence. Dárya Mikhaílovna
selected them, apparently in consonance with a
special system of her own. As a matter of fact,
she simply handed over to Natálya everything
which the French bookseller in Petersburg sent
her, with the exception, of course, of the novels
of Dumas fils, and Co. These novels Dárya
Mikhaílovna read herself. Mlle. Boncourt
glared through her spectacles with particular
severity and acidity when Natálya was perusing
historical books. According to the ideas of the
old Frenchwoman, all history was filled with un-
permissible things, although she herself, for some
reason or other, was acquainted with Cambyses
alone among the great men of antiquity; and,
among those of recent times, only with Louis
XIV and Napoleon, whom she could not abide.
But Natálya also read books whose very existence Mlle. Boncourt did not suspect: she knew
the whole of Púshkin by heart. . . .

Natálya blushed slightly on encountering Rúdin.

" Are you going for a stroll? " he asked her.

" Yes. We are going into the garden."

" May I go with you? "

Natálya glanced at Mlle. Boncourt.

" *Mais certainement, monsieur, avec plaisir,*"
the old spinster made haste to say.

Rúdin took his hat and went with them.

At first Natálya felt awkward at walking by
the side of Rúdin on one path; afterwards she
was more at her ease.   He began to question her
with regard to her occupations, and as to how she
liked the country.   She replied, not without
timidity, but without that hurried bashfulness
which is frequently passed off and mistaken for
modesty.   Her heart beat fast.

"You do not get bored in the country?" inquired Rúdin, taking her in with a sidelong
glance.

"How can one be bored in the country?   I am
very glad that we are here.   I am very happy
here."

"You are happy! . . . That is a great word.
However, that is comprehensible: you are
young."

Rúdin uttered this last word in a rather strange
manner, not precisely as though he envied Natásha, nor yet precisely as though he pitied her.

"Yes! Youth!" he added.   "The whole aim
of science is consciously to attain to that which
is bestowed gratuitously."

Natálya gazed attentively at Rúdin; she did
not understand him.

"I have spent this whole morning conversing
with your mother," he went on; "she is a remarkable woman.   I understand why all our
poets have prized her friendship.   And are you
fond of poetry?" he added, after a brief silence.

"He is putting me through an examination," thought Natálya, and said: "Yes, I am very fond of it."

"Poetry is the language of the gods. I myself love verses. But there is no poetry in ordinary verses; it is disseminated everywhere, it is all around us. . . . . Look at these trees, at this sky—from every direction emanate life and beauty; and where life and beauty are, there poetry is also."

"Let us sit down here, on this bench," he continued. "That's right. Somehow or other, it seems to me that when you shall have got accustomed to me" (and he looked into her face with a smile), "we shall become friends. What do you think?"

"He is treating me like a little girl," thought Natálya again, and, not knowing what to say, she asked him whether he intended to remain long in the country.

"All the summer, the autumn, and perhaps the winter also. As you know, I am far from being a wealthy man; my affairs are in disorder, and, moreover, I am tired of roaming about from place to place. It is time to rest."

Natálya was surprised.

"Is it possible that you think it is time for you to rest?" she asked him timidly.

Rúdin turned his face toward Natálya.

"What do you mean by that?"

"I mean to say," she returned, with some confusion, "that others may rest; but you . . . you ought to toil, to try to be of use. Who, if not you. . . ."

"I thank you for your flattering opinion," Rúdin interrupted her. "It is easy to say . . . . 'to be of use.'" (He passed his hand across his face.) "To be of use!" he repeated. "Even if I bore within me a firm conviction how I might be of use,—even if I had faith in my powers,—where am I to find sincere, sympathetic souls?"

And Rúdin waved his hand in so hopeless a manner, and drooped his head so sorrowfully, that Natálya involuntarily asked herself:—Was it really his rapturous speeches, breathing forth hope, which she had listened to on the preceding evening?

"But no," he added, suddenly shaking his long mane; "this is nonsense, and you are right. I thank you, Natálya Alexyéevna, I thank you sincerely." (Natálya decidedly did not know what he was thanking her for.) "That one word of yours has recalled me to my duty, has pointed out to me my path. . . . . Yes, I must act. I must not hide my talent, if I possess it; I must not waste my powers in empty chatter, useless chatter, in mere words. . . ."

And his words flowed forth in a stream. He talked very finely, fervently, convincingly, about the disgrace of cowardice and laziness, about the indispensability of doing deeds. He showered reproaches on himself, demonstrated that to argue beforehand about what one wants to do is as injurious as to stick a pin into a fruit overflowing with juice,—that this was only a vain waste of powers and of juices. He declared that there is no noble thought which does not win sympathy, that only those people remain misunderstood who either do not know themselves what they wish or are not worth understanding. He talked for a long time, and wound up by thanking Natálya Alexyéevna once more, and quite unexpectedly pressed her hand, saying: "You are a very beautiful, noble being!"

This liberty startled Mlle. Boncourt, who, in spite of her forty years' residence in Russia, understood Russian with difficulty, and merely admired the beautiful swiftness and fluency of the language in Rúdin's mouth. However, in her eyes he was something in the nature of a virtuoso or an artist; and from that sort of people, according to her ideas, it was impossible to demand the observance of decorum.

She rose, and, abruptly adjusting her gown, announced to Natálya that it was time to go home, that *Monsieur Volinsoff* (that was what she called Volýntzeff) was intending to come for breakfast.

" Yes, and there he is! " she added, glancing down one of the avenues which led to the house.

In fact, Volýntzeff made his appearance a short distance away.

He approached with an undecided gait, bowed to them all while still at a distance, and, addressing Natálya with a pained expression on his face, he said:

" Ah! Are you taking a stroll? "

" Yes," replied Natásha, " we are just going home."

" Ah! " ejaculated Volýntzeff. " Well, let us start."

And they all set off for the house.

" How is your sister's health? " Rúdin asked Volýntzeff, in a rather peculiarly caressing voice. He had been very amiable to him on the preceding evening also.

" I am obliged to you. She is well. Perhaps she will come hither to-day. . . . . I think you were discussing something when I came up."

" Yes. Natálya Alexyéevna and I had been having a chat. She said a word to me which has had a powerful effect upon me." . . .

Volýntzeff did not inquire what the word was, and all returned, in profound silence, to the house of Dárya Mikhaílovna.

Before dinner the salon was formed again. But Pigásoff did not come. Rúdin did not appear to advantage; he kept making Pandalévsky play selections from Beethoven. Volýntzeff maintained silence and stared at the floor. Natálya clung persistently to her mother's side, now immersed in thought, now devoting herself to her work. Basístoff never took his eyes from Rúdin, in the momentary expectation that the latter would say something clever. Three hours passed thus, rather monotonously. Alexándra Pávlovna did not come to dinner, and Volýntzeff, as soon as they rose from table, immediately ordered his calash to be brought round, and slipped away without taking leave of any one.

He felt heavy at heart. He had long loved Natálya, and was always on the verge of making her an offer of marriage. . . . . She favoured him,—but her heart remained calm; he perceived that clearly. He had no hope of inspiring in her a more tender sentiment, and was only awaiting the moment when she should become thoroughly accustomed to him—should draw nearer to him. What could have perturbed him? What change had he observed during those two days? Natálya had treated him exactly as heretofore. . . . .

Whether his soul was choked with the thought that, perhaps, he did not understand Natálya's character at all, that she was more alien to him than he had imagined, whether jealousy had awakened within him, whether he felt a dim fore-

RÚDIN

boding of something evil, ... at all events, he suffered, argue with himself as he might.

When he entered his sister's house, Lezhnyóff was sitting with her.

" What made you come home so early? " asked Alexándra Pávlovna.

" Because—I was bored."

" Is Rúdin there? "

" Yes."

Volýntzeff flung aside his cap and sat down. Alexándra Pávlovna turned to him with vivacity:

" Please, Seryózha, help me to convince this obstinate man " (she pointed at Lezhnyóff) " that Rúdin is remarkably clever and eloquent."

Volýntzeff muttered something.

" Why, I'm not disputing your statement in the least," began Lezhnyóff. " I have no doubt whatever as to Mr. Rúdin's cleverness and eloquence; all I say is that I do not like him."

" And do you mean to say that you have seen him? " asked Volýntzeff.

" I saw him this morning at Dárya Mikhaílovna's. You see, he is now her grand vizier. The time will come when she will part with him,— Pandalévsky is the only one with whom she will not part,—but he is reigning at present. Saw him? Of course I did! There he sat, and she pointed me out to him. ' Look, my dear sir,' says she, ' see what eccentric fellows we grow here.' I'm not a stud-horse—I'm not accus-

84

tomed to be trotted out on show, so I took and
marched off."

" But why wast thou at her house? "

" About the survey of the boundary-line; but
that 's nonsense. She simply wanted to have a
look at my physiognomy. She 's a fine lady—
every one knows what that means! "

" His superiority offends you. That 's what 's
the matter," said Alexándra Pávlovna, with ar-
dour. " That is what you cannot pardon him.
But I am convinced that, in addition to his mind,
he must also have an excellent heart. Just look
at his eyes when he . . . ."

" ' Of lofty uprightness he prates,' " . . . . interposed Lezhnyóff.

" You will provoke me, and I shall begin to
cry. I regret, from my soul, that I did not go
to Dárya Mikhaílovna's, and remained here with
you. You are not worthy of it. Do stop teasing
me," she added, in a plaintive voice. " You had
better tell me about his youth."

" About Rúdin's youth? "

" Yes, certainly. You know, you told me that
you knew him well, and had been acquainted with
him for a long time."

Lezhnyóff rose and paced the room.

" Yes," he began; " I do know him well. You
want me to tell you about his youth? Very well.
He was born in T . . . ., of poor parents of the
landed gentry class. His father soon died. He
was left alone with his mother. She was an ex-

tremely kind-hearted woman, and was perfectly infatuated with him; she subsisted on nothing but dried oatmeal, and used all the little money she possessed on him. He received his education in Moscow, first at the expense of some uncle or other, and later on, when he was grown and got his feathers, at the expense of a certain wealthy petty prince with whom he had sniffed up some sort of understanding . . . . well, pardon me, I will not do it again! . . . . with whom he had made friends. Then he entered the university. I knew him at the university, and became very intimate with him. Concerning our manner of life together at that epoch I will speak with you at some future time. At present I cannot. Then he went abroad. . . . ."

Lezhnyóff continued to stride up and down the room; Alexándra Pávlovna followed him with her eyes.

" From abroad," he went on, " Rúdin wrote to his mother very rarely, and never visited her but once, for about ten days. . . . . The old woman died in his absence—in the arms of strangers; but until the very moment of her death she never took her eyes from his portrait. I used to call on her when I lived in T . . . . . She was a good woman, and extremely hospitable. She loved her Mítya passionately. Gentlemen of the Petchórin [1]

---

[1] The hero of Lérmontoff's famous novel: "A Hero of Our Times."—TRANSLATOR.

school will tell you that we always love those
who themselves possess very little capacity for
loving; but it seems to *me* that all mothers love
their children, especially those who are absent.
Then I met Rúdin abroad. There a gentlewoman had tacked herself on to him—one of our
Russian women, a sort of blue-stocking, no longer
either young or pretty, as is fitting for a blue-
stocking. He bothered about with her for quite
a long time, and then abandoned her, or, no . . . .
what am I saying? . . . . pardon me!—she abandoned him. And then I dropped him. That is
all."

Lezhnyóff relapsed into silence, passed his
hand across his brow, and sank into an arm-chair
as though fatigued.

"Do you know what, Mikhaílo Mikhaílitch?"
began Alexándra Pávlovna. "I perceive that
you are a malicious man; really, you are no better than Pigásoff. I am convinced that everything you have said is true, that you have invented
nothing, and yet in what an unfavourable light
you have represented it all! That poor old
woman, her devotion, her lonely death! That
lady! . . . . What is the use of all that? . . . .
Do you know that it is possible to depict the life
of the best of men in such colours, and, without
adding anything, observe, that any one would be
horrified! Really, that also is calumny, in its
way."

Lezhnyóff rose, and again began to pace the room.

"I had not the slightest desire to make you feel horrified, Alexándra Pávlovna," he said at last. "I am not a calumniator. However," he added, after a little reflection, "there really is a certain amount of truth in what you say. I have not calumniated Rúdin; but—who knows? —perhaps he has succeeded in effecting a change in himself since then; perhaps I have been unjust toward him."

"Ah! There, you see! . . . . So now promise me that you will renew your acquaintance with him, that you will learn to know him well, and then you shall tell me your definitive opinion of him."

"So be it. . . . But why are you silent, Sergyéi Pávlitch?"

Volýntzeff started and raised his head, as though he had been awakened from sleep.

"What is there for me to say? I do not know him. And, besides, my head aches to-day."

"Thou really art rather pale to-day," remarked Alexándra Pávlovna; "art thou well?"

"My head aches," repeated Volýntzeff, and left the room.

Alexándra Pávlovna and Lezhnyóff gazed after him and exchanged a glance, but said nothing to each other. What was going on in Volýntzeff's heart was no secret either to him or to her.

VI

More than two months elapsed. During the whole course of that time Rúdin hardly left Dárya Mikhaílovna's house. She could not get along without him. It had become a necessity for her to talk to him about herself, to listen to his arguments. One day he made an attempt to depart, on the pretext that all his money was exhausted. She gave him five hundred rubles. He also borrowed a couple of hundred rubles from Volýntzeff. Pigásoff called upon Dárya Mikhaílovna much more rarely than before. Rúdin overwhelmed him with his presence. However, Pigásoff was not the only one to experience this sense of being overwhelmed.

" I don't like that clever fellow," he was wont to say; " he expresses himself unnaturally—for all the world like a personage in a Russian novel. He will say ' I,' and pause with emotion. . . . . ' I,' says he, ' I . . . .' He always uses such long words. If you sneeze, he will immediately begin to demonstrate to you precisely why you sneezed and why you did not cough. . . . . If he praises you, it 's exactly as though he were promoting you in rank. . . . . He will begin to revile him-

89

self, and will besmear himself with mud. Well, you think to yourself, now he will not look at God's daylight. Not a bit of it; he will even get jolly, as though he had been treating himself to bitter vodka."

Pandalévsky was afraid of Rúdin, and courted him cautiously. Volýntzeff found himself on strange terms with him. Rúdin called him a knight, and lauded him to his face and behind his back; but Volýntzeff could not bring himself to like Rúdin, and on every occasion experienced an involuntary impatience and vexation when the latter undertook, in his presence, to discuss his merits. " Is n't he laughing at me? " he thought, and his heart stirred within him with animosity. Volýntzeff tried to master his feelings, but he was jealous of him and Natálya. And Rúdin himself, although he always greeted Volýntzeff noisily, although he called him a knight and borrowed money from him, could hardly be said to be well disposed toward him. It would be difficult to define precisely what these two men felt when, as they shook each other's hands in friendly wise, they gazed into each other's eyes. . . . .

Basístoff continued to worship at Rúdin's shrine, and to catch every word of his on the fly. Rúdin paid very little attention to him. It happened, once, that he spent a whole morning with him, discussed with him the most important world-questions and -problems, and aroused in him the most lively enthusiasm; but then he dropped him. . . . . It was obvious that in words only did he seek pure and devoted souls. With Lezhnyóff, who had begun to frequent Dárya Mikhaílovna's house, Rúdin did not even enter into argument, and seemed to shun him. Lezhnyóff also treated him coldly, and had not yet pronounced a definitive opinion about him, which greatly disturbed Alexándra Pávlovna. She bowed down before Rúdin; but she also trusted Lezhnyóff. Every one in Dárya Mikhaílovna's house submitted to Rúdin's whims; his slightest wish was fulfilled. The order of the daily occupations depended upon him. Not a single *partie de plaisir* was made up without him. However, he was not very fond of all sorts of sudden trips and projects, and took part in them as adults take part in children's games, with affable and somewhat bored benevolence. On the other hand, he entered into everything: he discussed with Dárya Mikhaílovna the arrangements about the estate, the rearing of children, management of property, business affairs in general; he listened to her suggestions, was not annoyed even by details, proposed reforms and innovations. Dárya Mikhaílovna went into raptures over them,—in words,—and there it ended. In the matter of managing her estate she stuck to the counsels of her steward, an elderly, one-eyed little Russian, a good-natured and crafty knave. " Old things are fat, young things are lean," he was wont to say, grinning composedly, and blinking his single eye.

With the exception of Dárya Mikhaílovna herself, Rúdin chatted with no one so often or so long as with Natálya. He gave her books on the sly, confided to her his plans, read her the first pages of his projected articles and works. The sense of them frequently remained inaccessible to Natálya. But Rúdin did not appear to trouble himself much about her understanding him, so long as she listened to him. His intimacy with Natálya was not quite to the taste of Dárya Mikhaílovna. But, she thought, let her chatter with him in the country. She amuses him, like a little girl. There's no great harm in it, and she will grow cleverer. . . . . In Petersburg I will change all that. . . .

Dárya Mikhaílovna was mistaken. Natálya did not prattle like a little girl with Rúdin; she eagerly drank in his speeches; she tried to penetrate their meaning; she submitted all her thoughts, her doubts, to his judgment: he was her mentor, her guide. So far, only her head was seething . . . . but a young head does not seethe long alone. What sweet moments did Natálya live through when, in the park on a bench, in the light, transparent shadows of an ash-tree, Rúdin would begin to read aloud to her Goethe's

" Faust," Hoffmann, or the Letters of Bettina, or Novalis, pausing constantly and explaining that which seemed obscure to her! She spoke German badly, like nearly all of our young ladies, but understood it well, and Rúdin was completely immersed in German poetry, in the German romantic and philosophical world, and drew her after him into those interdicted regions. Novel, very beautiful, did they lie outspread before her attentive gaze; from the pages of the book which Rúdin held in his hands wondrous images, new, brilliant thoughts, fairly poured forth in tinkling streams into her soul and into her heart, agitated by the noble joy of grand sensations; the sacred spark of ecstasy quietly flashed up and grew into a blaze. . . .

" Tell me, Dmítry Nikoláitch," she began one day, as she sat at the window over her embroidery-frame; " you will go to Petersburg for the winter, will you not? "

" I do not know," replied Rúdin, dropping upon his knees the book whose pages he was turning over. " If I collect the means, I shall go."

He spoke languidly; he felt weary, and had remained indolent since the morning.

" It seems to me that you cannot fail to find the means? "

Rúdin shook his head.

" So it seems to you! "

And he glanced significantly aside.

RÚDIN

Natálya was on the point of saying something, but restrained herself.

"Look," began Rúdin, and pointed with his hand out of the window; "you see that apple-tree? It has broken down with the weight and multitude of its own fruit. It is the true emblem of genius." . . . .

"It broke because it had no support," replied Natálya.

"I understand you, Natálya Alexyéevna; but it is not so easy for a man to find that support."

"It seems to me that the sympathy of others . . . . in any case, isolation . . . ."

Natálya became slightly entangled, and blushed.

"And what shall you do in the country during the winter?" she hastily added.

"What shall I do? I shall complete my great article, you know, about the tragic in life and in art,—I narrated to you the plan of it day before yesterday,—and I shall send it to you."

"And you will print it?"

"No."

"Why not? For whom shall you toil?"

"How about toiling for you?"

Natálya dropped her eyes.

"That is beyond me, Dmítry Nikoláitch!"

"Permit me to ask, what is the article about?" modestly inquired Basístoff, who was sitting at a distance.

" About the tragic in life and in art," repeated Rúdin. " And Mr. Basístoff here shall read it also. However, I have not quite got the fundamental thought into shape yet. I have not yet rendered sufficiently clear to myself the tragic significance of love."

Rúdin gladly and frequently talked of love. At first, at the word " love " Mlle. Boncourt started and pricked up her ears, like an aged regimental horse who hears a bugle, but later on she got used to it, and only pursed up her lips and took snuff at intervals.

" It seems to me," remarked Natálya, timidly, " that the tragic thing about love is unhappy love."

" Not at all," returned Rúdin; " that is, rather, the comic side of love. . . . . That question must be posed in an entirely different manner . . . . one must go down deeper. . . . . Love! " he continued, " everything about it is a mystery: how it comes, how it develops, how it disappears. Now it makes its appearance suddenly, indubitably, joyous as the day; again it smoulders like fire under the ashes, and makes its way like a flame in the soul, when everything is already destroyed; now it creeps into the heart, like a serpent; again, it suddenly slips out of it. . . . . Yes, yes; it is a weighty question. Yes, and who loves in our day, who dares to love? "

And Rúdin relapsed into meditation.

"Why have we not seen Sergyéi Pávlitch this long time?" he suddenly asked.

Natálya flushed up, and bent her head over her embroidery-frame.

"I do not know," she whispered.

"What an extremely fine and noble man he is!" remarked Rúdin, rising. "He is one of the very best specimens of the genuine Russian nobleman." . . . .

Mlle. Boncourt gazed at him askance with her little French eyes.

Rúdin strolled about the room.

"Have you observed," he asked, making a sharp turn on his heels, "that on the oak—and the oak is a sturdy tree—the old leaves fall off only when the young ones begin to force their way through?"

"Yes," replied Natálya, slowly; "I have observed it."

"Exactly the same thing takes place with the old love in a strong heart; it is already dead, but it still hangs on; only another, a new love, can dislodge it."

Natálya made no reply.

"What does this mean?" she thought.

Rúdin stood still, shook his hair, and withdrew.

And Natálya went to her own room. For a long time she sat in perplexity on her little bed; for a long time she meditated on Rúdin's last words, and suddenly clasped her hands and fell to weeping. What she was weeping about God only knows. She did not know herself why her tears had flowed forth so suddenly. She wiped them away, but they streamed down afresh, like water from a spring which has long been accumulating.

On that same day a conversation about Rúdin took place, also, between Alexándra Pávlovna and Lezhnyóff. At first he maintained an obstinate silence, but she was determined to obtain a categorical answer.

" I see," she said, " that you do not like Dmítry Nikoláitch any more than before. I have deliberately refrained from interrogating you hitherto; but now you have had an opportunity to convince yourself whether any change has taken place in him, and I wish to know why you do not like him."

" Very well," retorted Lezhnyóff, with his wonted coolness; " if you cannot endure the present state of things; only, see here, you must not get angry." . . .

" Come, begin, begin."

" And you must let me say my say to the end."

" Very well, very well; begin."

" Well, then, ma'am," began Lezhnyóff, sinking down slowly on the divan. " I must inform you that I really do not like Rúdin. He is a clever man." . . .

" I should think so! "

" He is a strikingly clever man, although, in reality, frivolous." . . .

" It is easy to say that! "

" Although, in reality, frivolous," repeated Lezhnyóff; " but that's no harm; we are all frivolous people. I do not even blame him for being a despot in soul, lazy, not very well informed." . . .

Alexándra Pávlovna clasped her hands.

" Not very well informed! Rúdin! " she exclaimed.

" Not very well informed," repeated Lezhnyóff, in precisely the same tone as before; " he is fond of living at the expense of others, he is playing a part, and so forth . . . . all that is in the common order of things. But the ugly thing about it is that he is as cold as ice."

" He, that fiery spirit, cold! " interrupted Alexándra Pávlovna.

" Yes, cold as ice, and he knows it and pretends to be fiery. The bad part of it is," continued Lezhnyóff, gradually becoming animated, " that he is playing a dangerous game,—not dangerous for himself, of course; he would not stake a kopék or a hair on a card himself, but others stake their souls." . . .

" Of whom—of what are you talking? I do not understand you," said Alexándra Pávlovna.

" The bad point is that he is not honest; for

he is a clever man. He must know the worth of his own words; but he utters them as though they cost him something. He is eloquent, there is no disputing that; only his eloquence is not Russian. Yes, and, in conclusion, it is pardonable for a youth to talk eloquently, but at his age it is disgraceful to take pleasure in the sound of his own speeches. It is disgraceful to show off!"

"It seems to me, Mikhaílo Mikhaílitch, that for the hearer it makes no difference whether one shows off or not. . . ."

"Pardon me, Alexándra Pávlovna, it does make a difference. One person will say a word to me and it will pierce me through and through; another person will say the same word, or one even more eloquent, and I will not care a jot about it. Why is it thus?"

"That is to say, *you* will not care a jot," interrupted Alexándra Pávlovna.

"Yes, I will not care a jot," retorted Lezhnyóff. "I will not even prick up my ears, although, perhaps, I do possess large ears. The fact is that Rúdin's words remain mere words, and they never will become deeds; and, in the meanwhile, those same words may agitate, may ruin a young heart."

"But of whom—of whom are you speaking, Mikhaílo Mikhaílitch?"

Lezhnyóff paused.

"You wish to know of whom I am speaking? Of Natálya Alexyéevna."

Alexándra Pávlovna was disturbed for a moment, but immediately laughed.

"Good gracious!" she began, "what strange ideas you always have! Natálya is still a child; and, after all, if there should be anything in it, can you possibly suppose that Dárya Mikhaílovna . . . ."

"Dárya Mikhaílovna, in the first place, is an egoist, and lives for herself; and, in the second place, she is so confident of her skill in rearing children that it would never enter her head to feel uneasy about them. Fie! How can that be! One moment, one majestic glance, and all will be reduced to servile obedience. That's the idea of that lady, who imagines that she is a female Mæcenas, and a clever person, and God knows what besides; while, as a matter of fact, she is nothing but a horrid, worldly old woman. And Natálya is not a baby; believe me, she meditates more frequently and more profoundly than you and I do. And she—that honest, passionate, and fiery nature—must needs run up against such an actor, such a flirt! But that is the way things go."

"A flirt! Is it he that you are calling a flirt?"

"Of course it is he. . . . . Come, now, tell me yourself, Alexándra Pávlovna, what sort of part is he playing at Dárya Mikhaílovna's? To be an idol, an oracle in a house, to meddle with the arrangements, in the family scandals and gossip—is that worthy of a man?"

Alexándra Pávlovna gazed into Lezhnyóff's face with amazement.

"I do not recognise you, Mikhaílo Mikhaílitch," she said. "You have grown crimson; you are agitated. Really, there must be something else concealed under this." . . . .

"Well, and so there is! Just tell a woman something according to your conviction, and she will not rest easy until she devises some petty, irrelevant cause or other which makes you talk in precisely that way and not otherwise."

Alexándra Pávlovna waxed angry.

"Bravo, Monsieur Lezhnyóff! You are beginning to attack women to match Mr. Pigásoff; but, say what you please, however penetrating you may be, all the same it is difficult for me to believe that you can have understood everybody and everything in so brief a space of time. It seems to me that you are mistaken. According to you, Rúdin is a sort of Tartuffe."

"The point is that he is not even Tartuffe. Tartuffe at least knew what he was aiming at; but that fellow, with all his cleverness . . . ."

"What of him? What of him? Finish your sentence, you unjust, hateful man!"

Lezhnyóff rose.

"Listen, Alexándra Pávlovna," he began; "it is you who are unjust. It is not I. You are

vexed with me for my harsh judgment of Rúdin;
I have a right to speak sharply about him. It is
possible that I have purchased that right at anything but a small cost. I know him well; we lived
together for a long time. Remember that I
promised to narrate to you some time the story of
our life in Moscow. Evidently it must be done
now. But will you have the patience to hear me
out?"

"Speak, speak!"

"Well, at your service."

Lezhnyóff began to pace the room with deliberate strides, halting from time to time and
bending his head forward.

"Perhaps you know," he began, "and perhaps
you do not know, that I was early left an orphan,
and already in my seventeenth year I had no
older person in authority over me. I lived in my
aunt's house in Moscow, and did what I pleased.
I was rather a frivolous and selfish youngster,
was fond of showing off and of bragging. On
entering the university, I behaved like a school-
boy, and soon got into a row. I will not tell you
about that; it is not worth while. I lied, and lied
in a pretty odious way. . . . . The matter was
brought to light; I was convicted and disgraced.
. . . . I lost my self-control, and cried like a
child. This took place in the rooms of one of my
acquaintances, in the presence of many comrades.
All began to laugh loudly at me—all, with the

exception of one student, who, take note, had
been more indignant at me than the rest so long
as I was stubborn and would not confess my lie.
Whether he felt sorry for me, or for what reason,
at all events he put his arm in mine and led me to
his own quarters."

"That was Rúdin?" asked Alexándra Pávlovna.

"No; it was not Rúdin. . . . . It was a man;
he is dead now . . . . it was a remarkable man.
His name was Pokórsky. I am not able to describe him in a few words, but if one once begins
to talk about him he does not care to talk about
any one else. Pokórsky lived in a small, low-
ceiled chamber, in the upper story of a tiny, ancient wooden house. He was very poor, and eked
out his slender means, after a fashion, by giving
lessons. There were times when he could not
treat a guest even to a cup of tea, and his only
couch was so broken down that it resembled a
boat. But, in spite of these inconveniences, a
great number of persons visited him. Every one
loved him; he drew hearts to him. You will not
believe how sweet and merry it was to sit in his
poverty-stricken little chamber. At his quarters
I made acquaintance with Rúdin. He had already dropped his petty prince."

"What was there so peculiar about that Pokórsky?" asked Alexándra Pávlovna.

"How shall I explain it to you? Poetry and

truth—those were what attracted every one to
him. Though possessed of a clear, broad mind,
he was as amiable and amusing as a child. To this
day, the sound of his limpid laughter rings in my
ears; and, at the same time, he

> " Blazed like the midnight taper
> Before the shrine of good . . .

That was the way one half-crazy and most charming poet of our circle expressed himself about
him."

" But how did he talk? " Alexándra Pávlovna
put another question.

" He talked well when he was in the right
mood, but not astonishingly. Even then, Rúdin
was twenty times more eloquent than he."

Lezhnyóff halted and folded his arms.

" Pokórsky and Rúdin did not resemble each
other. There was a great deal more brilliancy
and crash about Rúdin, and, if you like, more
enthusiasm. He appeared to be far more gifted
than Pokórsky, but, as a matter of fact, he was
a wretched creature in comparison with him. Rúdin could develop any idea in a superior manner;
he argued in a masterly way, but his ideas did not
have their birth in his own head; he took them
from others, especially from Pokórsky. In aspect, Pokórsky was quiet and gentle, even weak,
was madly fond of women and of going on

sprees, and allowed no one to affront him. Rúdin appeared to be full of fire, boldness, life: but in his soul he was cold, and almost timid, until his self-love was wounded; then he became raving mad. He tried in every way to conquer people for himself, but he conquered them in the name of general principles and ideas, and really exercised a powerful influence on many. No one loved him, it is true; I was the only one, perhaps, who became attached to him. They endured his yoke. . . . All surrendered themselves to Pokórsky of their own accord. On the other hand, Rúdin never refused to talk and argue with the first person who came to hand. . . . . He had not read any too many books, but, at all events, many more than Pokórsky had, and than all the rest of us had; he had, in addition, a systematic mind, a vast memory, and you know that that takes effect on young people. 'Hey there, give me deductions, sum totals, no matter if they are incorrect, only give me totals!' A thoroughly conscientious man is not suited to that. Try to tell young people that you cannot give them the whole truth, because you yourself are not in possession of it, and the young people will not even listen to you. . . . . But neither can you deceive them. It is indispensable that you yourself should at least half believe that you are in possession of the truth. . . . . That is why Rúdin acted so powerfully on us fellows. You see, I just told you that he had read a little, but he had read philosophical books, and his head was so constructed that from what he had read he immediately extracted all the generalities, grasped the very root of the matter, and then traced straight, brilliant lines of thought from it in all directions, and threw open spiritual perspectives. Our circle then consisted, to speak the honest truth, of boys. Philosophy, art, science, life itself, were all mere words to us, if you like,—even illusory,—very beautiful, but scattered, isolated conceptions. We did not recognise any common bond between these conceptions, any common law of the universe. We felt none, although we talked about it in an obscure way, and endeavoured to form an idea of it. . . . . In listening to Rúdin, it seemed to us, for the first time, that we had grasped that common bond, that the curtain had at last been lifted. Let us admit that he did not utter his own ideas. What of that? Yet harmonious order was installed in all we knew, all the scattered facts suddenly became united, ranged themselves in order, waxed great before our eyes, like a building. Everything shone brightly, spirit breathed everywhere. . . . Nothing remained senseless, fortuitous; in everything an intelligent necessity and beauty were expressed, everything acquired a clear and, at the same time, mysterious significance; every separate phenomenon of life rang out in harmonious accord; and we ourselves, with a certain holy fear of adoration, with sweet quaking at the heart, felt ourselves to be living vessels of the eternal truth, its instruments, bound to something grand. . . . . You do not find all this ridiculous?"

"Not in the least!" replied Alexándra Pávlovna, slowly. "Why do you think so? I do not entirely comprehend you, but I do not find it ridiculous."

"Of course we have succeeded in gaining sense since those days," went on Lezhnyóff; "all that may now strike us as childish. . . . . But, I repeat it, we were then indebted to Rúdin for a great deal. Pokórsky was incomparably, indisputably above him; but he sometimes felt slothful, and held his peace. He was a nervous, sickly man; on the other hand, when he did unfold his wings—my God! whither did he not soar! Into the very depths and azure of heaven! But in Rúdin, in that handsome and stately young fellow, there was a lot of pettiness; he even indulged in gossip; he had a passion for meddling with everything, defining and explaining everything. His bustling activity never ceased . . . . a political nature, ma'am. I am speaking of him as I knew him then. But, unhappily, he has not changed. On the other hand, he has not altered his beliefs . . . . in thirty years! . . . . Not every one can say that of himself."

"Sit down," said Alexándra Pávlovna, "why

do you stalk back and forth in the room like a pendulum?"

"I feel better so," replied Lezhnyóff. "Well, ma'am, when I got into Pokórsky's set, I must inform you, Alexándra Pávlovna, I was completely regenerated: I became humble, I asked questions, I studied, I worshipped—in a word, it was exactly as though I had entered some temple or other. Yes; and, in fact, when I recall our meetings—well, by heavens! there was a great deal that was good, even touching, about them. Just imagine for yourself: five or six young fellows have gathered together; one tallow candle is burning, very bad tea is served, and with it ancient—very ancient—rusks; and you ought to have seen all our faces, you ought to have heard our speeches! In every man's eyes there is rapture, his cheeks flame, his heart beats, and we talk about God, about truth, about the future of mankind, about poetry. We sometimes talk nonsense, we wax enthusiastic over trifles; but where's the harm in that? . . . . Pokórsky sits, with his feet tucked up, with his pale cheek propped on his hand; but his eyes fairly flash. Rúdin stands in the middle of the room, and talks,—talks most beautifully,—precisely like the young Demosthenes before the roaring sea; the dishevelled poet, Subbótin, gives vent, from time to time, and as though in his sleep, to abrupt ex-

clamations; a student of forty, the son of the
German pastor Scheller, who bore among us the
reputation of a profound thinker, thanks to his
everlasting silence, which was never broken by
anything whatever, holds his peace somehow in a
peculiarly solemn way; even the jolly Shstchítoff,
the Aristophanes of our assemblies, is quiet and
merely grins; two or three novices are listening
with triumphant enjoyment. . . . . And the
night flies on softly and smoothly, as on wings.
And now the grey morning begins to appear
and we disperse, moved, cheerful, honest, sober
(liquor was not even mentioned among us then),
with a certain agreeable languor in the soul . . . .
and we even gaze at the stars in a confiding
sort of way, as though they had become nearer
and more comprehensible. . . . . Ekh! that was
a glorious time, and I am not willing to believe
that it was wasted. And it was not wasted—it
was not wasted, even for those whom life rendered commonplace later on. . . . . How many
times has it been my lot to encounter such men,
my former comrades! It seems as though a man
had become a perfect wild beast, but no sooner
do you mention Pokórsky's name in his presence
than all the remnants of nobility begin to stir
within him, just as though you had uncorked
a forgotten phial of perfume in a dark, dirty
room. . . . . "

Lezhnyóff ceased; his colourless face had become flushed.

" But why? When did you quarrel with Rúdin? " said Alexándra Pávlovna, gazing at Lezhnyóff in surprise.

" I did not quarrel with him, but I parted from him when I came to know him definitively abroad. But I might have quarrelled with him even in Moscow. He played me a nasty trick even then."

" What was it? "

" It was this: I . . . . how shall I express it to you? . . . . it does not suit my figure . . . . but I was always greatly inclined to fall in love."

" You? "

" Yes, I. It is strange, is it not? Nevertheless, so it is. . . . . Well, ma'am, so at that time I fell in love with a very charming young girl. . . . . But why do you look at me in that way? I might tell you a far more surprising thing about myself."

" What is that thing, permit me to ask? "

" Well, it was this sort of thing. In those Moscow days, I used to go to nocturnal rendezvous . . . . with whom do you suppose? . . . . with a young linden-tree at the end of my garden. I embraced its slender, shapely bole, and it seemed to me that I was embracing all nature, and my heart swelled and melted, as though, in actual fact, all nature were merged in it. . . . . That's the sort of fellow I used to be! . . . . But what of that? Perhaps you think that I did not write verses? I did, ma'am, and even composed a whole drama in imitation of ' Manfred.' Among the acting personages there was a spectre with blood on its breast,—and not its own blood either, observe, but the blood of mankind in general. . . . . Yes, ma'am; yes, ma'am; pray be not amazed. . . . . But I began to tell you about my love. I had made the acquaintance of a certain young girl. . . ."

" And you ceased to go to the tryst with the linden-tree? " asked Alexándra Pávlovna.

" I did. The girl was a very amiable and very pretty creature, with clear, merry little eyes and a ringing voice."

" You describe well," remarked Alexándra Pávlovna, with a smile.

" And you are a very severe critic," retorted Lezhnyóff. " Well, ma'am, this young girl lived with her old father. . . . . But I will not enter into details. I will merely tell you that the girl was, in reality, extremely amiable—she was forever pouring out three or four glasses of tea for you, when you had asked for only half a glass. . . . . On the third day after I had first met her I was already aglow, and on the seventh day I could contain myself no longer and made a clean breast of it all to Rúdin. It is impossible for a young man in love not to babble, and I confessed the whole thing to Rúdin. I was then completely under his influence, and that influence I will say, without circumlocution, was beneficial in many respects. He was the first one who did not scorn me, who rubbed the corners off me. I loved Pokórsky passionately, and felt a certain awe of his spiritual purity; but I stood nearer to Rúdin. On learning of my love, he went into indescribable raptures; he congratulated me, embraced me, and immediately set to work to instruct me, to explain to me the full importance of my new situation. I pricked up my ears. . . . . Well, you already know how he can talk. His words had a remarkable effect on me. I suddenly conceived an amazing respect for myself; I assumed a serious aspect, and ceased to laugh. I remember that I even began to walk more cautiously, as though I had in my bosom a vessel filled with precious liquid which I was afraid of spilling. . . . . I was very happy; the more so, as I was openly favoured. Rúdin expressed a desire to make the acquaintance of the object of my affections; and I myself almost insisted on introducing him."

"Well, I see—I see now what the point is," interrupted Alexándra Pávlovna. "Rúdin robbed you of the object of your affections, and you have not been able to forgive him for that to this day. . . . . I will wager that I am not mistaken."

"And you would lose your wager, Alexándra Pávlovna. You are mistaken. Rúdin did not rob me of the object of my affections, and he did not try to do so; but, nevertheless, he ruined my happiness,—although, judging the matter coolly, I am now ready to express my thanks to him for that. But at that time I nearly went crazy. Rúdin had not the slightest desire to injure me. On the contrary. But, as a consequence of his cursed habit of pinning down every movement in life—in his own life and in that of others —with a word, as one does a butterfly with a pin, he undertook to explain to both of us our selves, our relations, how we ought to behave; despotically made us render him an account of our feelings and thoughts; praised us, reproved us, even entered into correspondence with us. Just imagine! . . . . Well, he completely disconcerted us. I would hardly have married my young lady at that time (I had enough common sense left in me for that), but at least she and I might have passed a few glorious months together, after the fashion of Paul and Virginia; and then misunderstandings would have arisen, and all sorts of strained relations,—all sorts of nonsense would have come along, in short. It ended thus—that one fine morning Rúdin argued himself into the conviction that it was his most sacred duty, as a friend, to inform the old father of everything,— and he did it."

"You don't say so!" exclaimed Alexándra Pávlovna.

RÚDIN

" Yes, and observe that he did it with my consent—that's the remarkable thing about it! . . . .
I remember to this day what a chaos I carried about then in my head; everything was simply whirling round and presenting itself as though in a camera-obscura; white appeared to be black, and black white; falsehood seemed truth, and fantasy seemed duty. . . . . Eh! Even now I am ashamed to recall it. As for Rúdin, he was not cast down . . . . not a bit of it; he used to soar along, like a swallow over a pond, through all sorts of misunderstandings and complications."

" And so you parted from your young girl? " inquired Alexándra Pávlovna, ingenuously inclining her head on one side and elevating her eyebrows.

" I did . . . . and did it in a bad way, with insulting awkwardness, publicly, and that without any necessity for publicity. . . . I wept myself, and she wept, and the devil knows what took place. . . . . Some sort of a Gordian knot had got tied, and it was necessary to cut it,—and it hurt. But everything in the world settles itself for the best. She married a fine man, and is thriving now. . . ."

" But confess, you cannot yet pardon Rúdin . . . . ," Alexándra Pávlovna began.

" Not a bit of it! " . . . . interrupted Lezhnyóff. " I cried like a child when I saw him off

114

on his way abroad. But, to tell the truth, the seed was planted in my soul at that time. And when I met him afterward abroad, ... well, I had grown older then, ... Rúdin appeared to me in his true light."

" What, precisely, was it that you discovered in him? "

" Why, everything which I have been saying to you for about an hour past. But enough of him. I only wished to prove to you that if I judge him severely, it is not because I do not know him. . . . . As for Natálya Alexyéevna, I shall waste no superfluous words on her; but do you direct your attention to your brother."

" To my brother! What do you mean? "

" Why, look at him. Do you notice nothing? " Alexándra Pávlovna dropped her eyes.

" You are right," she said; " it is quite true . . . . for some time past . . . . my brother has not been like himself. But is it possible that you think . . . ."

" Hush! I think he is coming this way," ejaculated Lezhnyóff, in a whisper. " But Natálya is not a child, believe me, although, unfortunately, she is as inexperienced as a child. You will see, that young girl will astonish us all."

" In what way? "

" In this way . . . . do you know that it is precisely that sort of girls who drown themselves, take poison, and so forth? Never mind if she is quiet; her passions are strong, and her character—is the same, óï, óï!"

"Well, it strikes me that you are dropping into poetry. To such a phlegmatic man as you I appear like a volcano, I suppose."

"Well, no!" replied Lezhnyóff, with a smile. "And as for character,—you have no character at all, thank God!"

"What sort of impertinence is *this?*"

"This? It is the greatest compliment, I assure you. . . ."

Volýntzeff entered and looked suspiciously at Lezhnyóff and his sister. He had grown thin of late. Both of them began to talk to him, but he hardly smiled in response to their jests, and looked—as Pigásoff had once expressed himself concerning him—like a sorrowful hare. But, probably, there never yet has existed in the world a man who, at least once in his life, has not looked still worse than that. Volýntzeff felt that Natálya was receding from him, and, along with her, it seemed that the earth was slipping out from under his feet.

VII

THE next day was Sunday, and Natálya rose late. On the previous day she had been very taciturn until evening, being secretly ashamed of her tears, and she had slept very badly. As she sat, half dressed, before her little piano, she now struck chords which were barely audible in order not to awaken Mlle. Boncourt, now leaned her brow against the cold keys and remained motionless for a long time. She kept thinking all the while, not of Rúdin himself, but of some word which he had uttered, and was completely absorbed in her meditation. From time to time, Volýntzeff recurred to her mind. She knew that he loved her. But her thought instantly deserted him. . . . . She felt a strange agitation. In the morning she hastily dressed herself, went downstairs, and, after bidding her mother good morning, seized advantage of an opportunity and went off alone into the garden. . . . The day was a hot, bright, radiant day, in spite of showers at intervals. Athwart the blue sky low-hanging, smoke-coloured clouds floated swimmingly without concealing the sun, and from time to time dropped upon the fields abundant streams of a sudden and momentary downpour. The large, glittering drops showered down swiftly, with a certain sharp sound, like diamonds; the sun sparkled through the fine meshes of their network; the grass, shortly before agitated by the breeze, did not stir, thirstily drinking in the moisture; the soaked trees languidly trembled through all their little leaves; the birds did not cease singing, and it was a joy to hear their voluble chirping in the fresh rustle and murmur of the passing rain. The blazing roads smoked, and became somewhat streaked under the sharp blows of the frequent sprinklings. But now the thunder-cloud passed over, a little breeze began to flutter its wings, the grass began to be suffused with hues of emerald and gold, ... the leaves of the trees, clinging one to another, became transparent. A powerful odour arose everywhere around. . . . .

The sky had almost completely cleared when Natálya went into the garden. It breathed forth freshness and tranquillity—that gentle and happy tranquillity which reacts upon the heart of man with the sweet languor of mysterious sympathy and undefined desires. . . . .

Natálya walked along the edge of the pond, down the long avenue of silvery poplars. Suddenly, in front of her, as though from the earth, Rúdin started up.

She became confused. He gazed into her face.

" You are alone? " he asked.

" Yes, I am alone," replied Natálya; " but I came out only for a minute. . . . . I must go back to the house."

" I will accompany you."

And he walked by her side.

" You seem to be sad? " he said.

" I? . . . . And I was about to remark to you that you seem to be out of sorts."

" Perhaps. . . . . I am that way sometimes. It is more excusable in me than in you."

" Why? Do you think that I have nothing to feel sad about? "

" At your age one must enjoy life."

Natálya advanced several paces in silence.

" Dmítry Nikoláitch! " she said.

" What? "

" Do you remember . . . . do you remember the comparison which you made yesterday? You remember . . . . about the oak? "

" Well, yes; I remember it. What of it? "

Natálya cast a stealthy glance at Rúdin.

" Why did you . . . . what did you mean to say by that comparison? "

Rúdin bowed his head, and fixed his eyes on the distance.

" Natálya Alexyéevna! " he began, with that repressed and significant expression peculiar to him, which always made the hearer think that Rúdin was not uttering the tenth part of that

which was oppressing his soul.—" Natálya Alexyéevna! you may have observed that I speak
very little of my past. There are some strings
which I do not touch at all. My heart . . . .
what need is there for any one to know what has
taken place in it? To expose that on show has
always seemed to me a sacrilege. But with you
I am frank: you arouse my confidence. I
cannot conceal from you that I have lived and
suffered like every one else. . . . . When and
how? It is not worth while to talk about that;
but my heart has experienced many joys and
many sorrows."

Rúdin paused for a little.

" What I said to you yesterday," he went on,
" may be, in some degree, applied to me—to my
present position. But, again, this is not worth
mentioning. That side of my life has already vanished. All that remains for me now is to drag
myself along the sultry, dusty road, from posting-station to station, in a jolting peasant's
cart. . . . . When I shall arrive, and whether I
shall arrive,—God knows. . . . . Let us, rather,
talk about you."

" Is it possible, Dmítry Nikoláitch," Natálya
interrupted him, " that you expect nothing from
life? "

" Oh, no! I expect a great deal—but not for
myself. . . . . Activity, the bliss of activity, I
shall never renounce; but I have renounced en-

joyment. My hopes, my dreams, and my own personal happiness have nothing in common. Love " (at this word he shrugged his shoulders) —" love is not for me. I . . . . am not worthy of it. The woman who loves has a right to demand everything from a man, and I can no longer give everything. Moreover, pleasing is an affair of youth; I am too old. How should I turn other people's heads? God grant that I may keep my own on my shoulders! "

" I understand," said Natálya; " he who is striving toward a grand goal must no longer think of himself; but is not a woman capable of valuing such a man? It seems to me, on the contrary, that a woman will sooner turn her back on an egoist. All young men—those youths, according to you, are egoists—all are engrossed only with themselves, even when they love. Believe me, a woman is not only capable of understanding self-sacrifice: she herself understands how to sacrifice herself."

Natálya's cheeks flushed slightly, and her eyes sparkled. Until her acquaintance with Rúdin, she would never have uttered such a long speech and with such fervour.

" You have more than once heard my opinion as to the vocation of women," returned Rúdin, with a condescending smile. " You know that, in my opinion, Jeanne d'Arc alone could have saved France. . . . . But that is not the point. I

wanted to have a talk with you. You are standing on the threshold of life. . . . . To discuss your
future will be cheerful and not unfruitful. . . . .
Listen! You know that I am your friend; I take
in you almost the interest of a blood-relation
. . . . and, therefore, I hope you will not consider my question indiscreet. Tell me, is your
heart perfectly calm so far?"

Natálya blushed all over and said nothing.
Rúdin halted, and she halted also.

"You are not angry with me?" he asked.

"No," she said; "but I did not in the least
expect . . . ."

"However," he went on, "you need not answer me. Your secret is known to me."

Natálya glanced at him almost with terror.

"Yes . . . . yes; I know who pleases you.
And I must say that you could not have made a
better choice. He is a very fine man; he will
know how to prize you. He is not rumpled with
life—he is simple and transparent of soul—he
will make you happy."

"Of whom are you speaking, Dmítry Niko-
laítch?"

"As if you did not understand of whom I am
speaking! Of Volýntzeff, of course. Well, now,
is that incorrect?"

Natálya turned away a little from Rúdin. She
was completely disconcerted.

"Does not he love you? Good gracious! He never takes his eyes off you; he watches your every movement; yes—and, after all, can love be concealed? And can you be ill disposed toward him? So far as I can see, your mother also is pleased with him . . . . your choice. . . . "

"Dmítry Nikoláitch," Natálya interrupted him, in her confusion extending her hand to a bush which stood near by, "really, I find it so awkward to talk about this; but I assure you . . . you are mistaken."

"I am mistaken?" repeated Rúdin. . . . . "I think not. . . . . It is not long since I made your acquaintance; but I already know you well. What is the meaning of the change which I perceive in you—which I clearly perceive? Are you the same as I found you six weeks ago? . . . . No, Natálya Alexyéevna, your heart is not at ease."

"Possibly," replied Natálya, in a hardly audible tone; "but you are mistaken, nevertheless."

"How so?" inquired Rúdin.

"Leave me; do not ask me!" returned Natálya, and with swift steps she took her way homeward.

She was terrified at all which she suddenly felt within her.

Rúdin overtook and stopped her.

"Natálya Alexyéevna!" he began. "This conversation cannot end thus; it is too important for me also. . . . . How am I to understand you?"

"Leave me!" repeated Natálya.

"Natálya Alexyéevna, for God's sake!"

Agitation was depicted on Rúdin's countenance. He had turned pale.

"You understand everything; you must understand me, too!" said Natálya, tore her hand from him, and walked on without glancing back.

"Only one word!" cried Rúdin after her.

She paused, but did not turn round.

"You asked me what I meant to say by my comparison of yesterday. Know then—I will not deceive you. I was speaking of myself—of my past—and of you."

"What? Of me?"

"Yes, of you; I repeat it, I will not deceive you. . . . . You know now of what feeling—of what new feeling I was speaking then. . . . . Until to-day I could never have made up my mind . . . ."

Natálya suddenly covered her face with her hands, and ran toward the house.

She was so shaken by the unexpected outcome of the conversation with Rúdin that she did not notice Volýntzeff, past whom she ran. He was standing motionless, with his back resting against a tree. A quarter of an hour earlier he had arrived at Dárya Mikhaílovna's, and had found her in the drawing-room; he had said a word or two, then had retreated unobserved and set out in search of Natálya. Guided by the instinct peculiar to people in love, he had gone straight into the garden, and had hit upon her and Rúdin at the very moment when she tore her hand from him. Everything went dark before Volýntzeff's eyes. After following Natálya with his glance, he separated himself from the tree and took a couple of steps, not knowing whither he was going or why. Rúdin caught sight of him as he came on a level with him. Each man looked the other in the eye, bowed, and parted in silence.

"This shall not end so," both said to themselves.

Volýntzeff walked to the very end of the garden. He felt bitter and disgusted, and on his heart lay a burden of lead, and from time to time his blood rose viciously. A fine rain again began to patter down. Rúdin returned to his own room. And he was not at ease; his thoughts were circling round in a whirlwind. Unexpected contact with a young, honourable, trustful soul will perturb any one.

At table everything went wrong somehow. Natálya, ghastly pale, could hardly hold herself on her chair, and did not raise her eyes. Volýntzeff, as usual, sat beside her, and from time to time made a constrained remark to her. It so happened that Pigásoff was dining on that day with Dárya Mikhaílovna. He talked more at table than any one else. Among other things, he undertook to prove that men, like dogs, can be divided into bob-tailed and long-tailed. "People are bob-tailed," he said, "both by birth and through their own fault. The bob-tailed are badly off; nothing succeeds with them; they have not confidence in themselves. But the man who has a long, bushy tail is the happy man. He may be both worse and weaker than the bob-tailed man, but he has confidence in himself; he spreads out his tail and everybody admires it. And just that is deserving of amazement, for the tail is an utterly useless part of the body, you must admit; of what use can a tail be? But every one judges of your merits by your tail.

"I," he added, with a sigh, "belong to the category of the bob-tailed, and the most vexatious part of it all is that I cut off my own tail."

"That is, you mean to say," remarked Rúdin, carelessly, "that which La Rochefoucauld said long before your day: ' Believe in yourself, and others will believe in you.' What the object is in mixing a tail up with it, I do not understand."

"You must permit every one," began Volýntzeff, sharply— "you must permit every one to express himself as he sees fit. People talk about despotism. In my opinion, there is no worse despotism than that of the so-called clever people. May the devil take them!"

Volýntzeff's sally astonished everybody; all relapsed into silence. Rúdin tried to look at him, but could not sustain his gaze, turned away, smiled, and did not open his mouth.

" Ehe! and you 're a bob-tailed one also! " thought Pigásoff; but Natálya's soul sank within her for terror. Dárya Mikhaílovna stared at Volýntzeff for a long time in amazement, and at last was the first to speak. She began to tell a story about some remarkable dog or other belonging to Minister N. N. . . . .

Volýntzeff went away soon after dinner. As he was bidding farewell to Natálya, he could endure it no longer, and said to her:

" Why are you so confused, as though you were guilty? You cannot be guilty in any one's eyes! " . . . .

Natálya understood nothing, and only followed him with her eyes. Before tea, Rúdin approached her, and, bending over the table as though he were examining the newspapers, he whispered:

" All this is like a dream, is it not? I must see you alone, without fail, ... if only for a moment." He turned to Mlle. Boncourt. " Here," he said to her, " is the *feuilleton* which you were looking for." And, again bending toward Natálya, he added in a whisper: " Try to be by the terrace in the lilac arbour about ten o'clock. I shall be waiting for you." . . . .

Pigásoff was the hero of the evening. Rúdin

yielded the field to him. He greatly amused Dárya Mikhaílovna; first he told a story about one of his neighbours who, after having been henpecked by his wife for thirty years, had become so effeminate that one day, when he was crossing a small puddle in Pigásoff's presence, he put his hand behind him and pulled aside the skirts of his coat, as women do with their petticoats. Then he turned to another landed proprietor who had at first been a Freemason, then a misanthrope, and then had wanted to become a banker.

" How did you come to be a Freemason, Philípp Stepánitch? " Pigásoff asked him.

" Every one knows how: I wore a long nail on my fifth finger."

But Dárya Mikhaílovna laughed most of all when Pigásoff set out to argue about love, and to assert that women had sighed after him; also, that one fiery German girl had even called him "appetising little Afrikán" and "my dear little falcon." Dárya Mikhaílovna laughed, but Pigásoff was not lying; he really had a right to boast of his conquests. He declared that nothing can be easier than to make any woman you like fall in love with you. All that is necessary is to repeat to her, for ten days in succession, that paradise is in her lips and bliss in her eyes, and that all other women are simple rags in comparison with her; and on the eleventh day she herself will say that paradise is in her mouth and bliss in her eyes, and will fall in love with you. All sorts of things happen in the world. Who knows? Perhaps Pigásoff was right.

At half-past nine Rúdin was already in the arbour. The little stars had just come forth in the pale and distant depths of the sky; the west was still aglow—there the horizon seemed both clearer and purer; the crescent moon gleamed like gold athwart the black network of the weeping birch. The other trees either stood like surly giants, with a thousand apertures after the fashion of eyes, or were merged into dense, gloomy masses. Not a single leaf was stirring; the topmost branches of the lilacs and acacias seemed to be listening to something and stretching themselves out into the warm air. The house rose in a dark mass hard by; the long, illuminated windows in it were depicted as spots of reddish light. The evening was mild and still, but a repressed, passionate sigh seemed to hover in this stillness.

Rúdin stood with his arms folded on his breast and listened with strained attention. His heart beat violently, and he involuntarily held his breath. At last light, hurried footsteps became audible, and Natálya entered the arbour.

Rúdin rushed toward her, and seized her hands. They were as cold as ice.

"Natálya Alexyéevna!" he began, in an agitated whisper, "I wanted to see you . . . . I could not wait until to-morrow. I must tell you

—what I did not suspect—what I was not even conscious of this morning—I love you!"

Natálya's hand trembled weakly in his hands.

"I love you," he repeated; "and how could I so long deceive myself—how could I have failed long ago to divine that I love you! . . . . And you? . . . . Tell me, Natálya Alexyéevna, you?" . . . .

Natálya scarcely drew her breath.

"You see, I have come hither," she said at last.

"No; tell me, do you love me?"

"It seems to me . . . . that I do . . . ." she whispered.

Rúdin clasped her hands still more firmly, and tried to draw her to him.

Natálya cast a swift glance around her.

"Let me go!—I am afraid—It seems to me that some one is listening to us. . . . . For God's sake, be cautious. Volýntzeff divines the truth."

"Never mind him. You saw that I did not answer him to-day. . . . . Akh, Natálya Alexyéevna, how happy I am! Now nothing shall part us."

Natálya looked into his eyes.

"Release me," she whispered; "it is time for me to go."

"One moment—" began Rúdin. . . . .

"No; release me—release me!" . . . .

"You appear to be afraid of me?"

" No; but I must go . . . ."

" Then repeat at least once more that . . . ."

" You say that you are happy? " inquired Natálya.

" I? There is no happier man in the world than I! Can you doubt it? "

Natálya raised her head. Very beautiful was her pale face, so noble, youthful, and agitated, in the mysterious shadows of the arbour, in the faint light which fell from the nocturnal skies.

" Do you know," she said— " I will be yours! "

" Oh, God! " . . . exclaimed Rúdin.

But Natálya evaded him and departed. Rúdin stood still for a little while, then slowly emerged from the arbour. The moon brightly illuminated his face; over his lips strayed a smile.

" I am happy," he ejaculated in an undertone. " Yes, I am happy," he repeated, as though desirous of convincing himself.

He drew his body up erect, shook his curls, and walked briskly into the garden, joyously flourishing his arms.

But meanwhile the bushes were quietly parted in the lilac arbour, and Pandalévsky made his appearance. He glanced cautiously around, shook his head, compressed his lips, ejaculated significantly: " So that 's how it is, sir. This must be brought to the knowledge of Dárya Mikhaílovna," and disappeared.

VIII

On reaching home Volýntzeff was so downcast and gloomy, answered his sister so unwillingly, and so promptly locked himself up in his study, that she decided to send a mounted messenger for Lezhnyóff. She had recourse to him on all perplexing occasions. Lezhnyóff bade the man say to her that he would come to her on the morrow.

By morning, Volýntzeff had not cheered up. After tea he was on the point of setting out for his work, but stayed at home, lay down on the divan, and began to read a book, which infrequently happened with him. Volýntzeff did not feel attracted to literature, and he was simply afraid of poetry. "That is as incomprehensible as poetry," he was wont to say, and in support of his words he quoted the following lines from the poet Aibulat:

> "And till the end of sorrowful days
> Nor trial proud, nor reasoning,
> Shall crumple with its hand
> The life of bloody forget-me-nots."

Alexándra Pávlovna surveyed her brother with alarm, but did not disturb him with questions. A carriage drove up to the porch. "Well," she thought, "thank God! there is Lezhnyóff." . . . A servant entered and announced the arrival of Rúdin.

Volýntzeff flung his book on the floor and raised his head.

"Who has come?" he asked.

"Rúdin, Dmítry Nikoláitch," repeated the servant.

Volýntzeff rose.

"Ask him in," he said; "and do thou leave us, sister," he added, turning to Alexándra Pávlovna.

"But why?" she began. . . .

"I know why," he interrupted irritably; "I entreat thee."

Rúdin entered. Volýntzeff bowed coldly to him as he stood in the middle of the room, and did not offer him his hand.

"You did not expect me; confess it," began Rúdin, and laid his hat on the window-sill.

His lips quivered slightly. He felt awkward, but he endeavoured to conceal his confusion.

"I did not expect you, that is true," returned Volýntzeff; "after yesterday, I should sooner have expected some one—with a commission from you."

"I understand what you mean to convey," said Rúdin, seating himself; "and I am greatly delighted at your frankness. It is much better so.

133

I have come to you as to a man of noble character."

" Cannot we dispense with compliments? " remarked Volýntzeff.

" I wish to explain to you why I have come."

" You and I are acquaintances; why should you not come to my house? Moreover, this is not the first time that you have favoured me with a visit."

" I have come to you as to a noble man—as to a noble man," repeated Rúdin, " and I now wish to submit myself to your judgment. . . . . I have entire confidence in you. . . . ."

" But what is the point? " said Volýntzeff, who was still standing in his former position and staring gloomily at Rúdin, now and then tugging at the tips of his moustache.

" Permit me. . . . . I have come in order to have a definitive explanation; but, nevertheless, that cannot be done in an instant."

" Why not? "

" A third person is concerned here." . . .

" What third person? "

" Sergyéi Pávlitch, you understand me."

" Dmítry Nikoláitch, I do not understand you in the least."

" It suits you. . . . ."

" It suits me to have you speak without circumlocution! " put in Volýntzeff.

He was beginning to be seriously angry.

RÚDIN

Rúdin frowned.

" Very well . . . . we are alone. . . . I must tell you—however, you probably already divine " (Volýntzeff shrugged his shoulders impatiently) —" I must tell you that I love Natálya Alexyéevna, and have the right to assume that she loves me also."

Volýntzeff turned pale, but made no reply, walked to the window, and turned away.

" You understand, Sergyéi Pávlitch," went on Rúdin, " that if I were not convinced . . . ."

" Upon my word," interrupted Volýntzeff, hastily, " I have not the slightest doubt of it. . . . Very well! My good wishes! The only thing I am surprised at is, what the devil you should have taken it into your head for to favour me with a call to tell me this piece of news. . . . . What have I to do with it? What business is it of mine whom you love and who loves you? I simply cannot understand."

Volýntzeff continued to stare out of the window. His voice sounded dull.

Rúdin rose.

" I will tell you, Sergyéi Pávlitch, why I decided to come to you, why I did not even consider that I had a right to conceal from you our . . . . our mutual affection. I esteem you too profoundly—that is why I came. I did not wish . . . . neither of us wished—to play a comedy before you. Your sentiments toward Natálya

185

Alexyéevna were known to me. . . . . Believe
me, I know my own value; I know how little worthy I am to usurp your place in her heart; but if
it was fated to occur, can it possibly be better to
use cunning, to deceive, to dissimulate? Can it
possibly be better to subject one's self to misunderstandings, or even to the possibility of scenes
like the one which took place yesterday at dinner?
Tell me, Sergyéi Pávlitch?"

Volýntzeff folded his arms on his breast, as
though striving to subdue himself.

"Sergyéi Pávlitch!" went on Rúdin, "I have
grieved you; I feel it. . . . . But understand us
. . . . understand that we had no other means of
proving to you our esteem—of proving that we
know how to value your straightforward nobility.
Frankness—complete frankness—with any other
man would be out of place; but with you it becomes a duty. It is pleasant to us to think that
our secret is in your hands."

Volýntzeff laughed in a constrained way.

"Thanks for your confidence!" he exclaimed;
"although I beg you to note that I did not wish
to know your secret, or to betray my own to you;
you are making use of it as though it were your
own. But pardon me; you speak as though on
behalf of both. Consequently, I may assume that
Natálya Alexyéevna is aware of your visit, and
of the object of your visit?"

Rúdin became slightly confused.

"No; I did not communicate my intention to Natálya Alexyéevna; but I know that she shares my manner of thought."

"All that is very fine," began Volýntzeff, after a brief silence, during which he had drummed on the window-pane with his fingers; "although I must confess that it would have been a great deal better had you displayed less esteem for me. To tell the truth, I don't care a devil's rap for your respect; but what do you want of me now?"

"I want nothing .... or, no! I do want one thing: I want you not to regard me as a wily and crafty man; that you should understand me..... I hope that you already have no doubt as to my sincerity. .... I wish, Sergyéi Pávlitch, that we should part as friends .... that you should offer me your hand as heretofore." ...

And Rúdin stepped up to Volýntzeff.

"Excuse me, my dear sir," said Volýntzeff, turning away and retreating a pace. "I am ready to do full justice to your intentions; all that is very fine, we will assume,—even lofty,— but we are simple folks; we eat our gingerbread without decorations; we are not in a condition to follow the flight of such lofty intellects as yours. .... That which seems sincere to you, strikes us as intrusive and indiscreet. .... That which is simple and clear to you, is intricate and obscure to us. .... You make your boast that we dissemble; how are we to understand you?

137

You must excuse me. I can neither regard you
as a friend, nor will I give you my hand. . . . .
This may be petty; but then I am petty myself."

Rúdin took his hat from the window-sill.

" Sergyéi Pávlitch!" he said sorrowfully,
" farewell; I have been deceived in my expectations. My visit, in reality, is rather strange; but
I did hope that you . . . ." (Volýntzeff made an
impatient gesture) . . . . " Pardon me, I will say
no more about that. Taking everything into consideration, I see that it is true. You are in the
right, and you could not have acted otherwise.
Farewell, and permit me at least once more, for
the last time, to assure you of the purity of my
motives. . . . . I am convinced of your discretion. . . . ."

" This is too much!" exclaimed Volýntzeff,
and shook with rage. " I have not asked you for
your confidence in the least, and therefore you
have no right to rely on my discretion!"

Rúdin wanted to say something, but merely
flung his hands wide apart, bowed, and withdrew;
while Volýntzeff threw himself on the couch and
turned his face to the wall.

" May I come in?" Alexándra Pávlovna's
voice made itself heard at the door.

Volýntzeff did not immediately reply, and
stealthily drew his hand across his face. " No,
Sásha," he said, in a slightly unnatural voice;
" wait a little longer."

Half an hour later Alexándra Pávlovna again came to the door.

"Mikhaílo Mikhaílitch has come," she said; "wouldst thou like to see him?"

"Yes," replied Volýntzeff; "send him hither."

Lezhnyóff entered.

"What 's the matter—art thou ill?" he asked, as he seated himself in an arm-chair beside the couch.

Volýntzeff raised himself, leaned on his elbow, gazed for a long, long time into the face of his friend, and then and there imparted to him his entire conversation with Rúdin, word for word. Up to that time he had never given Lezhnyóff even a hint as to his feelings with regard to Natálya, although he had divined that they were no secret to him.

"Well, my dear fellow, thou hast amazed me," said Lezhnyóff, as soon as Volýntzeff had finished his narration. "I expected many queer things of him, but this is quite too. . . . However, I recognise him even here."

"Good heavens!" said the excited Volýntzeff; "this is downright insolence! Why, I came near flinging him out of the window! Did he want to brag to me, or has he turned coward? And on what grounds? How could he bring himself to go to a man!" . . . .

Volýntzeff threw his arms behind his head and relapsed into silence.

" No, my dear fellow, that's not it," returned
Lezhnyóff, calmly. " Thou wilt not believe me,
but he did it from a good motive. Really, ... it
is noble and frank, thou seest,—well; and an opportunity presents itself to talk, to launch into
eloquence; and that's what we require, that's
what we are not capable of living without. . . .
Okh, his tongue is his enemy, ... Well; and, on
the other hand, it is his servant."

" Thou canst not imagine the triumph with
which he entered and talked! " . . . .

" Well, he couldn't get along without that.
He buttons up his coat as though he were fulfill-
ing a sacred duty. I'd like to put him in an un-
inhabited prison, and watch him from round the
corner, to see how he would manage there. And
he prates of simplicity! "

" But tell me, my dear fellow, for God's sake,"
asked Volýntzeff, " what this is? Is it philosophy? "

" How shall I explain it to you? On the one
hand, if you like, philosophy is precisely what it
is; but, on the other hand, it is not that at all.
It is not proper to unload all sorts of trash, even
on philosophy."

Volýntzeff cast a glance at him.

" And was he lying, think you? "

" No, my son; he was not lying. But dost thou
know what? We have talked enough about this.
Come on, my dear fellow; let's smoke our pipes

and invite Alexándra Pávlovna hither. . . . . In her presence it will be pleasanter to talk and easier to hold our tongues. She will give us some tea."

" Very well," returned Volýntzeff. " Sásha, come in!" he shouted.

Alexándra Pávlovna entered. He seized her hand and pressed it firmly to his lips.

Rúdin returned home in a confused and strange state of mind. He was vexed with himself; he reproached himself for unpardonable rashness, for boyish behaviour. Some one has truthfully said: There is nothing more painful than the consciousness that one has just perpetrated a piece of stupidity.

Repentance gnawed Rúdin.

" The devil possessed me," he whispered through his teeth, " to go to that country squire. A pretty inspiration I had, truly. I merely invited insolence!" . . . .

But something unusual had taken place in Dárya Mikhaílovna's house. The mistress of the house herself had not made her appearance during the entire morning, and she did not come out to dinner. According to the assertion of Pandalévsky, the sole person who was admitted to her presence, she had a headache. Of Natálya, also, Rúdin hardly caught a glimpse; she sat in her own room with Mlle. Boncourt. . . . . When she met him in the dining-room she looked at him so sadly that his heart shuddered. Her face was distorted, as though a calamity had befallen her since the preceding day. The anguish of ill-defined forebodings began to torment Rúdin. In order to distract his thoughts in some manner, he busied himself with Basístoff, chatted a great deal with him, and found in him an ardent, vivacious young fellow with enthusiastic hopes and a faith as yet unshaken. Toward evening, Dárya Mikhaílovna showed herself for a couple of hours in the drawing-room. She treated Rúdin amiably, but held herself, in some sort, aloof, and smiled and frowned by turns, talked through her nose, and chiefly in hints. . . . . She fairly reeked with the atmosphere of the court lady. Of late she had, as it were, grown rather cool toward Rúdin. " What enigma is this? " he said to himself, as he gazed askance at her, with her head erect and even thrown backward.

He had not long to wait for the solution of this enigma. On his way to his room, at midnight, he passed along a dark corridor. Suddenly some one thrust a note into his hand. He glanced round. A young girl—Natálya's maid, it seemed to him—was retreating. He reached his room, dismissed his man, opened the note, and read the following lines traced by Natálya's hand:

" Come to-morrow morning, not later than seven o'clock, to Avdiúkh's pond, behind the oak forest. No other time is possible. This will be our last meeting;

everything will be at an end if. . . . Come.   We must reach a decision. . . . .

" P.S.—If I do not come it will mean that we shall not meet again; in that case I shall let you know."

Rúdin became thoughtful, turned the note about in his hands, laid it under his pillow, undressed, got into bed but did not soon fall asleep, slept lightly, and it was not yet five o'clock when he awoke.

IX

AVDIÚKH's pond, beside which Natálya had fixed
the meeting with Rúdin, had long since ceased to
be a pond. Thirty years before the dam had
given way, and since that time it had been abandoned. .Only from the flat, even bottom of the
ravine, formerly covered with greasy slime, and
from the remains of the dam, could it be divined
that a pond had once existed there. There had,
also, once been a farm-house there. It had long
since disappeared. Two huge pine-trees called it
to remembrance; the wind was forever rustling
and humming in their lofty, sparse verdure.
Mysterious rumours were in circulation among
the country-people about a terrible crime which
was said to have been perpetrated at their base.
It was even asserted that neither of them would
fall without causing the death of some one; that
a third pine had once stood there in former days,
which had fallen during a tempest and had
crushed a little girl. The whole locality round
about the ancient pond was regarded as accursed: empty and bare, but obscure and gloomy
even on a sunny day, it seemed still more obscure and gloomy from the vicinity of the de-

crepit oak forest, which had long since died out
and dried up. The sparse grey skeletons of the
vast trees rose aloft like melancholy spectres
above the low undergrowth of bushes. It was
painful to look at them; they seemed like malicious old men who had met together and were
plotting something evil. A narrow, barely indicated path wound about on one side. No one
passed Avdiúkh's pond without special necessity.
Natálya had deliberately selected this isolated
place. It was not more than half a verst distant
from Dárya Mikhaílovna's house.

The sun had long been up when Rúdin arrived
at Avdiúkh's pond; but it was not a cheerful
morning. Dense clouds of a milky hue covered
the whole heavens; the wind, whistling and moaning, was driving them swiftly onward. Rúdin began to pace to and fro along the dam, which was
covered with adhesive burdock and blackened net-
tles. These meetings, these new sensations, engrossed yet also agitated him, especially after the
note of the night before. He perceived that a
catastrophe was approaching, and he was secretly
perturbed in spirit, although no one would have
thought so on observing the concentrated decision wherewith he folded his arms upon his
breast and rolled his eyes about. Pigásoff had
once observed, quite justly, concerning him, that
his head was incessantly nodding about, like that
of a Chinese idol. But from the head alone, no

matter how powerful it may be, it is difficult for a man to find out what is taking place within himself. . . . . Rúdin—clever, penetrating Rúdin—was not in a position to say with certainty whether he really loved Natálya, whether he were suffering, whether he would suffer on parting with her. Why, without pretending to be a Lovelace,—one must render him that justice,—had he led astray a poor young girl? Why was he waiting for her with secret trepidation? To this there is but one answer: No one is so easily carried away as the unimpassioned people.

He walked on the dam, but Natálya hastened toward him, straight across the meadow, on the damp grass.

"My lady! My lady! you will wet your feet," said her maid Másha, who could hardly keep up with her.

Natálya paid no heed to her, and ran on without looking back.

"Akh, if only no one sees us!" Másha kept repeating. "And 't is a wonder how we got out of the house. If only mam'zell does not wake up! . . . . Luckily, it is n't far. . . . . And there he is already—waiting," she added, suddenly catching sight of Rúdin's stately form, standing in a picturesque attitude on the dam. "Only, he ought n't to stand so on the mound; he ought to have descended into the ravine."

Natálya halted.

"Wait here, Másha, by the pine-trees," she said, and descended to the pond.

Rúdin approached her, and stopped short in amazement. Never yet had he beheld such an expression on her face. Her brows were contracted, her lips were tightly compressed, her eyes gazed straight forward, and sternly.

"Dmítry Nikoláitch," she began, "we have no time to lose. I have come for five minutes. I must tell you that mama knows all. Mr. Pandalévsky was watching us day before yesterday, and has told her about our meeting. He always has been a spy for mama. Last night she summoned me to her."

"My God!" exclaimed Rúdin. "This is terrible!.... What did your mother say to you?"

"She was not angry with me; she did not scold me—she only upbraided me for my giddiness."

"Is that all?"

"Yes; and she announced to me that she would rather see me dead than your wife."

"Can she have said that?"

"Yes; and she added that you yourself were not in the least desirous of marrying me; that you had only been paying court to me idly, out of ennui, and that she had not expected this of you; that, moreover, she herself was to blame for having permitted me to see so much of you .... that she had had confidence in my good sense,—that I had greatly astonished her . . . . and I do not remember all she said to me."

Natálya uttered all this in a certain even, almost toneless voice.

" And you, Natálya Alexyéevna, what reply did you make to her? " asked Rúdin.

" What reply did I make to her? " repeated Natálya. . . . . " What do *you* mean to do now? "

" My God! My God! " returned Rúdin. " This is cruel! So soon! . . . . such a sudden blow! . . . . And your mother went into such a rage? "

" Yes . . . . . yes, she will not hear of you."

" This is dreadful! So there is no hope? "

" None whatever."

" Why are we so unhappy! That abominable Pandalévsky! . . . . You ask me, Natálya Alexyéevna, what I intend to do? My head is in a whirl—I can make no plans. . . . . I am conscious only of my misfortune. . . . I am amazed that you can preserve your coolness! "

" Do you think I find it easy? " said Natálya.

Rúdin began to pace the dam. Natálya never took her eyes from him.

" Your mother did not question you? " he said at last.

" She did ask me whether I loved you."

" Well . . . . and you? "

Natálya remained silent for a little. " I did not tell a falsehood."

Rúdin took her hand.

" Always, in everything, noble and magnanimous! Oh, the heart of a young girl is pure gold! But did your mother really announce to you so decisively her will in regard to the possibility of our marriage? "

" Yes, decisively. I have already told you; she is convinced that you yourself are not thinking of marrying me."

" So she regards me as a deceiver! How have I deserved this? "

And Rúdin clutched at his head.

" Dmítry Nikoláitch," said Natálya, " we are wasting time to no purpose. Remember, we are seeing each other for the last time. I have not come hither to weep, to complain —you see, I am not weeping—I came for advice."

" But what advice can I give you, Natálya Alexyéevna? "

" What advice? You are a man. I am accustomed to trust you, I shall trust you to the end. Tell me, what are your intentions? "

" My intentions? Your mother will, in all probability, turn me out of the house."

" Possibly. She announced to me yesterday that I must break off acquaintance with you. . . . . But you do not answer my question."

" What question? "

" What do you think we ought to do now? "

"What ought we to do?" returned Rúdin. "Submit, of course."

"Submit!" repeated Natálya, slowly, and her lips paled.

"Submit to fate," went on Rúdin. "What is there to do? I know but too well how bitter, painful, intolerable it is; but judge for yourself, Natálya Alexyéevna. I am poor. . . . I can work, it is true; but even were I a wealthy man, would you be capable of enduring the enforced rupture with your family, the wrath of your mother? . . . . No, Natálya Alexyéevna; that is not to be thought of. Obviously, we are not fated to live together, and the happiness of which I dreamed is not for me!"

Natálya suddenly covered her face with her hands, and fell to weeping. Rúdin approached her.

"Natálya Alexyéevna! Dear Natálya!" he began, with fervour. "Do not weep, for God's sake! Do not torture me; cheer up."

Natálya raised her head.

"You tell me to cheer up," she began, and her eyes flashed through her tears. "I am not weeping over that which you suppose. . . . . That does not pain me; what pains me is, that I have been deceived in you. . . . . What! I come to you for advice, and at what a moment!—and your first word is—'Submit.' Submit! . . . . So that is the way you apply to practice your explanations of freedom, of sacrifices which. . . ."

Her voice broke.

"But, Natálya Alexyéevna," began the disconcerted Rúdin, "remember . . . . I do not renounce my words . . . . only. . . ."

"You asked me," she went on, with renewed force, "what answer I made to my mother when she declared to me that she would sooner consent to my death than to my marriage with you. I answered her that I would sooner die than marry any one else. . . . . But you say, ' Submit ' ! So she was right; you really have been making sport of me, through the lack of something to do, because you were bored. . . ."

"I swear to you, Natálya Alexyéevna, ... I assure you. . . . " repeated Rúdin.

But she did not listen to him.

"Why did not you stop me? Why did you yourself. . . . Or did you not anticipate any obstacles? I am ashamed to speak of this—but, you see, everything is at an end now."

"You must calm yourself, Natálya Alexyéevna," Rúdin began. "We must consider together what means. . . ."

"You have talked so often of self-sacrifice," she interrupted; "but, do you know, if you had said to me to-day, just now, ' I love thee, but I cannot marry thee; I cannot answer for the future. Give me thy hand and follow me '—do you know that I would have gone with you; do you know that I had made up my mind to everything? But, in truth, it is a long way from words to deeds, and you have lost courage now, just as you did day before yesterday, at dinner, in the presence of Volýntzeff."

The colour flew to Rúdin's face. Natálya's unexpected enthusiasm had astounded him; but her last words had stung his self-love.

"You are too much irritated now, Natálya Alexyéevna," he began. "You cannot understand how cruelly you are wounding me. I hope that, in time, you will do me justice; you will understand what it has cost me to reject that happiness which, as you yourself have said, imposed upon me no obligations. Your peace of mind is more precious to me than anything in the world, and I should be the vilest of men if I could make up my mind to take advantage of . . . ."

"Perhaps, perhaps," interrupted Natálya; "perhaps you are right; I do not know what I am saying. But hitherto I have trusted you, I have believed your every word. . . Henceforth, be so good as to weigh your words, do not utter them to the winds. When I told you that I loved you, I knew what that word meant: I was ready for anything. . . . Now, all that remains for me to do, is to thank you for the lesson—and to bid you farewell!"

"Stop, for God's sake, Natálya Alexyéevna, I entreat you. I do not deserve your scorn, I swear to you that I do not. Put yourself in

my position. I am responsible for you to myself also. If I did not love you with devoted
affection—yes, my God! I would, myself, have
immediately proposed to you to elope with
me. . . Sooner or later, your mother would forgive us . . . and then . . . But before thinking of
my own happiness . . ."

He paused. Natálya's gaze, fixed straight
upon him, confused him.

"You are trying to prove to me that you are
an honest man, Dmítry Nikoláitch!" she said:—
"I do not doubt it. You are not capable of acting from calculation; but did I wish to convince
myself of that, was it for that that I came
hither. . . ."

"I did not expect, Natálya Alexyéevna . . . ."

"Ah! There you have made a slip of the
tongue! Yes, you did not expect all this—you
did not know me. Do not disturb yourself . . . .
you do not love me, and I force myself on no
one."

"I do love you!" exclaimed Rúdin.

"Possibly; but how do you love me! I remember all your words, Dmítry Nikoláitch.
Remember, you said to me: 'without complete
equality, there is no love. . You are too high for
me, we are not mates. . . . I am rightly punished. Occupations more worthy of you are
awaiting you. I shall not forget this day. . .
Farewell . . ."

"Natálya Alexyéevna, you are going? Can we part thus?"

He stretched out his arms toward her. She halted. His beseeching voice, it seemed, had made her waver.

"No," she said at last:—"I feel that something within me is broken. . . I came hither, I talked with you, in a sort of fever; I must recover my senses. You yourself have said that this must not be, and it shall not be. My God, when I came hither, I mentally bade farewell to my home, to my past,—and what then? whom have I encountered here? a cowardly man. . . . And how did you know that I would be not capable of enduring the separation from my family? 'Your mother does not consent . . . this is terrible!' That is all that I have heard from you. Is this you, is this you, Rúdin? No! farewell. . . . Akh! if he had loved me, I should have felt it now, at this moment. . . No, no, farewell!" . . . .

She turned swiftly round, and ran to Másha, who had long since begun to be uneasy, and to make signs to her.

"It is *you* who have lost courage, not I!" Rúdin shouted after Natálya.

She no longer paid any attention to him, and hastened, across the field, in the direction of home. She reached her own bed-chamber in safety; but no sooner had she crossed the threshold, than her forces deserted her, and she fell senseless into Másha's arms.

But Rúdin remained for a long time standing on the dam. At last he started, reached the path with short strides, and walked quietly along it. He was greatly mortified . . . and embittered. " Is that the sort of girl she is? " he said to himself. " At eighteen years of age! . . . . No, I did not know her. . . . She is a remarkable girl. What strength of will! . . . . She is right; she is worthy of a different sort of love from that which I felt for her . . . . Felt? . . ." he asked himself. " Is it possible that I no longer feel love? So this is how it was all bound to end! How pitiful and insignificant I was in her presence! "

The light rumble of a racing-gig caused Rúdin to raise his eyes. Lezhnyóff was driving toward him, with his inevitable trotter. Rúdin made him a silent bow, and, as though struck by a sudden thought, turned aside from the road, and walked swiftly in the direction of Dárya Mikhaílovna's house.

Lezhnyóff allowed him to depart, gazed after him, and after a brief reflection, also turned his horse round—and drove back to Volýntzeff, with whom he had spent the night. He found him asleep; gave orders that he was not to be wakened, and while waiting for tea, seated himself on the balcony, and smoked his pipe.

X

VOLÝNTZEFF rose about ten o'clock, and on hearing that Lezhnyóff was sitting on his balcony, was greatly amazed, and gave orders that he should be invited to his room.

"What has happened?" he inquired of him. "Surely, thou didst intend to drive home?"

"Yes, I did, but I met Mr. Rúdin. . . He was walking alone in the fields, and his face was so disturbed. I took and came back."

"Thou hast returned, because thou hast met Rúdin?"

"That is, to tell the truth, I do not know myself why I turned back; probably, because I recalled thee to mind; I wanted to sit a while with thee; and I shall get home in good season. . . . ."

Volýntzeff smiled haughtily.

"Yes, it is impossible to think of Rúdin now, without also thinking of me . . . . Servant!" he shouted loudly,—"give us some tea."

The friends began to drink tea. Lezhnyóff undertook to talk about farming, about a new method of roofing storehouses with paper. . . .

Suddenly, Volýntzeff sprang from his chair, and brought his fist down on the table, with so much force, that the cups and saucers rattled.

"No!" he exclaimed:—"It is beyond my power to endure this any longer! I will challenge that clever man, and let him shoot me, or I will try to lodge a bullet in his learned forehead!"

"What ails thee, what ails thee, for heaven's sake!" muttered Lezhnyóff:—"how canst thou yell so! I have dropped my pipe! . . . . What's the matter with thee?"

"The matter is, that I cannot listen to his name with indifference: all the blood in my body fairly boils."

"Enough of that, brother, enough of that! art not thou ashamed of thyself!" returned Lezhnyóff, picking his pipe up from the floor. "Drop it!—Devil take him!"

"He has insulted me," went on Volýntzeff, striding about the room. . . "yes! he has insulted me. Thou must agree to that. At first, I did not have command of myself: he stunned me; and who could have expected that? But I'll show him that he cannot jest with me. I'll shoot him down like a partridge, the cursed philosopher!"

"Much wilt thou gain by that, certainly! I am not speaking of thy sister now. Of course, thou art tempest-tossed with passion . . . how can one expect thee to think of thy sister! And so far as the other person is concerned, thinkest thou that, by killing the philosopher, thou wilt set thine own affairs right?"

Volýntzeff flung himself into an easy chair.

"Then I'll go off somewhere! For her my heart is overwhelmed with anguish; I simply cannot find a place anywhere."

"Thou wilt go off . . . that is quite another matter! I agree to that. And dost thou know what I would like to propose to thee. Let us go together—to the Caucasus, or simply to Little Russia, to eat dumplings. That's splendid, my dear fellow!"

"Yes; but with whom shall we leave my sister?"

"And why should not Alexándra Pávlovna go with us? By heavens, that's a capital expedient. As for looking after her—I'll undertake to do that! She shall not want for anything; if she takes a fancy, I will arrange a serenade under her window every evening; I'll scent the postilions with eau de cologne, I'll stick flowers all along the roads. And thou and I, brother, will simply begin life over again; we'll enjoy ourselves so, we'll come back with such fat paunches, that no love whatever will pierce us!"

"Thou art always jesting, Mísha!"

"I'm not jesting at all. That was a brilliant thought that occurred to thee."

"No! nonsense!" cried Volýntzeff again;—"I want to fight, to fight with him!" . . .

"What, again! Well, brother, thou certainly
hast the blind staggers to-day!" . . .

A man-servant entered with a letter in his
hand.

"From whom?" inquired Lezhnyóff.

"From Rúdin, Dmítry Nikoláevitch. The
Lasúnskys' man brought it."

"From Rúdin?" repeated Volýntzeff:—"to
whom?"

"To you, sir."

"To me? . . . give it here."

Volýntzeff seized the letter, hastily broke the
seal, and began to read. Lezhnyóff watched
him attentively: a strange, almost joyful surprise was depicted on Volýntzeff's face; he
dropped his hands.

"What is it?" asked Lezhnyóff.

"Read it," said Volýntzeff in a low voice, and
handed him the letter.

Lezhnyóff began to read. This is what Rúdin
had written:

"Dear Sir, SERGYÉI PÁVLOVITCH!

"To-day I leave Dárya Mikhaílovna's house, and I
leave it forever. This will, probably, surprise you,
especially after what took place yesterday. I cannot
explain to you precisely what causes me to act thus; but
it seems to me that, for some reason or other, I ought
to inform you of my departure. You do not like me,
and you even regard me as a bad man. I have no in-

RÚDIN

tention of justifying myself : time will justify me. In
my opinion, it is both unworthy and useless for a man
to demonstrate to a prejudiced person the injustice of
his prejudice. He who wishes to understand me, will
pardon me, and he who will not, or cannot understand—
that person's accusations do not affect me. I have been
mistaken in you. In my eyes, you will remain, as heretofore, a noble and honourable man ; but I had supposed
that you would know how to stand on a higher level than
the sphere in which you have grown up I
was in error. What is to be done? It is not the first, and
it will not be the last time. I repeat to you : I am going
away. I wish you happiness. You must agree with me,
that that wish is thoroughly disinterested, and I hope,
that you will now be happy. Perhaps, in the course of
time, you will change your opinion about me. Whether
we shall ever meet again, I know not, but, in any case,
I remain, yours with sincere respect—

"D. R."

"P.S. I will send you the two hundred rubles which
I owe you, as soon as I reach my own home, in the
country, in the Government of T * * * I will also request you not to mention this letter in the presence of
Dárya Mikhaílovna.

"P.P.S. One last, but important request : as I am
now going away, I trust that you will not mention my
visit to you, in Natálya Alexyéevna's presence. . . . "

"Well, what hast thou to say? " inquired Volýntzeff, as soon as Lezhnyóff had finished the
letter.

"What is there to say!" returned Lezh-

160

nyóff,—"exclaim, in Oriental fashion: 'Allah! Allah!' and thrust your finger into your mouth with amazement—that is all that one can do. He is going away . . . . Well! May his path be as smooth as a table-cloth! But here's the curious part of it: he regarded it as *his duty*, to write you this letter, and he presented himself to you, from a sense of duty. . . . . . It is duty at every step, with these gentlemen,—and duty," added Lezhnyóff, pointing, with a grin, to the postscript.

"And what phrases he gets off!" exclaimed Volýntzeff.—"'He has been mistaken in me: he expected that I would stand on a higher level than the sphere. . .' What nonsense, oh, Lord! it's worse than poetry!"

Lezhnyóff made no reply; only his eye smiled. Volýntzeff rose.

"I wish to go to Dárya Mikhaílovna's," said he:—"I want to find out what all this means . . . ."

"Wait, brother: give him a chance to take himself off. What's the use of thy coming into collision with him again? He's going to vanish, you see, and what more dost thou want? Better lie down and take a nap; for thou hast been tossing from side to side all night long. But now, thy affairs are mending . . . ."

"From what dost thou draw that conclusion?"

" Why, it seems so to me. Really, it will be better to take a nap; and I will go to thy sister, and sit with her."

" I have not the slightest desire to sleep. Why should I sleep? I had better go and survey the field," said Volýntzeff, adjusting the skirts of his coat.

" All right, go along, my dear fellow, go along, survey the field." . . .

And Lezhnyóff betook himself to Alexándra Pávlovna's part of the house. He found her in the drawing-room. She greeted him amiably. She was always delighted at his arrival; but her face remained sad. Rúdin's visit of the day before had disquieted her.

" Do you come from my brother? " she asked Lezhnyóff:—" how is he to-day? "

" All right, he is going to survey the field."

Alexándra Pávlovna said nothing for a while.

" Tell me, please," she began, attentively inspecting the border of her handkerchief:—" do not you know, why . . . ."

" Rúdin came? " interpolated Lezhnyóff:—" Yes, I know: he came to say farewell."

Alexándra Pávlovna raised her head.

" What—to say farewell? "

" Yes. Have n't you heard? He is leaving Dárya Mikhaílovna's."

" He is leaving? "

" Forever: at all events, so he says."

" But, good gracious, how am I to understand that, after all that . . . ."

" But that 's another matter! It is impossible to understand it, but so it is. Something must have happened there. He drew the chord too tight—and it broke."

" Mikhaílo Mikhaílitch!" began Alexándra Pávlovna:—" I understand nothing; it seems to me, that you are laughing at me . . . . ."

" But I am not, God is my witness. . . . I tell you, that he is going away, and he has even announced it by letter to his acquaintances. It 's not a bad thing, if you like, from certain points of view; but his departure has prevented the realisation of one astonishing enterprise, which your brother and I had begun to discuss."

" What is that? What enterprise? "

" Why, this. I suggested to your brother to go away, for diversion, to travel, and to take you with him. I took it upon myself to attend upon you . . ."

" Very fine, indeed! " exclaimed Alexándra Pávlovna:—" I can imagine how you would attend upon me. You would starve me to death."

" You say that, Alexándra Pávlovna, because you do not know me. You think that I am a perfect booby, or some sort of a wooden thing; but are you aware, that I am capable of melting like sugar, of spending whole days on my knees? "

RÚDIN

"I must confess, I should like to see that!"

Lezhnyóff suddenly rose.—"Then marry me, Alexándra Pávlovna, and you shall see it all."

Alexándra Pávlovna blushed to her very ears.

"What do you mean, Mikhaílo Mikhaílitch?" she repeated, in confusion.

"Why, what I said," replied Lezhnyóff:— "what has already been on the tip of my tongue a thousand times. I have blurted it out at last, and you may act as you see fit. But, in order not to embarrass you, I will withdraw now. If you will be my wife . . . I will retire. If it is not repulsive to you, only have me called: I shall understand. . ."

Alexándra Pávlovna tried to detain Lezhnyóff, but he briskly left the room, and went into the garden, without his hat, where he leaned his arms on the wicket-gate, and began to stare off somewhere in the distance.

"Mikhaílo Mikhaílitch!" rang out the maid's voice behind him:—"Please come to my lady. She has ordered me to summon you."

Mikhaílo Mikhaílitch turned round, took the maid's head in his hands, to her great amazement, kissed her on the brow, and went to Alexándra Pávlovna.

XI

On reaching home, immediately after his encounter with Lezhnyóff, Rúdin locked himself up in his chamber and wrote two letters:—one to Volýntzeff (which is already known to the reader), and the other to Natálya. He sat for a long time over this second letter, crossed out and re-wrote a great deal of it, and after carefully copying it on a thin sheet of note-paper, folded it into as small a compass as possible, and placed it in his pocket. With sorrow in his face, he walked back and forth several times through the room, sat down in an arm-chair near the window, and propped himself on his elbows; the tears started softly out upon his eyelashes. . . He rose, buttoned his coat to the throat, summoned a man-servant, and ordered him to inquire of Dárya Mikhaílovna, whether she could see him.

The man speedily returned and announced, that Dárya Mikhaílovna had given commands that he should be invited to come to her. Rúdin went to her.

She received him in her boudoir, as on the first occasion, two months previously. But this time, she was not alone; Pandalévsky was sitting by her side, modest, fresh, neat and full of emotion, as usual.

Dárya Mikhaílovna greeted Rúdin with amiability, and Rúdin saluted her amiably, but, at the first glance into the faces of both, a person of any experience whatever, would have understood, that something unpleasant had taken place between them, even if it had not been put into words. Rúdin knew that Dárya Mikhaílovna was angry with him. Dárya Mikhaílovna suspected that he was already informed of everything.

Pandalévsky's denunciation had disturbed her greatly. Worldly pride had begun to stir within her. Rúdin, poor, without official rank, and, so far, an unknown man, had dared to make an appointment for a meeting with her daughter—the daughter of Dárya Mikhaílovna Lasúnsky! ! !

"Let us admit that he is clever, that he is a genius!" she had said:—"Yet, what does that prove? After this, any man may hope to become my son-in-law?"

"For a long time, I could not believe my eyes," Pandalévsky had interpolated. "I am amazed that he should not know his place!"

Dárya Mikhaílovna had been extremely agitated, and she had made Natálya smart for it.

She invited Rúdin to take a seat. He sat down, but no longer in the manner of the former Rúdin, almost as though he were the master of the house, not even like a close acquaintance, but like a visitor, and not even like an intimate visitor. All this had been accomplished in one instant. . . . Just so does water become converted into firm ice.

"I have come to you, Dárya Mikhaílovna!" began Rúdin:—"to thank you once more for your hospitality. I have received news to-day from my little country place, and must go thither this very day, without fail."

Dárya Mikhaílovna gazed intently at Rúdin.

"He has forestalled me; it must be, that he divines the truth," she thought. "He is relieving me of a painful explanation; so much the better! Long live the clever people!"

"Really?" she said aloud. "Akh! how disagreeable! Well, what is to be done? I shall hope to see you next winter in Moscow. We shall soon leave here ourselves."

"I do not know, Dárya Mikhaílovna, whether I shall manage to be in Moscow; but if my means admit of that, I shall regard it as my duty to call upon you."

"Aha, my good fellow!" thought Pandalévsky in his turn: "it was n't so very long ago that thou wert playing the master here, and now see how thou art forced to express thyself!"

"So you have received unsatisfactory news

from your village?" he said, with his habitual
drawl.

" Yes," returned Rúdin curtly.

" A bad harvest, perhaps?"

" No . . . . something else. . . Believe me,
Dárya Mikhaílovna," added Rúdin:—" I shall
never forget the time I have spent in your house."

" And I, Dmítry Nikoláitch, shall always recall with pleasure my acquaintance with you.
. . . When do you set out?"

" To-day, after dinner."

" So soon! . . . Well, I wish you a prosper-
ous journey. But, in case your affairs do not
detain you, perhaps you will still find us here."

" It is hardly likely that I shall have time,"
replied Rúdin and rose. " Pardon me," he
added:—" I cannot repay my debt to you at the
present moment; but as soon as I reach my
estate . . . ."

" Stop, Dmítry Nikoláitch!" Dárya Mikhaílovna interrupted him:—" aren't you ashamed
of yourself! . . . But what time is it?" she
asked.

Pandalévsky pulled a gold enamelled watch
from his waistcoat pocket, and looked at it, cautiously, leaning his rosy cheek upon his firm,
white collar.

" Thirty-three minutes past two," he said.

" It is time to dress," remarked Dárya Mikhaílovna. " Farewell for the present, Dmítry
Nikoláitch!"

RÚDIN

Rúdin rose. The whole conversation between him and Dárya Mikhaílovna had borne a peculiar imprint. In this fashion do actors rehearse their parts, in this fashion do diplomats at conferences exchange phrases which have been agreed upon in advance. . .

Rúdin left the room. He knew now, by experience, how society people do not even cast aside, but simply drop a man, who has become unnecessary to them: like a glove, after a ball, like the wrapper from confects, like a ticket in a society lottery, which has not drawn a prize.

He hastily packed his things, and began impatiently to await the moment of departure. Every one in the household was greatly surprised, on learning his intention; people even stared at him in astonishment. Basístoff did not hide his grief. Natálya openly shunned Rúdin. She tried to avoid meeting his gaze; nevertheless, he succeeded in thrusting his letter into her hand. After dinner, Dárya Mikhaílovna once more repeated, that she hoped to see him again before their departure for Moscow, but Rúdin made her no reply. Pandalévsky addressed him more frequently than any one else. More than once, Rúdin felt strongly inclined to fling himself upon him, and cleave open his blooming, rosy face. Mlle. Boncourt cast frequent glances at Rúdin, with a crafty and strange expression in her eyes; that sort of expression can sometimes be seen in aged, very in-

telligent setter dogs. . . . "Ehe!" she appeared
to be saying to herself:—"you 've caught it
now!"

At last, six o'clock struck, and Rúdin's tarantás was brought round to the door. He began
hastily to take leave of them all. His spirit was
in a very evil plight. He had not anticipated
that he would make his exit from that house
after this fashion: it was as though he were being
expelled. . . . "How has all this come to pass!
and what need was there for me to hurry? However, it 's all the same in the end"—that is what
he was thinking, as he bowed on all sides, with a
constrained smile. For the last time, he looked
at Natálya, and his heart was stirred within him:
her eyes were fixed upon him in sorrowful, farewell reproach.

He ran briskly down the steps, and sprang
into his tarantás. Basístoff had offered to escort him to the railway station, and took his seat
beside him.

"Do you remember," began Rúdin, as soon as
the tarantás had emerged from the courtyard
upon the broad road, bordered with fir-trees:—
"do you remember what Don Quixote said to
his squire, when he emerged from the Duchess's
palace? 'Liberty,' said he, 'my friend Sancho,
is one of man's most precious possessions, and
happy is he on whom heaven hath bestowed a
morsel of bread, who is not compelled to be in-

debted for it to any one!' What Don Quixote
felt then, I feel now. . . . . God grant, my
good Basístoff, that you may some day experience this feeling!"

Basístoff squeezed Rúdin's hand, and the
heart of the honest young fellow beat violently
in his deeply affected breast. Rúdin discoursed
all the way to the railway station, on the dignity
of man, on the significance of genuine freedom,—
discoursed fervently, nobly and justly—and
when the moment of parting came, Basístoff
could endure it no longer, flung himself on his
neck, and burst out sobbing. Tears streamed
down Rúdin's face also; but he did not weep because he was parting with Basístoff, and his
tears were the tears of self-love.

Natálya went to her own room and read Rúdin's letter.

"My dear Natálya Alexyéevna—" he had written to
her—"I have decided to go away. There is no other
issue for me. I have decided to go away, before I am
told, in plain terms, to begone. With my departure, all
misunderstandings will come to an end; and it is hardly
likely that any one will pity me. What else could I expect? . . . All this is so; but why should I write to
you?

"I am parting from you, probably forever, and it
would be too bitter to leave you a memory of myself still
worse than that which I merit. That is why I am
writing to you. I do not wish either to defend myself,

171

RÚDIN

or to blame any one except myself: I wish, so far as possible, to explain myself . . . . . The events of the last few days have been so unexpected, so sudden. . . .

" Our meeting of to-day will serve me as a memorable lesson. Yes, you are right: I did not know you, but I thought I knew you! In the course of my life, I have had to deal with all sorts of people, I have been closely acquainted with many women and young girls; but when I met you, I met, for the first time, a *perfectly* honourable and upright soul. I was not accustomed to this, and I did not know how to appreciate you. I felt drawn towards you, from the very first day of our acquaintance —you may have noticed it. I passed hours and hours in your society, and yet I did not learn to know you; I hardly even tried to know you . . . . and I could imagine that I had fallen in love with you!! For that sin I am now punished.

" Once before, I loved a woman, and she loved me. . . . My feeling for her was complicated, as was hers for me; but, as she herself was not simple, it was fitting. The truth did not make itself felt by me then: I did not recognise it, and now, when it stood before me, ... I recognised it, at last, but too late. . . . The past cannot be brought back. . . . Our lives might have been merged in one—and they will never be merged. How can I prove to you, that I might have loved you with real love—with the love of the heart, not of the imagination—when I myself do not know whether I am capable or not of such a love!

" Nature has endowed me with much—that I know, and I will not assume an air of modesty to you, out of false shame, especially now, in moments so bitter, so

172

shameful for me. . . . Yes, nature has given me much; but I shall die, without having done anything worthy of my powers, without having left behind me a single beneficent trace. All my wealth will perish in vain; I shall behold no fruits from my seeds. I lack . . . I myself cannot say precisely what is lacking in me. . . What I lack is, in all probability, that without which it is as impossible to move the hearts of men, as it is to subdue the hearts of women; and sovereignty over minds alone is both uncertain and useless. Strange, almost comic is my fate: I surrender the whole of myself, eagerly, completely—and cannot surrender myself. I shall end by sacrificing myself for some nonsense or other, in which I shall not even believe. . . My God! the idea of being still engaged, at the age of thirty-five, in preparing to do something! . . .

" I shall never again speak out my sentiments to any one—this is my dying confession.

" But enough about me. I wish to speak about you, to give you a few counsels: I am fit for nothing else . . . . you are still young, but no matter how long you may live, always follow the intuitions of your heart, do not surrender yourself to your own mind, nor to the mind of any one else. Believe me, the more simple, the more restricted the circle in which life flows on, the better; the important point does not lie in seeking out new sides of it, but in having all its transitions accomplished in their proper season. ' Blessed is he, who has been young from his youth ' . . But I observe, that these counsels apply much more to me, than they do to you.

" I will confess to you, Natálya Alexyéevna, that I am very heavy at heart. I have never deceived myself, as to the character of the feeling which I inspired in Dárya Mikhaílovna; but I hoped, that I had found, at least a temporary harbour. . . . Now, once more, I must roam about the world. What will compensate to me for your conversation, your presence, your attentive, and intelligent gaze? . . . I myself am to blame; but you must agree with me, that fate has seemed deliberately to mock at us. A week ago, I hardly suspected that I loved you. . Day before yesterday evening, in the garden, I heard, for the first time, from you . . . but why recall to you that which you then said—and now, to-day, I am going away, going away in disgrace, after a cruel explanation with you, and bearing with me not the slightest hope. . . And even yet, you do not know to what an extent I am to blame towards you. . . There is in me a certain stupid frankness, a certain loquacity. . . . But why speak of that? I am going away forever."

(Here Rúdin had an idea of recounting to Natálya his visit to Volýntzeff, but changed his mind, and erased all that passage, but added the second postscript to his letter to Volýntzeff).

" I shall remain alone on earth, in order to devote myself, as you said to me this morning, with a cruel sneer, to occupations more suited to me. Alas! if I could really devote myself to those occupations, conquer my indolence at last. . . . . But no! I shall remain the same incomplete creature as I have been hitherto. . . . At the very first obstacle—I am completely scattered to the winds; the affair with you has demonstrated that to me. If I had, at least, but offered my love as a sacrifice

to my future occupation, to my vocation; but I was
simply frightened at the responsibility, which had fallen
upon me, and therefore, in very truth, I am unworthy
of you. I am not worthy of your wresting yourself out
of your sphere for me. . . And, after all, perhaps it is
all for the best. Perhaps I shall emerge from this trial
purer and stronger.

"I wish you the fulness of happiness. Farewell!
Think of me, now and then. I hope that you will yet
hear of me.

"RÚDIN."

Natálya dropped Rúdin's letter on her lap,
and sat for a long time motionless, with her eyes
riveted on the floor. This letter, more clearly
than all possible arguments, proved to her how
thoroughly in the right she had been when, on
parting from Rúdin that morning, she had involuntarily exclaimed, that he did not love her!
But she felt none the more at ease for that. She
sat motionless; it seemed to her, as though some
sort of dark waves were closing in, without a
plash, above her head, and she was sinking to the
bottom, growing stiff and dumb as she went.
Every one finds the first disillusionment painful;
but for the sincere soul, which does not wish to deceive itself, which is alien to frivolity and exag-
geration, it is almost beyond endurance. Natálya recalled her childhood, when, during her
evening strolls, she was always striving to go
in the direction of the bright rim of the sky,

thither where the glow of sunset burned, and not toward the dark. Life now stood dark before her, and she had turned her back on the light. . . .

Tears sprang to Natálya's eyes. Tears are not always beneficent. They are consoling and healing, when, after having, for a long time, seethed in the breast, they flow at last—first violently, then more and more gently, more sweetly; they dissolve the dumb torture of grief. . . . But if they be cold tears which flow sparingly: the woe which lies like a heavy, immovable burden on the heart, crushes them out, drop by drop; they are devoid of consolation, and they bring no relief. Want weeps with such tears as these, and he has not yet been unhappy who has not shed them. Natálya made acquaintance with them on that day.

Two hours elapsed. Natálya mustered her courage, rose, wiped her eyes, lighted a candle, burned Rúdin's letter to the end in its flame, and flung the ashes out of the window.

Then she opened Púshkin at haphazard, and read the first lines which met her eye (she often told her fortune in this manner with him). This is what turned up:

> He who hath felt, that man doth trouble
> The wraith of days forever gone. . . .
> For there is no witchery more, . . .
> Him doth memory's serpent,
> Him doth repentance gnaw. . . . . .

She stood, and gazed at herself in the mirror, with a cold smile, and after making a small movement with her head, downwards from above, she went to the drawing-room.

Dárya Mikhaílovna, as soon as she saw her, bade her come into her boudoir, seated her by her side, tapped her affectionately on the cheek, and in the meantime, peered attentively, almost curiously, into her eyes. Dárya Mikhaílovna felt a secret perplexity: for the first time it had entered her head, that, in reality, she did not know her own daughter. On hearing from Pandalévsky about her meeting with Rúdin, she had felt not so much incensed as amazed, that sensible Natálya could make up her mind to such a step. But when she had summoned her to her, and had undertaken to scold her—not in the least as might have been expected from a European woman, but in a decidedly shrill and inelegant manner—Natálya's firm replies, the decision of her glances and movements, had disconcerted, even alarmed, Dárya Mikhaílovna.

Rúdin's abrupt and not entirely comprehensible departure, had removed a great weight from her heart; but she had expected tears, hysterical attacks. . . . Natálya's outward composure again baffled her.

" Well, my child," began Dárya Mikhaílovna: —" how art thou to-day? "

Natálya looked at her mother.

" He has gone, you know, the object of your

affections. Dost thou not know, why he made ready so hastily?"

"Mama!" began Natálya, in a quiet voice:— "I pledge thee my word, that if thou thyself wilt not mention his name, thou wilt never hear anything from me."

"So thou acknowledgest, that thou wert to blame toward me?"

Natálya drooped her head, and repeated: "Thou wilt never hear anything from me."

"Well, see that I do not!" returned Dárya Mikhaílovna, with a smile. "I believe thee. But day before yesterday, dost thou remember how. . . . Well, I will not do it again. It is ended, settled and buried. Isn't it? Here now, I recognise thee again; but I was pretty nearly at an utter loss. Come, kiss me, my wise one!" . . .

Natálya raised Dárya Mikhaílovna's hand to her lips, and Dárya Mikhaílovna kissed her on her bowed head.

"Always heed my counsels, do not forget that thou art a Lasúnsky and my daughter," she added:—"and thou wilt be happy. And now go."

Natálya withdrew in silence. Dárya Mikhaílovna gazed after her, and thought: "She takes after me—she also will fall in love: *mais aura moins d'abandon.*" And Dárya Mikhaílovna immersed herself in memories of the past . . . . of the distant past . . . .

Then she ordered Mlle. Boncourt to be summoned, and sat for a long time with her, the two locked in together. On dismissing her, she called in Pandalévsky. She insisted upon knowing the real cause of Rúdin's departure . . . but Pandalévsky completely reassured her. That was part of his business.

On the following day Volýntzeff came with his sister to dinner. Dárya Mikhaílovna was always very amiable to him, and on this occasion, she treated him in a particularly caressing manner. It was intolerably painful to Natálya: but Volýntzeff was so respectful, talked to her so timidly, that she could not but thank him in her soul.

The day passed quietly, in a rather tiresome way, but all, on separating, felt that they had got back into their ordinary rut; and this means a great deal, a very great deal.

Yes, all had got back into their former rut . . . . all, except Natálya. When, at last, she was alone, she dragged herself, with difficulty, to her bed, and weary, broken, fell face down upon the pillows. Living seemed to her so bitter, and repulsive, and insipid, she felt so ashamed of herself, of her love, of her sorrow, that, at that moment, she would, probably, have consented to die. . . . Many painful days still lay before her, many sleepless nights, of torturing agitation, but she was young—life was only just beginning for her, and sooner or later, life asserts itself. Whatever blow has been dealt to a man, on the very same day, or on the next day at latest—pardon the vulgarity of the comparison—he will begin to eat, and there you have the first consolation. . . . .

Natálya suffered tortures, she was suffering for the first time. . . But first sufferings, like first love, are not repeated,—and God be thanked for that!

XII

ABOUT two years have elapsed. The first days
of May had arrived. On the balcony of her house
sat Alexándra Pávlovna, only no longer Lípin
but Lezhnyóff; it was more than a year since
she had married Mikhaílo Mikhaílitch. As in
the past, she was charming, but had grown stout
of late. In front of the balcony, from which
steps led into the garden, a nurse was walking,
holding in her arms a baby, in a little white cloak,
and with a white pompon on its hat.

Alexándra Pávlovna kept glancing at it.
The baby was not crying, but was sucking its
thumb with dignity, and staring about it. The
worthy son of Mikhaílo Mikhaílitch was already
asserting itself in him.

Beside Alexándra Pávlovna, on the balcony,
sat our old acquaintance, Pigásoff. He has
grown noticeably grey, since we parted from
him, has become bent and thin, and hisses when
he talks; the hissing imparts still more venom to
his speeches. . . His spite has not diminished
with the years, but his witticisms have lost their
point, and he repeats himself more frequently
than of yore. Mikhaílo Mikhaílitch was not at

home; they were expecting him for tea. The sun had already set. In the place where it had gone down, a strip of pale-gold, of lemon colour, stretched along the horizon; in the opposite quarter, there were two streaks: one, the lower, blue, the other, the higher up, brilliant purple. Light clouds were melting into the zenith. Everything foreboded steady weather.

All at once, Pigásoff broke out laughing.

" What are you laughing at, Afrikán Semyónitch? " inquired Alexándra Pávlovna.

" Oh, because . . . Yesterday, I heard a peasant say to his wife—she, the fool, was chattering:—' Don't squeak!' . . . That pleased me greatly. Don't squeak! Yes, and as a matter of fact, what can a woman argue about? You know, that I never talk about present company. Our elders were wiser than we. In their fairy-tales, the beauty sits at the window, on her brow is a star, but she never utters a sound. That's the way it ought to be. But otherwise, judge for yourself: day before yesterday, the wife of our marshal of .the nobility, as good as fired a pistol into my brains: she said to me, that she did not like my *tendency!* Tendency! Come now, would n't it be better for her, and for everybody, if somehow, by some beneficent arrangement of nature, she could have suddenly been deprived of the use of her tongue? "

" You are just the same as ever, Afrikán

Semyónitch: you are always attacking us poor women. . . . Do you know, that really is a misfortune, in its way. I am sorry for you."

"A misfortune? What are you pleased to mean by that? In the first place, in my opinion, there are only three misfortunes in the world: to live in cold lodgings in the winter, to wear tight boots in summer, and to spend the night in a room where a baby is screaming, which cannot be put to sleep with Persian powder; and, in the second place, I have become the most peaceable of men now. You might even use me as a model in a copy-book! I behave in such a moral way."

"You do behave well, there's no denying it! Not longer ago than yesterday evening, Eléna Antónovna complained of you to me."

"You don't say so, ma'am! And what did she tell you, permit me to inquire?"

"She told me, that during the whole course of the morning, the only reply you had made to her questions, was, 'What, ma'am? what, ma'am?' and that in such a squeaking voice, to boot."

Pigásoff broke into a laugh.

"And that was a fine idea, you must agree, Alexándra Pávlovna . . . . hey?"

"Remarkably! How can you be so impolite to a woman, Afrikán Semyónitch?"

"What? Is Eléna Antónovna a woman, in your opinion?"

"What is she, then, in yours?"

"A drum, good gracious, a common drum, the sort that is thumped with sticks." . .

"Akh, yes!" interrupted Alexándra Pávlovna, wishing to change the conversation:—"I am told that you are to be congratulated?"

"On what?"

"On the ending of your law-suit. The Glinóvsky meadows remain your property."

"Yes, they do," returned Pigásoff gloomily.

"You have been trying to accomplish this for years, and now you seem to be dissatisfied."

"I will inform you, Alexándra Pávlovna," said Pigásoff deliberately:—"that nothing can be worse and more offensive than happiness which comes too late. It cannot afford you any satisfaction, and, on the other hand, it deprives you of a precious right,—the right to scold and to curse fate. Yes, madam, belated happiness is a bitter and offensive thing."

Alexándra Pávlovna merely shrugged her shoulders.

"Nurse," she began:—"I think it is time to put Mísha to bed. Bring him hither."

And Alexándra Pávlovna busied herself with her son, while Pigásoff took himself off, growling, to another corner of the balcony.

All at once, Mikhaílo Mikhaílitch made his appearance, in his racing-gig, a short distance off, on the road which skirted the garden. In

front of his horse ran two huge yard-dogs: one
yellow, the other grey; he had lately provided
himself with them. They were incessantly fight-
ing, and dwelt in inseparable friendship. An
aged mastiff emerged from the gate to meet
them, opened his mouth, as though preparing to
bark, and wound up by yawning and returning,
wagging his tail in a friendly way.

"Look, Sásha,—" shouted Lezhnyóff from
afar to his wife;—"see whom I am bringing to
thee." . . .

Alexándra Pávlovna did not, on the instant,
recognise the man, who was sitting with his back
to her husband.

"Ah! Mr. Basístoff!" she cried, at last.

"'T is he, 't is he," replied Lezhnyóff:—"and
what splendid news he has brought. Just wait,
thou wilt hear directly."

And he drove into the yard.

A few moments later, he made his appearance
with Basístoff on the balcony.

"Hurrah!" he exclaimed, and embraced his
wife.—"Seryózha is going to be married!"

"To whom?" asked Alexándra Pávlovna,
with agitation.

"To Natálya, of course. . . . Our friend,
here, has brought the news from Moscow, and
there is a letter for thee. . . Dost thou hear, Mi-
shúk!" he added, catching his son in his arms;—
"thine uncle is to be married! . . . Ekh, what

villainous apathy! he does nothing but blink his eyes!"

"He is sleepy," remarked the nurse.

"Yes, madam," said Basístoff, approaching Alexándra Pávlovna:—"I have arrived from Moscow to-day, with a commission from Dárya Mikhaílovna—to audit the accounts of the estate. And here is the letter."

Alexándra Pávlovna hastily broke the seal of her brother's letter. It consisted of a few lines. In his first transport of joy, he informed his sister, that he had offered himself to Natálya, had received her consent and Dárya Mikhaílovna's, and promised to write further with the first post, and, though absent, he embraced and kissed them all. It was evident that he had written under a sort of spell.

Tea was served, and Basístoff was made to sit down. He was pelted with a hail of questions. Every one, even Pigásoff, was delighted at the news he had brought.

"Tell me, please," said Lezhnyóff, among other things:—"Rumours have reached us concerning a certain Mr. Kortchágin,—of course, it was nonsense?"

(Kortchágin was a handsome young man—a society lion, extremely inflated with pride and importance: he bore himself in a remarkably majestic manner, as though he were not a live man, but his own statue, erected by public subscription.)

" Well, no, it's not entirely nonsense," returned Basístoff, with a smile. " Dárya Mikhaílovna favoured him greatly; but Natálya Alexyéevna would not hear to him."

" Yes, and I know him," interpolated Pigásoff: " he's a double-flowered blockhead, a thundering blockhead . . . . good gracious! Why, if all people were like him, it would be necessary to demand a lot of money, before one would consent to live . . . upon my word! "

" Perhaps so," replied Basístoff:—" but he plays a far from insignificant part in society."

" Well, that makes no difference! " exclaimed Alexándra Pávlovna:—" I want to have nothing to do with him! Akh, how glad I am for my brother! . . . And is Natálya cheerful, happy?"

" Yes, madam,—she is composed, as usual— you know her, of course—but, apparently, she is contented."

The evening passed in pleasant and vivacious conversation. They sat down to supper.

" Yes, by the way," inquired Lezhnyóff of Basístoff, as he poured him out some claret:— " do you know where Rúdin is?"

" I do not know for certain, at present. He came to Moscow last winter, for a short time, then he went off to Simbírsk with a family; he

and I corresponded for a time: in his last letter,
he informed me, that he was leaving Simbírsk—
he did not say whither he was going—and since
then, I have heard nothing about him."

" He won't get lost! " interpolated Pigásoff:
—" he's sitting somewhere, and preaching.
That gentleman will always find two or three
worshippers, who will listen to him, with gaping
mouths, and lend him money. You 'll see, he 'll
end by dying somewhere in Tzarevokokosháisk,
or in Tchukhlóm, in the arms of a very aged
spinster, in a wig, who will think of him as the
greatest genius in the world. . ."

" You express yourself very harshly with regard to him," remarked Basístoff in an undertone, and with displeasure.

" I 'm not in the least harsh! "—retorted Pigásoff:—" but perfectly just! In my opinion, he 's
nothing more than a lickspittle. I had forgotten
to tell you," he continued, addressing Lezhnyóff:—" you see, I made the acquaintance of
that Terlakhóff, with whom Rúdin went abroad.
I should think I did! I should think I did! You
cannot imagine what he told me about him—it
was enough to make you die with laughing, simply! It is a notable fact, that all Rúdin's friends
and followers become, in time, his enemies."

" I beg that you will except me from the number of those friends," interrupted Basístoff,
hotly.

" Well, you—that's another matter! We are not talking about you."

" But what was it that Terlakhóff told you?" inquired Alexándra Pávlovna.

" Why, he told me a great deal: I cannot recall all of it. But the very best anecdote of all that happened to Rúdin, is this. Uninterruptedly developing himself (that sort of gentleman always develops: others, for example, simply sleep, or eat—but they find themselves in the moment of development of sleeping or of eating; isn't that so, Mr. Basístoff?"—Basístoff made no reply). . . . " And so, constantly developing, Rúdin arrived, by the road of philosophy, at the argument, that he ought to fall in love.

" He began to look up an object, who should be worthy of such a remarkable syllogism. Fortune smiled upon him. He made the acquaintance of a French woman, a very pretty little milliner. The affair took place in a German town, on the Rhine, please to note. He began to call on her, to carry her various books, to talk to her about Nature and Hegel. Can you imagine the situation of the milliner? She took him for an astronomer. But, you know, he's a fairly good-looking young fellow; well, he was a foreigner, a Russian, and he caught her fancy. So, at last, he appointed a tryst, and a very poetical tryst: in a gondola, on the river. The

French woman consented; she dressed herself in her best, and set off with him in the gondola. Thus they rowed about for a couple of hours. And how do you think he spent all that time? He kept stroking the French woman on the head, gazing meditatively at the sky, and repeating, several times, that he felt a paternal affection for her. The French woman returned home in a rage, and told the whole thing herself, afterwards, to Terlakhóff. That's the sort of gentleman he is!"

And Pigásoff laughed.

"You are an old cynic!" remarked Alexándra Pávlovna, with vexation:—"and I am more and more convinced that even those who revile Rúdin, can say nothing bad of him."

"Nothing bad? Upon my word! and how about his forever living at the expense of other people, his borrowing? . . . Mikhaílo Mikhaílitch, he certainly must have borrowed money from you?"

"See here, Afrikán Semyónitch!" began Lezhnyóff, and his face assumed a serious expression:—"listen to me: you know, and my wife knows, that I have not felt particularly well disposed toward Rúdin of late years, and that I have even frequently condemned him. Nevertheless" (Lezhnyóff poured champagne into the glasses), "this is what I propose to you: we have just drunk the health of our dear brother

190

and his affianced bride; I now propose to you that we shall drink the health of Dmítry Rúdin!"

Alexándra Pávlovna and Pigásoff stared at Lezhnyóff with amazement, but Basístoff gave a great start, flushed crimson with delight, and opened his eyes wide.

" I know him well," pursued Lezhnyóff:— " his defects are well known to me. They are the more apparent, because he, himself, is not a petty man."

" Rúdin has the temperament of a genius," interpolated Basístoff.

" There is some genius in him, I admit," returned Lezhnyóff;—" but as for temperament .... Therein lies his whole misfortune, that there is no temperament whatever about him.... But that is not the point. I wish to speak of that which is good and rare in him. He has enthusiasm; and that, believe me, for a phlegmatic man, is the most precious quality of all in our day. We have all become intolerably reasonable and languid: we have fallen asleep, we have congealed, and we owe thanks to any man who will, even for an instant, move us and warm us up! It is high time! Dost thou remember, Sásha, how I once was talking to thee about him, and reproached him with coldness? I was both right and wrong then. That coldness is in his blood— he is not to blame for that—but not in his

head. He is not an actor, as I termed him, he
is not a deceiver, nor a rogue; he lives at other
people's expense not like an intriguer, but
like a child. . . . Yes, he really will die somewhere in poverty and need; but can one hurl a
stone at him for that? He will do nothing himself, precisely because he has no temperament, no
blood; but who has a right to say, that he will not
be, has not already been, of use? that his words
have not sown many good seeds in young souls,
to whom nature has not denied, as it has to him,
the power of action, the capacity for carrying
out their own projects? Yes, I myself, I was the
first to undergo all that experience on myself. . .
Sásha knows what Rúdin was to me in my youth.
I remember, that I, also, asserted that Rúdin's
words could not affect people; but I was talking then about people like myself, at my present age, of people already elderly and broken
by life. A single false tone in a speech—and
all its harmony has vanished for us; but in a
young man, happily, the ear is not yet so highly
developed, not so spoiled. If the essence of
what he hears seems fine to him, what cares he
for the tone! He will find the right tone within
himself."

  "Bravo! bravo!" exclaimed Basístoff:—
"how justly that was said! As far as Rúdin's
influence is concerned, I swear to you, that that
man not only understood how to shake you to

the depths, he moved you from your place, he did not let you halt, he converted you from the very foundations, he set you on fire!"

"Do you hear that!" went on Lezhnyóff, turning to Pigásoff:—"what more proof do you need? You attack philosophy; in speaking of it, you cannot find words sufficiently scornful. I do not favour it much myself, and understand very little about it: but our principal misfortunes do not arise from philosophy! The artful devices and ravings of philosophy will never get inoculated into the Russian: he possesses too much sound sense for that; but attacks upon every aspiration toward the truth and knowledge, under the name of philosophy, cannot be permitted. Rúdin's misfortune consists in the fact, that he does not know Russia, and that, really, is a great misfortune. Russia can get along without any one of us, but no one can get along without her. Woe to him who thinks so, twofold woe to him who really does get along without her. Cosmopolitanism is nonsense, the cosmopolite is a cipher, worse than a cipher; outside of nationality, there is neither art, nor truth, nor life, there is nothing. Without physiognomy, there is not even an ideal face; only a commonplace face is possible without physiognomy. But I will say it again, that is not Rúdin's fault: it is his fate, a bitter and heavy fate, for which we will not blame him. It would lead us very far

193

afield, if we were to undertake to examine into the question—why do Rúdins make their appearance among us. But let us be grateful to him for what good there is in him. That is easier than it is to be unjust to him, and we have been unjust to him. It is not our business to punish him and it is not necessary: he has punished himself far more harshly than he has deserved. . . And God grant, that unhappiness has expelled all evil from him, and left in him only what is fine! I drink to the health of Rúdin! I drink to the health of the comrade of my best years, I drink to youth, to its hopes, to its aspirations, to its truthfulness and honesty, to everything which made our hearts beat high at the age of twenty, and anything better than that we have not known and we never shall know in life. . . I drink to thee, O golden age, I drink to the health of Rúdin! "

All clinked glasses with Lezhnyóff. Basístoff, in his fervour, came near smashing his glass, and drained it off at one draught, while Alexándra Pávlovna pressed Lezhnyóff's hand.

" I did not suspect you, Mikhaílo Mikhaílitch, of being so eloquent," remarked Pigásoff:— " you are fairly the equal of Mr. Rúdin himself; it even penetrated me."

" I am not in the least eloquent," replied Lezhnyóff, not without vexation;—" and I think it would be difficult to penetrate you. However, enough of Rúdin; let us talk of something else. . .

What . . . . what the deuce is his name? . . . Is Pandalévsky still living at Dárya Mikhaílovna's?" he added, turning to Basístoff.

" Of course he is still with her! She has procured a very good position for him."

Lezhnyóff grinned.

" There 's a fellow who will not die in poverty, you may bet on that."

Supper came to an end. The guests separated. When she was left alone with her husband, Alexándra Pávlovna looked into his face with a smile.

" How fine thou wert to-day, Mísha," she said, caressing his brow with her hand,—" how cleverly and nobly thou didst speak! But confess, that thou wert a little carried away in favour of Rúdin, just as, formerly, thou wert carried away against him."

" One does not strike a man who is down . . . . but I was afraid, then, that he might turn thy head."

" No," answered Alexándra Pávlovna ingenuously:—" he always seemed to me too learned. I was afraid of him, and did not know what to say in his presence. But Pigásoff sneered at him quite maliciously to-day, did n't he?"

" Pigásoff!" said Lezhnyóff. " That is exactly why I stood up so hotly for Rúdin, because Pigásoff was there. He dares to call Rúdin a lickspittle! But in my opinion, his rôle, the rôle of a Pigásoff, is a hundred times worse. He is in independent circumstances, he jeers at everybody, and how he clings to the distinguished and the rich! Do you know, that that Pigásoff, who reviles everything and everybody with so much rancour, and attacks philosophy and women,— do you know, that he, when he was in the service, took bribes, and did other things of that sort? Ah! And that is precisely the reason!·"

"Is it possible?" exclaimed Alexándra Pávlovna. "I did not expect that in the least! . . . . Listen, Mísha," she added, after a brief silence:— "I want to ask thee something." . . .

"What is it?"

"What dost thou think? Will my brother be happy with Natálya?"

"How can I tell . . . there is every probability that he will. . . She will command— there's no use in making a secret of that between ourselves—she is cleverer than he; but he's a splendid fellow, and loves her with all his soul. What more would you have? Why, here are we—we love each other and are happy, are n't we?"

Alexándra Pávlovna smiled, and pressed Mikhaílo Mikhaílitch's hand.

On that same day, when all that we have narrated took place in Alexándra Pávlovna's house,—in one of the distant governments of

RÚDIN

Russia, a wretched basket kibítka[1] was jogging
along, in the very sultriest part of the day, on the
highway, drawn by a tróïka[1] of peasants' horses.
On the box, with his legs braced slantwise against
the whiffletree, towered up a miserable, grey-
haired peasant in a tattered coat, who incessantly
jerked at the rope reins, and flourished his small
whip; and in the kibítka, on a lean trunk, sat a
man of lofty stature, in a foraging cap, and an
old, dusty cloak. It was Rúdin. He sat with
drooping head, and with the visor of his cap
pulled down over his eyes. The uneven jolts of
the kibítka tossed him from side to side; he seemed
entirely insensible, as though in a doze. At last
he straightened himself up.

" When shall we reach the station? " he asked
the peasant, who was sitting on the box.

" Why, dear little father," replied the peasant,
and tugged more vigorously than ever at the
reins:—" when we get up the hill, there will be
two versts left, not more. . . Come, thou beast!
use thy brains. . . . I 'll use them for thee! " he
added in a shrill voice, and began to lash the off
horse.

" It seems to me, that thou drivest very badly,"
remarked Rúdin:—" we have been dragging
along ever since early morning, and cannot reach

[1] A team of three horses abreast: the middle horse, a trotter, is
between the shafts, connected by a wooden arch over his head. The
side horses, attached by traces, gallop, with heads bent downward
and backward. *Kibítka*, a covered travelling waggon.—TRANSLATOR.

our destination. Thou hadst better sing something."

" Why, what 's to be done, dear little father!
the horses, as you see for yourself, are starved to
death . . . and then again, there 's the heat.
And we can't sing: we 're not a postilion. . . .
You snipe, hey there, you snipe," the peasant
suddenly exclaimed, addressing a passer-by in a
grey smock and patched bast slippers:—" get
out of the way, snipe! "

" A pretty sort of coachman thou art! " muttered the wayfarer after him, and halted. " Vile
little Moscow bone! " he added, in a voice filled
with censure, shook his head, and hobbled onward.

" What art thou about? " put in the wretched
little peasant, with pauses, pulling at the shaft-
horse:—" Akh, thou art a sly one! truly, a sly
one. . . ."

The exhausted nags finally managed to crawl
to the posting-station. Rúdin got out of the kibítka, paid the peasant (who did not salute him,
and who turned the money over in his palm for
a long time—which meant, that he had not received enough for liquor), and himself carried his
trunk into the posting-house room.

One of my acquaintances, who has roamed a
great deal about Russia in his time, once made
the remark, that if on the walls of the station-
room hang pictures representing scenes from the
" Prisoner of the Caucasus," or Russian Gener-

als, then one can promptly procure horses; but
if the pictures present the life of the well-known
gambler, Georges de Germanie, then the traveller need not hope for a speedy departure: he
will have an opportunity to admire the curled
crest, the white, open-breasted waistcoat, and the
extremely tight and short trousers of the gambler
in his youth, and his fanatical physiognomy when
he, now already an old man, slays his own son,
with a chair brandished aloft, in a hovel with a
steep roof. In the room which Rúdin entered,
hung precisely these pictures from " Thirty
Years, or the Life of a Gambler." At his shout,
the superintendent made his appearance, sleepy
(by the way—has anyone ever beheld a superintendent who was not sleepy?), and, without even
awaiting Rúdin's question, announced, in a languid voice, that there were no horses.

" How can you tell that there are no horses,"
said Rúdin:—" when you do not even know
whither I am going? I came hither with peasant
horses."

" We have no horses for any direction," replied
the superintendent. " But whither are you
going? "

" To * * * sk."

" There are no horses," repeated the superintendent, and left the room.

Rúdin, in irritation, stepped to the window, and
flung his cap on the table. He had not changed

RÚDIN

much, but had grown sallow during the last two years; silver threads gleamed here and there among his curls, and his eyes, which were still very handsome, seemed, somehow, to have grown dull; tiny wrinkles, the traces of bitter and agitating emotions, lay around his mouth, on his cheeks, and on his temples.

His clothing was threadbare and old, and no linen was anywhere visible. Evidently, the time of his bloom was past: as the gardeners express it, he had gone to seed.

He set about reading the inscriptions on the walls . . . . the familiar diversion of bored travellers . . . . when, all of a sudden, the door squeaked, and the superintendent entered.

"There are no horses for * * * sk, and there will not be any for a good while," he began, " but there are some going back to * * * off."

"To * * * off?" said Rúdin. "But, good heavens, that is not on my road at all. I am on my way to Pénza, but * * * off lies in the direction of Tambóff, I think."

"What of that? Then you can cross over from Tambóff, or, if not, you can turn off from * * * off, somehow or other."

Rúdin reflected.

"Well, all right," he said at last:—" order them to harness the horses. It's all the same to me; I will go to Tambóff."

The horses were soon brought round. Rúdin

200

carried out his trunk, got into the peasant cart, seated himself, drooped his head as before. There was something helpless and sadly submissive in his bent figure. . . . And the tróïka crawled along at a leisurely trot, spasmodically jingling its bells.

EPILOGUE

(Several more years have elapsed.)

IT was a chill, autumnal day. A travelling calash drove up to the porch of the chief inn
in the Government capital S * * * ; from it,
slightly stretching and yawning, alighted a gentleman, who was not yet elderly, but who had
already succeeded in acquiring that corpulence
of body which it has become the custom to desig-
nate as respectable. Ascending the stairs to the
second storey, he halted at the entrance to a
broad corridor, and seeing no one in front of
him, he asked for a room, in a loud voice. A door
somewhere banged, a long lackey sprang out
from behind a small screen, and advanced with a
brisk, sidelong gait, flashing through the half-
dark corridor with his shining back and tucked-up
sleeves. On entering his room, the newcomer
immediately threw off his overcoat and scarf,
seated himself on the divan, and resting his closed
fists on his knees, first took a look around him,
then gave orders that his servant should be called.
The lackey made an evasive movement, and vanished. The traveller was no other than Lezh-

202

nyóff. The recruiting had called him forth from his country estate to S * * *.

Lezhnyóff's servant, a curly-headed and rosy-cheeked young fellow, with a sky-blue girdle, and soft felt boots, entered the room.

"Well, here now, brother, we have arrived," went on Lezhnyóff:—" but thou wert in constant fear lest the tire should fly off the wheel."

"We have arrived!" returned the servant, trying to smile, through the upturned collar of his overcoat;—" but why that tire did n't fly off. . . ."

"Is there no one here?" sang out a voice in the corridor.

Lezhnyóff started, and began to listen.

"Hey, there! Who's there?" repeated the voice.

Lezhnyóff rose, went to the door, and hastily opened it.

Before him stood a man of lofty stature, almost completely grey and bent, in an old velveteen coat with bronze buttons. Lezhnyóff instantly recognised him.

"Rúdin!" he exclaimed with emotion.

Rúdin turned round. He could not distinguish the features of Lezhnyóff, who was standing with his back to the light, and he gazed at him in perplexity.

"Don't you know me?" said Lezhnyóff.

"Mikhaílo Mikhaílitch!" cried Rúdin, and stretched out his hand, but was smitten with con-

RÚDIN

fusion, and was on the point of drawing it back
again. . . .

Lezhnyóff hastily grasped it in both of his.

" Come in, come in to my room! " he said to
Rúdin, and led him in.

" How you have changed! " ejaculated Lezhnyóff, after a pause, and involuntarily lowering
his voice.

" Yes, they tell me so! " returned Rúdin, as
his gaze roamed about the room. " It is the years.
. . But here are you—the same as ever. How is
Alexándra . . . . your wife? "

" Thanks,—she is well. But how do you chance
to be here? "

" I? It would take a long time to tell the story.
To tell the truth, I came hither quite by accident.
I was looking up an acquaintance. However,
I am very glad. . ."

" Where are you going to dine? "

" I? I don't know. In some eating-house or
other. I must leave here to-day."

" You must? "

Rúdin smiled significantly.

" Yes, sir, I must. I am being sent home, to
my country estate, for residence."

" Dine with me."

Rúdin, for the first time, looked Lezhnyóff
straight in the eye.

" You are proposing that I should dine with
you? " he said.

" Yes, Rúdin, in our old way, in comradely fashion. Will you? I had not expected to encounter you, and God knows when we shall see each other again. You and I must not part thus! "

" Very well, I accept."

Lezhnyóff shook Rúdin by the hand, called the servant, ordered dinner, and gave orders that a bottle of champagne should be put on the ice.

During the dinner, Lezhnyóff and Rúdin, as though by common consent, talked constantly of their student days, recalled many things, many persons—both dead and living. At first, Rúdin was reluctant to talk, but he drank several glasses of wine, and his blood began to warm up. At last, the lackey carried out the last dish. Lezhnyóff rose, locked the door, and returning to the table, seated himself directly opposite Rúdin, and quietly rested his chin on both hands.

" Well, now," he began:—" tell me everything that has happened to you, since I saw you last."

Rúdin looked at Lezhnyóff.

" My God!—" Lezhnyóff said to himself once more—" how he has changed, poor fellow! "

Rúdin's features had undergone little change, especially since we saw him at the posting-station, although the stamp of approaching old age had already become imprinted on them; but their expression had become different. His eyes had another look; in all his being, in his movements, now leisurely, now incoherently abrupt, and in his chilled, as it were, broken speech, weariness spoke, a secret and quiet grief, very different from that semi-assumed sadness, of which he had been wont to make a display, as youth in general does while full of hope and of confident self-love.

" Tell you everything that has happened to me?" he said. "I cannot tell you all, and it is not worth the while. . . I have worn myself out greatly, I have wandered not with the body alone, I have roamed with the soul also. In what and in whom have I not been disenchanted, my God! with whom have I not come in contact! Yes, with whom!" repeated Rúdin, observing that Lezhnyóff was looking into his face with a certain special sympathy. "How many times have not my own words become repulsive to me —I am not speaking of them in my own mouth, but on the lips of people who shared my views! How many times have not I passed from the irritability of a baby, to the dull insensibility of a horse, which no longer twitches its tail when it is cut with the whip. . . How many times have not I rejoiced, hoped, grown hostile and humbled myself in vain! How many times have I soared with the flight of a falcon—and returned crawling, like a snail, whose shell has been crushed! . . . Where have I not been, by what roads have I not wandered! . . . And the roads are sometimes dirty," added Rúdin, and slightly turned aside. " You know, ..." he went on. . . .

" See here," Lezhnyóff interrupted him;— " once on a time, we used to call each other ' thou ' . . . . Wouldst thou like it? let us resume our old habit. . . Let 's drink to *thou!* "

Rúdin started, half rose, and in his eyes flashed something which words cannot express.

" Let us drink!" said he:—" I thank thee, brother, let us drink!"

Lezhnyóff and Rúdin drank off a glass.

" *Thou* knowest," began Rúdin once more, with emphasis on ' thou ' and with a smile:—" there is some sort of a worm within me, which gnaws me, and swallows, and will give me no peace to the end. It brings me into contact with people— at first, they yield to my influence, and later on . . . ."

Rúdin waved his hand in the air.

" Since I parted from you . . . from thee, I have experienced and learned much. . . . I began to live, I undertook something new twenty times—and here I am!—thou seest!"

" Thou hadst no staying power," remarked Lezhnyóff, as though to himself.

" How canst thou say, that I had no staying power! . . . I have never known how to construct anything; yes, and 't is difficult to construct, brother, when there is no ground under one's feet, when one is compelled to create one's own foundation! I will not describe to thee all my peregrinations, that is, properly speaking, all my failures. I will give thee two or three instances . . . those incidents in my life when, apparently, success was smiling on me, when I had begun to have hopes of success,—which is not quite the same thing. . . ."

Rúdin tossed back his grey hair, already thin, with the same movement of the hand wherewith, in days gone by, he had been wont to throw aside his thick, dark curls.

"Well, listen," he began. "In Moscow, I became connected with a decidedly peculiar gentleman. He was very wealthy, and owned extensive estates; he was not in government service. His chief, his sole passion, was a love for science, for science in general. Up to this moment, I cannot comprehend how that passion made its appearance in him! It was as suitable for him as a saddle is for a cow. By dint of exertion alone did he keep himself on the heights of mind, and he hardly knew how to talk, but merely rolled his eyes expressively, and shook his head significantly. I have never met, my dear fellow, any one less gifted and poorer by nature than he was. . . In the Government of Smolénsk, there are spots where there is sand—and nothing else, save here and there grass, which not a single animal will eat. He did easily nothing, everything regularly crawled away from him as far as possible: he was crazy over making everything easy difficult. Had it depended on his management, people would have eaten with their heels, indeed they would. He worked, wrote and read indefatigably. He courted science with a certain obstinate persistency, with strange patience; his self-love was huge, and he had a character of iron. He lived alone, and bore the reputation of an eccentric. I made his acquaintance . . . . well, and he liked me. I must confess, that I soon saw through him; but his zeal touched me. Moreover, he possessed such great means, so much good could be done through him, so much real service could be rendered. . . I settled down in his house, and, at last, went off with him to his country place. My plans, brother, were vast: I dreamed of various improvements, innovations. . . . ."

"As at Mme. Lasúnsky's, thou wilt remember," remarked Lezhnyóff, with a good-natured smile.

"The idea! there, I knew in my own soul, that nothing would come of my words; but in this case . . . a totally different field opened out before me. . . I took with me agronomical books . . . it is true, . . that I had never read a single one of them through to the end . . . . well, and I set to work. At first, things did not go just as I had expected; but afterwards, they did seem to be moving. My new friend continued to hold his tongue, and to look on; he did not interfere with

me,—that is to say, to a certain degree he did
not interfere with me. He accepted my sugges-
tions, and carried them out, but obstinately, stiffly,
with secret distrust, and gave everything a turn
of his own. He set especial value on every
thought of his own. He would climb up it, with
an effort, as a lady-bug crawls up a blade of
grass; and he would sit and sit on it, as though
he were pluming his wings, and getting ready to
fly—and, all of a sudden, he would tumble
down, and then crawl up again. . . Be not surprised at all these comparisons: they fairly
seethed in my soul even then. Well, so I struggled along in that way for two years. Matters
were progressing badly, despite all my pains. I
began to grow weary, my friend bored me, I
began to say caustic things to him, he smothered
me, like a feather-bed; his distrust passed into
dull irritation, an unpleasant feeling took possession of both of us, we could no longer con-
verse about anything; he was underhandedly but
incessantly trying to prove to me, that he was not
submitting to my influence, my arrangements
were either distorted or entirely set aside. . . . . .
I noticed, at last, that I stood toward Mr.
Landed Proprietor in the quality of a hanger-on
in the department of mental exercises. It was
bitter for me to waste my time and strength in
vain, it was bitter to feel that I had again and
again been deceived in my expectations. I knew

very well what I should lose by going away; but I could not conquer myself, and one day, as the result of a painful and exciting scene, of which I was a witness, and which showed me my friend from an altogether too unfavourable side, I quarrelled with him definitively and went away, abandoning the gentleman-pedant moulded of common prairie flour, with an admixture of German molasses. . . . ."

" That is to say, thou didst fling away thy bit of daily bread," remarked Lezhnyóff, and laid both hands on Rúdin's shoulders.

" Yes, and found myself again light and naked in empty space. ' Fly whithersoever thou wilt,' said I . . . Ekh, let 's have a drink!' "

" To thy health!" said Lezhnyóff, rising and kissing Rúdin on the brow.—" To thy health, and in memory of Pokórsky. . . . He, also, knew how to remain poor."

" There 's number one, for you, of my peregrinations," began Rúdin, after a little.—" Shall I go on?"

" Go on, pray."

" Ekh! but I don't feel like talking. I am weary, I tell thee, brother. . . Well, however, so be it. After knocking about in various places— by the way, I might tell thee how I came near getting the post of secretary to a well-intentioned dignitary, and what came of it; but that would take us too far. . . . After knocking about in

various places, I decided, at last, to become . . . .
don't laugh, please . . . a man of business, a
practical man. It happened in this way: I got
connected with a certain . . . . perhaps thou
hast heard of him . . . . with a certain Kurbyéeff . . . . no? "

" No, I have not heard of him. But, good gracious, Rúdin, how is it, that, with thy intelligence,
thou didst not guess that it was no business of
thine to be . . . . pardon the pun . . . a man of
business? "

" I know, brother, that it is not; besides, in what
does it consist? . . . . But if thou hadst only
seen Kurbyéeff! Please do not imagine that he
was a sort of empty babbler. People used to say
that I was eloquent, in days gone by. But, in
comparison with him, I count for nothing. He
was wonderfully learned, well informed, with a
head, brother, a creative head, in matters of industry and commercial enterprises. His brain
was fairly swarming with the boldest, the most
unexpected projects. He and I joined company,
and decided to use our forces for a matter of
public benefit. . . . ."

" What was it, may I ask? "
Rúdin dropped his eyes.
" Thou wilt laugh."
" Why? No, I will not laugh."
" We decided to convert one of the rivers in the

Government of K * * * into a navigable stream,"
said Rúdin, with an awkward smile.

" You don't say so! Then that Kurbyéeff
must have been a capitalist? "

" He was poorer than myself," returned Rúdin, and softly hung his grey head.

Lezhnyóff burst out laughing, but suddenly
stopped, and took Rúdin's hand.

" Forgive me, brother, pray do," he said to
him:—" but I did not, in the least, expect that.
Well, and so that enterprise of yours remained
on paper? "

" Not altogether. There was a beginning of
fulfilment. We hired labourers . . . . well, and
they set to work. But then we encountered divers obstacles. In the first place, the proprietors
of mills would not understand us, and, in addition to that, we could not deal with the water
without machinery, and we had not the money
for machinery. Six months we lived in earth
huts. Kurbyéeff subsisted on bread alone, and
I did not eat my fill either. However, I do not
regret that: nature is wonderful there. We
struggled and struggled, exhorted the merchants,
wrote letters and circulars. It ended in my
spending my last copper on that project."

" Well! " remarked Lezhnyóff:—" I do not
think it was difficult to spend your last copper."

" It was not difficult, exactly so."

213

Rúdin stared out of the window.

" But the project, by heaven, was not a bad one, and might have produced enormous profits."

" And what became of Kurbyéeff?" inquired Lezhnyóff.

" Of him? He is in Siberia now, he has turned gold-miner. And thou wilt see, he will acquire a competence. He will not go to the wall."

" Possibly; but thou wilt certainly not acquire a competence."

" I? What is to be done! However, I know: I always have been an empty man in thine eyes."

" Thou? Hush, brother! . . . . . There was a time, really, when only thy dark sides were apparent to my eye; but now, believe me, I have learned to value thee. Thou wilt not acquire a fortune. . . Yes, and for that I love thee . . . . upon my word! "

Rúdin smiled faintly.

" Really? "

" I respect thee for that!" repeated Lezhnyóff;—" dost thou understand me? "

Both remained silent for a space.

" Well, shall we proceed to number three?" asked Rúdin.

" Do me that favour."

" At your service. Number three, and the last. I have only just got rid of that number. But am not I boring thee? "

" Go on, go on."

" Well, you see," began Rúdin:—" one day I was meditating at leisure. . . I have always had plenty of leisure—and I thought: I have considerable knowledge, my desires are good . . . . see here, thou surely wilt not deny that my desires are good? "

" I should think not! "

" On all other points, I have suffered more or less defeat . . . why should not I turn pedagogue, or, to put it more simply, teacher . . . rather than live thus in vain. . ."

Rúdin paused and sighed.

" Rather than live in vain, would it not be better to endeavour to communicate to others what I know: perchance, they will derive some benefit from my knowledge. My capacities are not ordinary, in short, I am a master of language. . . So I determined to devote myself to this new business. I had a good deal of trouble in finding a place; I did not wish to give private lessons; there was nothing for me to do in the lower schools. At last, I succeeded in obtaining the post of lecturer in the gymnasium here."

" Lecturer—on what? " asked Lezhnyóff.

" Lecturer on Russian literature. I will tell thee this,—never have I undertaken a single affair with so much zeal as in this case. The thought of acting on youth inspired me. Three weeks did I spend over the composition of my first lecture."

"Hast thou not got it with thee?" inquired Lezhnyóff.

"No; it got lost somewhere. It turned out quite well, and pleased people. I seem to behold, now, the faces of my auditors,—kind, young faces, with an expression of open-hearted attention, even of amazement. I mounted the tribune, read my lecture in a fever; I thought there was enough of it to last more than an hour, and in twenty minutes I had finished it. The inspector was sitting there—a dry old man, in silver-mounted spectacles, and a short wig,—he inclined his head in my direction from time to time. When I had finished, and had sprung from my chair, he said to me: 'Very good, sir, only a trifle high-flown, rather obscure, and, moreover, there was very little said about the subject itself.' But the gymnasium pupils gazed after me with respect . . . . really they did. That's the precious thing about young people. I delivered my second lecture from manuscript, and the third in the same way . . . and after that, I began to improvise."

"And wert successful?" inquired Lezhnyóff.

"I was very successful. I imparted to my hearers everything that was in my soul. Among them there were three or four lads, who were really remarkable; the rest did not understand me well. However, I must admit, that even those who did understand me sometimes disconcerted me by their questions. But I did not become despondent. As for loving me, they all did that. But then an intrigue was begun against me . . . . or no! there was no intrigue whatever; but I, simply, had got out of my sphere. I embarrassed the others, and they embarrassed me. I lectured to the gymnasium lads, in a manner different from that in which students are always lectured to; my hearers carried but little away from my lectures; . . . I was but badly acquainted with facts myself. Moreover, I did not content myself with the circle of action which had been prescribed for me . . . . thou knowest that that is my weakness. I wanted radical reforms, and I give thee my word of honour, that these reforms were practical and easy. I hoped to carry them out through the director, upon whom I at first had some influence. His wife helped me. I have met very few such women in the course of my life, brother. She was nearly forty years of age; but she believed in good, she loved everything that was excellent, like a young girl of fifteen, and was not afraid to speak out her convictions before any one whatsoever. I shall never forget her noble enthusiasm and purity. By her advice, I began to write out a plan. . . But at this point I was undermined, my reputation was blackened to her. I was particularly injured by the teacher of mathematics, a sharp, bilious little man, who believed in nothing, after the fashion of Pigásoff, only much more active than he. . . . By the way, what has become of Pigásoff, is he still alive?"

"Yes, and just imagine, he has married a woman of the petty burgher class, who beats him, they say."

"And serve him right! And is Natálya Alexyéevna well?"

"Yes."

"Is she happy?"

"Yes."

Rúdin said nothing for a while.

"What the deuce was I talking about? . . . . oh, yes! about the teacher of mathematics. He conceived a hatred for me; he compared my lectures to fireworks, he caught up on the fly every expression that was not entirely clear, he once even contradicted me about some monument or other of the XV century . . . but the chief point was, that he suspected my intentions; my last soap-bubble hit against him, as against a pin, and broke. The inspector, with whom I had not got on from the first, stirred up the director against me; a row ensued; I would not yield, I waxed angry, the matter was brought to the knowledge of the authorities; I was forced to resign. I did not stop there, I tried to prove that they could not treat me like that . . . . but they can treat me as they please . . . I am now compelled to leave this place."

RÚDIN

A silence followed. Both friends sat with drooping heads.

Rúdin was the first to speak.

" Yes, brother," he began:—" now I can say with Koltzóff: ' Whither hast thou led me, hounded me, O my youth, that no longer have I where to set my foot!' . . . And, nevertheless, am I good for nothing, is there really no work for me on earth? I have frequently put that question to myself, and, strive as I might to humble myself in my own eyes, I nevertheless could not but be conscious of powers within myself, which are not given to all men! Then why do these powers remain sterile? And here is another thing: dost thou remember, when thou and I were abroad, I was self-conceited and false. . . . The fact was, that I had not then comprehended what I wished, I intoxicated myself with words, and believed in phantoms; but now, I give thee my word of honour, I can declare aloud, in the presence of all the world, everything which I desire. I positively have nothing to conceal: I am thoroughly, and in the most essential meaning of the word, a well-meaning man; I abase myself, I wish to adapt myself to circumstances, I wish for little, I wish to attain to a proximate goal, I wish to be of even the slightest use. No! I cannot succeed! What is the meaning of this? What is it that prevents my living and being active like other people?... That is the only thing I dream of now. But no sooner do I emerge into a definite position, no sooner do I halt at a fixed point, than fate fairly thrusts me off to a distance. . . . I have begun to fear it—my fate. . . . Why is all this? Solve this riddle for me! "

"Riddle!" repeated Lezhnyóff. "Yes, it is true. Thou hast always been a riddle for me also. Even in thy youth, when, after some petty sally or other, thou wouldst suddenly begin to talk in such a way that the heart quivered, and then wouldst begin again . . . . well, thou knowest what I mean to say . . . even then, I did not understand thee: that was precisely the reason why I ceased to love thee—there was so much power in thee, so much indefatigable aspiration toward the ideal. . . ."

"Words, nothing but words! there were no deeds!" broke in Rúdin.

"There were no deeds! What deeds. . . ."

"What deeds? To support a blind peasant woman and all her family by my labours, as Pryázhentzoff did, thou wilt remember. . . . There's a deed for thee."

"Yes; but a good word is a deed also."

Rúdin gazed in silence at Lezhnyóff, and slowly shook his head.

Lezhnyóff tried to find something to say, and passed his hand over his face.

"And so, thou art going to thy estate?" he asked, at last.

" Yes."

" But hast thou still an estate belonging to thee? "

" There is something of that sort left yonder. Two souls and a half. There is a corner wherein to die. Perchance, thou art thinking, at this moment: ' And even now, he could not get along without flowery phrases! ' Phrases, in point of fact, have been my undoing; they have devoured me to the very end, I have not been able to rid myself of them. But what I have just said is not a mere phrase. These white locks, these wrinkles, are not phrases, brother; these ragged elbows are not phrases. Thou hast always been stern with me, and thou wert just; but this is no time for sternness, when everything is already at an end, and there is no more oil in the lamp, and the lamp itself is shattered, and the wick is on the very verge of smoking itself out. . . . . Death, brother, must reconcile, at last. . . . ."

Lezhnyóff sprang to his feet.

" Rúdin! " he exclaimed, " why dost thou say this to me? How have I deserved this from thee? What sort of a judge, and what sort of a man should I be, if, at the sight of thy hollow cheeks and wrinkles, the word ' phrases ' could enter my mind? Dost thou wish to know what I think of thee? Very well! I think: here is a man . . . with his capacities, what might not he attain to, what earthly benefits might not he now possess, if he only willed it! . . . . but I meet him hungry, without a shelter. . . . ."

" I arouse thy pity," said Rúdin in a dull voice.

" No, there thou art mistaken. Thou inspirest me with respect—that 's what I mean. Who prevented thy spending years and years with that landed proprietor, thy friend, who, I am fully convinced, if thou hadst but been willing to knuckle under to him, would have given thee a secure position? Why couldst thou not live in harmony at the gymnasium, why—O strange man!—with whatever designs thou didst begin a thing, hast thou, in every case, inevitably wound up by sacrificing thy personal interests, hast not struck root in evil soil, however rich it might be? "

" I was born a rolling stone," continued Rúdin with a melancholy smile. " I cannot stop myself."

" That is true; but the reason why thou canst not stop thyself is not, that in thee lives a worm, as thou hast said to me at the beginning of this conversation. . . 'T is not a worm that lives in thee, 't is not the spirit of idle uneasiness,—it is the fire of love for the truth, it burns within thee, and it is evident, despite all thy talk, that it burns in thee more powerfully than in many who do not even regard themselves as egoists, but, in all probability, call thee an intriguer. Yes, I would have been the first, had I been in thy place, to have forced that worm, long ago, to hold its peace within me, and I would have reconciled myself to everything; but in thee there has not even been an access of bile, and thou, I am convinced of it, art ready this very day, this very moment, to set about some new undertaking, like a young lad."

" No, brother, I am weary now," said Rúdin. " I have had enough."

" Weary! Any one else would have died long ago. Thou sayest that death reconciles; but does not life reconcile, thinkest thou? He who has lived long, and has not become lenient towards others, does not deserve leniency himself. And who can say, that he does not stand in need of leniency? Thou hast done what thou couldst, thou hast striven as long as thou wert able. . . . What more can be demanded? Our roads have lain apart . . . ."

" Thou art an entirely different man from me, brother," interposed Rúdin, with a sigh.

" Our roads have lain apart," pursued Lezhnyóff:—" perhaps, that is precisely the reason why, thanks to my position, to my cold blood, and to other fortunate circumstances, nothing has prevented my becoming a stay-at-home, and remaining a spectator, with arms folded; but thou hast been forced to go forth into the field, with sleeves stripped up, to toil and work. Our roads have lain apart . . . but observe, how near we are to each other. For we talk almost an identical language, we understand each other at half a hint; we grew up on the same sentiments. Not many of us are left now, brother; for thou and I are the last of the Mohicans! We might get angry, even quarrel, in the olden years, when we had a great deal of life ahead of us; but now, when the throng is thinning around us, when the new generations are sweeping past us, to goals which are not our goals, we must cling fast to each other. Let us clink glasses, brother, and let us sing, as of old: ' Gaudeamus igitur!' "

The friends touched glasses, and sang in deeply moved, real Russian voices out of tune, the ancient student song.

" So, now thou art going to thy village," began Lezhnyóff again. " I do not think thou wilt remain there long, and I cannot imagine how, where and when thou wilt wind up. . . But remember this: whatever may happen to thee, thou hast always a place, there is always a nest, where thou mayest take refuge. That is my house . . . . dost thou hear me, old fellow? Thought also has its invalid soldiers: they must have an asylum."

Rúdin rose.

" I thank thee, brother," he went on. " I thank thee! I will not forget this of thee. Only, I am not worthy of an asylum. I have ruined my own life, and I have not served thought as I should have done."

" Hush!" continued Lezhnyóff. " Every one remains what nature made him, and nothing more can be demanded of him! Thou hast called thyself the Wandering Jew. . . . And how dost thou know, perhaps thou also must wander eternally thus, perhaps thou wilt, thereby, fulfil a higher destination, of which thou thyself knowest nothing: not for nothing has the wisdom of the people declared, that we all go as God wills."

" Art thou going?" went on Lezhnyóff, perceiving that Rúdin was picking up his cap. " Wilt thou not spend the night here?"

" I am going! farewell. Thanks. . . But I shall end badly."

" God only knows about that. . . Thou art determined to go?"

" Yes. Good-bye. Bear me no ill-will."

" Well, and do thou bear me no ill-will . . . and do not forget what I have told thee. Good-bye. . . . ."

The friends embraced. Rúdin swiftly left the room.

Lezhnyóff paced up and down the room for a long time, halted in front of the window, reflected, muttered, in an undertone: " Poor fellow!" and seating himself at the table, began to write a letter to his wife.

Outside, the wind rose, and howled with an ominous roar, beating heavily and spitefully against the rattling window-panes. The long, autumnal night closed in. It is well with him, who, on such nights is sitting under the shelter of a house, who has a warm nook. . . And may the Lord help all shelterless wanderers!

At the sultry noonday of July 26, 1848, in Paris, when the insurrection of the " national working-men " had been almost suppressed, in one of the narrow alleys of the Faubourg Saint Antoine a battalion of the line captured a barricade. It had already been shattered by several cannon-shots; those of its defenders who remained alive, had abandoned it, and were thinking only of their safety, when, all of a sudden, on its very crest, upon the crushed body of an overturned omnibus, there appeared a tall man in an old coat, girt about with a red scarf, and with a straw hat on his grey, dishevelled locks. In one hand he grasped a red flag, in the other, a curved, dull sword, and shouted something in a strained, shrill voice, as he scrambled upwards and waved the flag and the sword. A sharpshooter of Vincennes took aim at him,—and fired. . . . The tall man dropped the flag, and fell face downward, like a sack, exactly as though he were bowing down to some one's feet. . . . The bullet had passed straight through his heart.

" *Tiens!* " said one of the fleeing insurgents to another: " *On vient de tuer le Polonais.*"

"*Bigre!*" replied the latter, and both flung themselves into the cellar of a house, all of whose shutters were closed, and its walls streaked with the traces of bullets and cannon-balls.

That " Polonais " was—Dmítry Rúdin.

END

A KING LEAR OF
THE STEPPES

(1870)

A KING LEAR OF
THE STEPPES

SIX of us were assembled one winter evening
at the house of an old comrade of university
days. A discussion arose about Shakespeare,
about his types, about the profundity and fidelity
with which they have been delineated from the
very inmost recesses of human " nature." We
particularly admired their vivid truth, their
everyday character; each of us enumerated the
Hamlets, the Othellos, the Falstaffs, even the
Richard the Thirds and the Macbeths—(these
last, it is true, only as possibilities)—with whom
he had happened to come in contact.

" And I, gentlemen,"—exclaimed our host,
a man already elderly,—" have known a King
Lear! "

" What do you mean? "

" Precisely that. If you like, I will tell you
the story."

" Pray do."

And our friend immediately began his narrative.

231

I

My entire childhood, and my early youth, up to
the age of twenty, he began,—I spent in the
country, on the estate of my mother, a wealthy
landowner of the * * * Government. Perhaps the
most clear-cut impression of that already distant
epoch, which remains in my memory, is the figure
of our nearest neighbour, a certain Martýn Petróvitch Kharlóff. And it would be difficult
indeed to erase that impression: I have never, in
all the course of my life since then, encountered
anything like Kharlóff. Picture to yourselves
a man of gigantic stature! On his huge trunk
sat a monstrous head, somewhat awry, and without the slightest trace of a neck: above it rose a
regular hay-cock of tangled, yellowish grey hair,
starting almost from his bristling eyebrows. On
the broad expanse of his bluish, as it were flayed
face jutted forth a robust, wen-like nose, diminutive blue eyes glared arrogantly, and a mouth
gaped, equally tiny, but crooked and cracked, of
the same colour as the rest of the face. The voice
emitted from this mouth, although hoarse, was
extremely powerful and sibilant . . . . . . Its
sound reminded the hearer of the clatter of iron

232

bars which are being transported in a cart along a bad pavement—and Kharlóff talked as though he were shouting at some one on the other side of a broad chasm, in a high wind. It was difficult to say precisely what Kharlóff's face expressed, so vast was it. . . . It could not be taken in with a single glance! But it was not disagreeable— a certain majesty was even discernible in it, only it was prodigious and remarkable. And what hands he had—regular pillows! what fingers, what feet! I remember, that I could not gaze without alarm at Martýn Petróvitch's back, two arshíns [1] in length, at his shoulders, which resembled millstones; but his ears, in particular amazed me! regular kalátches [2] they were, with all the folds and turns: his cheeks fairly thrust them up on both sides. Martýn Petróvitch wore —both winter and summer—a coat, tightly fitted to his figure, of green cloth, girt with a narrow Tcherkessian belt of leather, and oiled boots; I never saw a neckerchief on him, and what was there for him to tie a neckerchief about? He breathed slowly and heavily, like an ox, but he walked noiselessly. One might have supposed that, when he happened to find himself in a room, he lived in constant terror of smashing and over-turning everything, and therefore moved from place to place cautiously, chiefly sideways, as

[1] An arshín is twenty-eight inches.—TRANSLATOR.
[2] A favourite hot wheaten roll of peculiar shape.—TRANSLATOR.

though by stealth. He was possessed of genu-
inely herculean strength, and in consequence enjoyed great respect in the neighbourhood: our
people, down to the present day, worship epic
heroes. Legends were even invented about him:
it was narrated, that he had once encountered a
bear in the woods, and almost vanquished him;
that having caught a strange peasant among his
beehives, he flung him, together with his cart
and horse, over the wattled fence, and other
things of the same sort. Kharlóff himself never
bragged of his strength. " If I have a blessed
right hand,"—he was accustomed to say,—" it is
because such is the will of God!"—He was
proud: only, he was not proud of his strength,
but of his station, of his good birth, of his brains.

" Our family is Vshedish " (he always pronounced Swedish in that manner), " descended
from the Vshede Kharlus," he asserted:—" during the reign of Prince Iván Vasílievitch the
Blind—(just think of that!) he came to Russia;
and that Vshede Kharlus did not want to be a
Finnish Count—but he wanted to be a Russian
noble, and he inscribed himself in the Golden
Book.[1] So that's where we Kharlóffs come
from! . . . . And, for the same reason, all we
Kharlóffs are born with fair hair, with light eyes,
and with clear skins! because we are snow-men!"

" But, Martýn Petróvitch,"—I tried to re-

[1] The official genealogy.—TRANSLATOR.

tort,—" Iván Vasílievitch the Blind never existed
at all, but there was an Iván Vasílievitch the
Terrible. The Blind was the appellation of a
certain Prince Vasíly Vasílievitch." [1]

" Go on with thine idle chatter! "—Kharlóff
answered me calmly:—" if I say it, it was so! "

Once upon a time, my mother took it into her
head to praise Kharlóff, to his face, for his really
remarkable disinterestedness.

" Ekh, Natálya Nikoláevna! "—he said, almost
angrily,—" a pretty thing you have found to
praise me for! We gentle born cannot be otherwise: let no low-born rapscallion, bee-keeper, or
dependent dare to think ill of us! I am Kharlóff,
yonder is the place whence I derive my de-
scent . . . . ." (here he pointed with his finger
to some place very high above him—to the ceiling),—" and the idea that there should not be
honour in me! Why, how is that possible? "

On another occasion a dignitary who was the
guest of my mother, took it into his head to make
fun of Martýn Petróvitch. The latter again began to talk about the Vshede Kharlus who had
come to Russia. . . . .

" In the days of Tzar Pea? " [2]—interrupted
the dignitary.

" No, not in the days of Tzar Pea,—but in

[1] Literally: The Dark, 1425–1462. He was the first Grand Prince
crowned at Moscow.—TRANSLATOR.
[2] Equivalent to "King David," or any other absurdly remote an·
cestor.—TRANSLATOR.

the days of Grand Prince Iván Vasílievitch the Blind."

" Why, I had supposed,"—went on the dignitary,—" that your race was much more ancient, and went back even to antediluvian times, when there were mastodons and megalotheriums....."

These learned terms were totally unknown to Martýn Petróvitch; but he understood that the dignitary was ridiculing him.

" Perhaps it does,"—he burst out,—" our race is really very ancient: at the time when my ancestor arrived in Moscow, they say that a fool, the equal of your Excellency, dwelt there, and only one such fool is born in a thousand years."

The dignitary flew into a rage, but Kharlóff threw back his head, thrust out his chin, snorted, and took himself off. Two days later, he made his appearance again. My mother began to reprove him. " Read him the lesson, madam,"—interrupted Kharlóff:—" don't dash forward headlong, inquire, first of all, with whom you are dealing. He's very young still, he needs teaching." The dignitary was nearly of the same age as Kharlóff; but that giant had acquired the habit of looking upon everybody as a stripling. He had the greatest confidence in himself, and feared absolutely no one. " Can they do anything to me? Where in the world is there such another man "—he was wont to ask, and suddenly he would burst into a curt, but deafening laugh.

II

My mother was very fastidious about her acquaintances, but she received Kharlóff with particular cordiality, and overlooked many things in him: five and twenty years before, he had saved her life, by holding her carriage on the brink of a deep abyss, into which the horses had already fallen. The traces and breech-straps gave way, but even then Martýn Petróvitch did not let go of the wheel which he had seized in his grasp—although the blood spurted from beneath his finger-nails. My mother even arranged his marriage: she gave him to wife an orphan girl of seventeen, who had been reared in her house: he was over forty at the time. Martýn Petróvitch's wife was weak in health,—it was said that he had carried her into his house on his palms,—and she did not long survive the wedding; but she bore him two daughters. Even after her death, my mother continued to show her good-will to Martýn Petró-vitch: she got the eldest daughter into one of the Government boarding-schools, then she found her a husband—and already had her eye on another for the second daughter. Kharlóff was an excellent farmer, his little estate consisted of about

three hundred desyatínas,[1] and he had added to
it somewhat; and as for the way in which his serfs
obeyed him,—it simply is useless to discuss it!
Owing to his obesity, Kharlóff hardly ever went
on foot: he was too heavy. He rode about everywhere in a low racing-drozhky, and drove the
horse himself, a raw-boned mare thirty years old,
with the scar of a wound on her shoulder: that
wound she had received in the battle of Borodinó,
as the mount of the quartermaster in the Cheva-
lier Guards regiment. This horse constantly
limped, on all four feet simultaneously, it seemed:
she could not go at a walk, but meandered along
at a jog-trot, with a skip and a jump; she ate
mugwort and wormwood from the grass strips
between the cultivated fields, a thing which I have
never observed any other horse do. I remember
that I always wondered how that half-alive horse
could draw about such a frightful burden. I
dare not repeat how many puds [2] our neighbour
weighed. Behind Martýn Petróvitch in the racing-gig his swarthy little page, Maxím, took his
place. Cuddling his whole body and face up
against his master, and bracing his bare feet
against the hind axle of the drozhky, he seemed
a tiny leaf, or a worm, which was leaning against
the gigantic carcass that towered up in front of
him. This same page, once a week, shaved Mar-

---

[1] A desyatína is 2.70 acres.—TRANSLATOR.
[2] A pud is 36 pounds.—TRANSLATOR.

týn Petróvitch. For the accomplishment of this operation, he stood on the table, so they said: some jesters asserted, that he was forced to run around his master's chin. Kharlóff was not fond of staying at home for long at a time, and, therefore, he was quite frequently to be seen driving about in his inevitable equipage,[1] with the reins in one hand (the other, he deftly, with elbow crooked out, propped on his knee), with a tiny, old cap of military shape on the very apex of his head. He gazed alertly about him with his little, bear-like eyes, shouted in stentorian tones at all the peasants, petty burghers, and merchants whom he met: he launched strong epithets at the priests, whom he was very far from loving, and one day, as he came alongside me, (I had gone out for a stroll with my gun), he began to halloo so vociferously at a hare which was lying by the roadside, that the moaning and din stuck in my ears until evening.

---

[1] The racing-drozhky, used also for rough work in the country, consists of a board, with or without a cushion, attached without springs to four small wheels, all of the same size. The driver sits astride the board, with his feet braced against the shafts. — TRANSLATOR.

239

III

My mother, as I have already said, was wont to give Martýn Petróvitch a cordial welcome; she knew what profound respect he cherished for her. " She 's a gentlewoman! a lady! one of our own sort! "—was the way in which he was accustomed to refer to her. He called her his benefactress, and she looked upon him as a devoted giant, who would not have hesitated to defend her single-handed against a whole horde of peasants:—and, although not even the possibility of such a clash was apprehended, still, according to my mother's views, in the absence of a husband (she had been early widowed), such a defender as Martýn Petróvitch was not to be despised. Moreover, he was an upright man, he fawned on no one, he did not borrow money, he did not drink liquor—and neither was he stupid, although he had received no education whatever. My mother trusted Martýn Petróvitch. When she took it into her head to make her last will and testament, she summoned him as a witness, and he drove home for the express purpose of getting the circular, iron spectacles, without which he was unable to write; and with these spectacles on his nose, he barely contrived, in the course of a quarter of an hour, panting and puffing, to jot down his rank, name, patronymic, and surname, and, withal, he made his letters huge, square, with flourishes and tails; and having completed his labour, he announced that he was weary, and that writing was, for him, as hard work as catching fleas. Yes, my mother respected him . . . . but he was not allowed any further than the dining-room in our house. A very strong odour emanated from him: he reeked of the earth, of forest thickets, of marsh mire. "A regular forest-demon!" my old nurse averred. At dinner, a special table was placed in the corner for Martýn Petróvitch—and he was not offended at this—he knew that it was awkward for others to sit beside him—and moreover, he himself could eat in greater comfort; and he ate as, I suppose, no one has eaten since the days of Polyphemus. By way of precaution, a pot of buckwheat groats, containing about six pounds, was always provided for him at the very beginning of the dinner: "otherwise, thou wilt certainly eat me out of house and home!"—my mother used to say. "Exactly, madam, I shall eat you out of house and home!" Martýn Petróvitch would answer, with a grin.

My mother loved to listen to his arguments on any point of domestic management; but she could not endure his voice very long.

"Well, good heavens!"—she would exclaim:

241

—"you ought to get cured of that, I think! you have completely deafened me. What a trumpet!"

"Natálya Nikoláevna—Benefactress!"—Martýn Petróvitch generally replied:—"I have no control over my throat. And what medicine could I take?—please to judge for yourself. I had better hold my peace for a bit."

As a matter of fact, I don't suppose that any medicine could have penetrated Martýn Petróvitch. He had never been ill.

He could not narrate, and did not like to do so. "Asthma is caused by long speeches," he remarked reprovingly. Only when he was got upon the subject of the war of 1812, (he had served in the militia, and had received a bronze medal, which he wore with the ribbon of the Order of St. Vladimir on festive occasions), when he was interrogated about the French, did he impart a few anecdotes, although he kept asserting, at the same time, that no genuine Frenchmen had come to Russia; but that, impelled by hunger, marauders had made an incursion, and that he had administered a thrashing to many of that rabble.

IV

YET this invincible, self-reliant giant had his
hours of melancholy and irresolution. Without
any visible cause, he would suddenly begin to suffer from depression: he would lock himself up
alone in his room and buzz—precisely that, buzz
like a whole swarm of bees: or he would summon
his page, Maxím, and order him either to read
aloud from the only book which had strayed into
his house, an odd volume of Nóvikoff's "The
Labourer at Rest,"—or to sing. And Maxím,
who, by a strange freak of fate, could read by
spelling out, would set to work with the usual dis-
location of words, and transference of the accent,
to shout out phrases, in the nature of the following: " But a pas-siónate hu-mán being deducés
from that empty place, which he finds in crea-
túres, utterly conflicting in-ferénces. Any crea-
túre se-par-átely, he says, has not the power of
rendér-ing me hap-pý!" and so forth,[1] or he
would strike up, in the shrillest sort of a little
voice, some mournful ditty, of which nothing
could be distinguished except: " I .... i .... e
.... i .... e .... i .... Aa .... ska! ... O
.... ou .... ou .... bi .... i .... i .... i ....

1 "The Labourer at Rest," a periodical publication, etc. Moscow,
1785, Part III., p. 23, line 11 from the top.

la!" And Martýn Petróvitch would sway his head, to and fro, and allude to the instability of life, to the fact that everything will turn to dust, will wither like unto the grass of the field: it will pass away—and cease to exist! In some manner, there had fallen into his hands a picture which depicted a burning taper, on which the winds are blowing from all four points of the compass, with distended cheeks; underneath was the inscription: "Such is human life!" This picture pleased him greatly; he hung it up in his private study;—but in ordinary, non-mournful periods he was accustomed to turn it with its face to the wall, in order that it might not worry him. Kharlóff, that colossus, was afraid of death! Yet, even in his fits of melancholy, he rarely resorted to religion, to prayer, for aid: he placed more reliance on his own wits in that case also. He was not particularly devout; he was not often seen in church; to tell the truth, he said that he did not go there because, on account of the size of his body, he was afraid of crushing everybody out. The fit usually ended in Martýn Petróvitch's beginning to whistle—and, all at once, in a thundering voice, he would order his drozhky to be harnessed up, and he would drive off somewhere in the neighbourhood, waving his free hand with considerable dash above the visor of his cap, as though desirous of saying, "I don't care a rap about anything now!" He was a Russian man.

V

VERY strong men, like Martýn Petróvitch, are generally of a phlegmatic temperament; he, on the contrary, was rather easily irritated. The person who, in particular, drove him out of patience was the brother of his deceased wife, a certain Bytchkóff, who lived in our house, not precisely in the quality of a jester, nor yet quite in that of a hanger-on; having received the nickname of Souvenir in his earliest years, every one still called him so, even the servants who, it is true, addressed him as Souvenir Timoféitch. His real name was not even known to himself, apparently. He was a miserable little man, despised by every one: a parasite, in short. All his teeth were lacking on one side of his mouth, hence his tiny, wrinkled face appeared to be distorted. He was forever bustling and fidgeting about: he would drop in at the maids' hall, or the estate office, to see the priests in the village, or the village-elder in his cottage; he would be driven out everywhere, and would merely shrug his shoulders, and screw up his little eyes,—and emit a pitiful, thin little laugh, like the sound of a bottle being rinsed. It always seemed to me, that if

Souvenir had had money, he would have turned out the worst possible sort of a man, immoral, vicious, even cruel. Poverty had " tamed " him down willy-nilly. He was allowed to drink liquor only on festive occasions. He was neatly clothed, in accordance with my mother's orders, as he played piquet or boston with her in the evenings. Souvenir kept incessantly reiterating: " Here, I, permit me, I will immejutly, immejutly." " But what is *immejutly?* " my mother would ask him with vexation. He would instantly fling back his hands, grow timid, and stammer: " What you please, madam! " He had no occupations, except to eavesdrop at doors, talk scandal, and, chief of all, "nag" or "tease"; and he " nagged " as though he had a right to do so, as though he were avenging himself for something or other. He called Martýn Petróvitch " brother," and bored him to death. " Why did you kill my sister Margaríta Timoféevna? "—he besieged him, capering about in front of him and snickering. One day, Martýn Petróvitch was sitting in the billiard-room, a cool apartment, in which no one had ever beheld a fly,—and which our neighbour, who detested heat and sunlight, was greatly addicted to for that reason. He was sitting between the wall and the billiard-table. Souvenir slipped hastily past his "paunch," jeered at him, and played antics. . . . . . Martýn Petróvitch wanted to brush him aside, and thrust out both hands in front of him. Luckily for Souvenir, he contrived to get out of the way—his dear brother's hands landed on the supports of the billiard-table,—and the heavy wooden table-top flew clear off its six screws. . . What a pan-cake Souvenir would have been converted into, if he had fallen under those mighty hands!

VI

I HAD long been curious to see how Martýn Petróvitch had arranged his dwelling, what sort of
a house he had. One day, I offered to escort
him on horseback as far as Es'kovo (that was the
name of his estate).—" Really now! Thou wish-
est to inspect my domain,"—said Martýn Petróvitch.—" All right! I 'll show thee the garden, and the house, and the threshing-floor—and
everything. I have lots of every sort of property! "—We set out. The distance from our village to Es'kovo was reckoned at not more than
three versts.[1]—" Here it is, my domain! "—
suddenly thundered Martýn Petróvitch, en-
deavouring to turn his immovable head, and
pointing to right and left.—" It 's all mine! "—
Kharlóff's manor-house lay on the crest of a
sloping hillock; at the foot, clinging close to a
small pond, were several miserable peasants' cots.
At the pond, by the dam, an old peasant woman
in a plaid petticoat of homespun was pounding
clothes twisted into a roll, with a beater.

" Aksínya! "—roared Martýn Petróvitch, so
that the daws rose in a flock from a neighbouring

[1] A verst is two thirds of a mile.—TRANSLATOR.

field of oats. . . . "Art washing thy husband's trousers?"

The woman wheeled round instantly, and made a reverence to the girdle.

"Yes, dear little father,"—her weak voice made itself heard.

"Just so! See there,"—went on Martýn Petróvitch, making his way at a trot along a half-rotten wattled fence,—"this is my hemp-patch; and that one, yonder, belongs to the peasants; thou perceivest the difference! And here is my garden; I set out the apple-trees myself, and the willow-trees also. There did not use to be any trees here. So look at that—and learn a lesson!"

We turned into the courtyard, enclosed in a hedge; directly opposite the gate stood a very, very aged little wing, with a straw thatch, and a tiny portico on pillars; on one side stood another, somewhat newer, and with a tiny partial second storey—but also on "chicken's legs."— "Here's another lesson for thee,"—said Kharlóff:—"thou seest, in what sort of little manor-houses our forefathers lived; but this is the sort of residence I have built fór myself now."— The residence resembled a house of cards. Five or six dogs, each more shaggy and hideous than the other, greeted us with howls.—"Sheep-dogs!"—remarked Martýn Petróvitch.—"Genuine Crimean sheep-dogs! Get out, you damned beasts! I'll take and string you all up, one after

the other, the first you know!" On the little
porch of the new wing a young man in a long,
peasant dust-coat of crash made his appearance,
the husband of Martýn Petróvitch's eldest daughter. Skipping lightly to the drozhky, he respectfully supported his father-in-law by the elbow, as
he alighted—and even made a motion with one
hand, as though he were about to grasp the gigantic foot, which the latter, bending his body
forward, threw over the seat with a flourish;—
then he aided me to alight from my horse.

"Anna!" — shouted Kharlóff: — "Natálya
Nikoláevna's little son has been so good as to
visit us; we must entertain him. And where 's
Evlámpiushka?" (The eldest daughter was
named Anna—the younger, Evlámpiya.)

"She 's not at home; she has gone to the fields
for corn-flowers,"—replied Anna, making her
appearance at a tiny window by the door.

"Are there any curds?" asked Kharlóff.

"Yes."

"And is there cream?"

"There is."

"Well, fetch them to the table, and, meanwhile,
I 'll show him my study.—Please come this way—
this way," he added, turning to me, and beckon-
ing me on with his forefinger. In his own
house, he did not address me as "thou"; the
master of the house must be polite. He led me
along a corridor.—"Here 's where I live,"—he

said, stepping sideways across the threshold of a broad doorway,—" and here's my study. Please enter."

This study proved to be a large room, unplastered and almost empty; along the walls, on nails driven in at irregular intervals, hung two Kazák riding-whips, a rusty three-cornered hat, a single-barrelled gun, a sword, a strange sort of horse-collar with metal discs, and the picture representing the candle attacked by the winds; in one corner stood a wooden couch, covered with a motley-hued rug. Hundreds of flies were buzzing thickly close to the ceiling; but the room was cool; only, it smelled particularly strong of the peculiar forest odour which accompanied Martýn Petróvitch everywhere.

" Well, isn't my study nice? "—Kharlóff asked me.

" Very nice."

" See, I have a horse-collar from Holland hanging up yonder,"—went on Kharlóff, again relapsing into " thou."—" A splendid collar! I bought it of a Jew. Just take a good look at it! "

" It 's a good collar."

" The most practical sort! Just smell of it. . . . What dost thou think of that for leather? "—I smelled the collar; there was an odour of rancid oil, nothing more.

" Come, sit down—yonder, on that little chair, be my guest," said Kharlóff, and dropped down

251

himself on the couch, and, as though he were dozing, closed his eyes, and even snored. I stared at him in silence, and could not recover from my amazement: he was a mountain—and that's all there was to be said! Suddenly he started up.

"Anna!"—he shouted, and therewith his huge paunch rose and fell, like a wave of the sea:— "what art thou about? Hurry up! Didst not thou hear me?"

"Everything is ready, dear father; pray come,"—resounded his daughter's voice.

I inwardly marvelled at the celerity with which Martýn Petróvitch's orders had been executed, and followed him to the dining-room, where, on the table, spread with a red table-cloth with white patterns, the luncheon stood ready: curds, cream, wheat bread, even powdered sugar with ginger. While I was vanquishing the curds, Martýn Petróvitch, after affectionately growling:—"Eat, my little friend, eat, my dear little dove, despise not our rustic viands,"—seated himself once more in the corner, and once more seemed to fall into a doze! In front of me, motionless, with downcast eyes, stood Anna Martýnovna, and through the window I could see her husband walking my cob up and down in the yard, wiping off the chain of the snaffle with his own hands.

VII

My mother did not like Kharlóff's oldest daughter; she called her a haughty chit. Anna Martýnovna almost never came to call on us, and in
my mother's presence she bore herself staidly
and coldly, although she was indebted to her for
having received her education in the boarding-
school and got married, and on the wedding day
had received from her a thousand rubles, and a
yellow Turkish shawl,—somewhat worn, it is
true. She was a woman of medium stature, thin,
very vivacious and quick in her movements, with
thick, reddish-blonde hair, a handsome, dark-com-
plexioned face, and narrow, pale-blue eyes; she
had a thin, straight nose, her lips were thin also,
and her chin was " spike-shaped." Any one, to
look at her, would certainly have thought: " Well,
you 're a clever—and an ill-tempered woman! "
And yet, there was something attractive about
her; even the dark moles, scattered like grains of
buckwheat over her face, were becoming to her,
and augmented the feeling which she evoked.
Thrusting her hands under her kerchief, she
stealthily inspected me from above (I was sitting,
she was standing) ; a malicious smile hovered over

her lips, and over her cheeks, under the shadow of her long eyelashes.

" Okh, thou spoiled little gentleman! " that smile seemed to be saying. Every time she drew a breath, her nostrils dilated slightly—that, also, was rather strange; but, nevertheless, it seemed to me, that if Anna Martýnovna would only fall in love with me, or merely wish to kiss me with her thin, hard lips,—I would leap up to the ceiling with rapture. I knew that she was very stern and exacting, that the peasant matrons and maids feared her like fire,—but what of that! Anna Martýnovna mysteriously excited my imagination. However, I was only fifteen years old at that time,—and at that age! . . . . .

Again Martýn Petróvitch started up.— " Anna! "—he shouted:—" thou hadst better jingle the piano. . . . . Young gentlemen like that."

I glanced round: a pitiful similitude of a piano stood in the room.

" Very well, father,"—replied Anna Martýnovna.—" Only, what shall I play to him? It will not interest him."

" Then why wert thou taught in the *pin*sion? "

" I 've forgotten it all completely . . . . and the strings are broken."

Anna Martýnovna's little voice was very pleasant, resonant and plaintive, as it were . . . . . such a voice as birds of prey have.

" Well,"—said Martýn Petróvitch, and became thoughtful.—" Well,"—he began again,— " would n't you like to inspect the threshing-floor, to satisfy your interest? Volódka will show you the way.—Hey, Volódka!"—he shouted to his son-in-law, who was still walking my horse up and down the yard,—" here, escort this gentleman to the threshing-floor, . . . and, in general, ... show him my farm. But I must have a nap! Ta-ta! Good luck to you!"

He left the room, and I followed him. Anna Martýnovna immediately began to clear the table, briskly and with a vexed sort of manner. On the threshold, I turned and bowed to her: but she appeared not to notice my salute, only she smiled again, and more maliciously than before.

I took my horse from Kharlóff's son-in-law, and led it by the bridle. He and I went to the threshing-floor,—but as we found nothing particularly curious about it, and as he could not presuppose any special love for farming in me, a young lad, we returned through the garden to the highway.

VIII

I WAS well acquainted with Kharlóff's son-in-law: his name was Slétkin, Vladímir Vasílievitch; he was an orphan, the son of a petty official, my mother's attorney, and she had reared him. At first he had been placed in the county school, then he had entered the " office of patrimonial estates," then he had been inscribed in the service, in the department of government warehouses, and, finally, he had been married to the daughter of Martýn Petróvitch. My mother called him the little Jew, and, as a matter of fact, with his crisp curls, his black, eternally moist eyes, like stewed prunes, his hawk-like nose and wide, red mouth, he did recall the Hebrew type; only, his skin was white, and, altogether, he was a very good-looking fellow. He was of an obliging disposition, if only his own personal profit were not concerned. If that were the case, he immediately became frantic with greed, he even went as far as tears: he was ready to beg all day long for the sake of a rag, to recall a promise once given a hundred times. waxing indignant and shrieking shrilly if it were not immediately fulfilled. He loved to lounge across the fields with his gun; and when he

.256

succeeded in bagging a hare or a duck, he put his booty into his hunting-pouch with a peculiar feeling, saying the while: "Well, now frolic away, thou shalt not escape! Now thou shalt serve *me!*"

" That 's a nice little nag of yours,"—he said, in his lisping voice, as he helped me to get into the saddle:—" I wish I had just such a horse! But where am I to get it! I have no such luck. You might ask your mamma . . . . remind her. . . . ."

" But has she made you a promise? "

" If she only had! No; but I thought, that in her benignity . . . . ."

" You had better apply to Martýn Petróvitch."

" To Martýn Petróvitch! " repeated Slétkin, in a slow drawl. " In his eyes, I am of about as much consequence as that insignificant page Maxím. He keeps us under his thumb, and we never have even a peep at a reward from him for all our labours."

" Really? "

" Yes, God is my witness. When he says: ' My word is sacred!'—well, it 's just like cutting you off with an axe. You may implore and implore,—it has no result. And there is Anna Martýnovna, my wife, she has no such advantage in his eyes as Evlámpiya Martýnovna.

" Akh, good heavens! " he suddenly interrupted himself, and wrung his hands in despair. " Look: what is that? Some scoundrel has cut a whole half-eighth [1] of oats—of our oats. What do you think of that? A pretty world this! Thieves! thieves! You see, people actually speak the truth when they say, there's no trusting És'kovo, Bés'kovo, Érino, Byélino!" (These were the names of the four neighbouring villages.) "Akh, akh! Just think of it! Here's a loss of a ruble and a half—or, perhaps, even of two rubles!"

Something akin to sobs was audible in Slétkin's voice. I touched my horse's side, and rode away from him.

Slétkin's exclamations had not yet ceased to reach my ear when, suddenly, at a turn in the road, I came upon that same second daughter of Kharlóff, Evlámpiya, who, according to Anna Martýnovna's statement, had gone to the fields for corn-flowers. A thick wreath of those flowers encircled her head. We exchanged a silent greeting. Evlámpiya, also, was very pretty, quite as good-looking as her sister, but in another style. She was tall and stout; everything about her was large: her head, and her feet, and her hands, and her snow-white teeth, and especially her eyes, which were prominent, languishing, dark-blue, like glass beads; everything about her was monumental, even (not for nothing was she the daughter of Martýn Petróvitch), but handsome. Evidently, she did not know what to do with her

[1] An "eighth" is equal to 11.55 pecks.—TRANSLATOR.

thick, flaxen hair, and had wound it thrice round her head. Her mouth was charming, fresh as a rose, of a deep-crimson colour, and when she spoke, the centre of her upper lip was lifted in a very pretty way. But in the gaze of her huge eyes there was something wild and almost harsh. " A free lance, Kazák blood,"—that was the way Martýn Petróvitch expressed himself about her. I was afraid of her. . . . That imposing beauty reminded me of her father.

I rode on a little further, and heard her begin to sing, in an even, powerful, rather sharp, regular peasant voice: then she suddenly ceased. I glanced round, and from the summit of the hill I descried her, standing by the side of Kharlóff's son-in-law, in front of the eighth of rye which had been reaped. The man was flourishing his hands and pointing, but she did not move. The sun illumined her tall figure, and the wreath of corn-flowers on her head gleamed blue.

IX

I THINK I have already told you, gentlemen, that
my mother had provided a husband for this second daughter of Kharlóff also. He was one of
the poorest of our neighbours, a retired army
Major, Gavrílo Fedúlitch Zhitkóff, a man no
longer young, and, as he himself expressed it, not
devoid of licentiousness, and, as though it were a
recommendation: " beaten and broken." He
barely knew how to read and write, was stupid,
but cherished a secret hope of obtaining the position of manager to my mother, for he felt himself
to be possessed of " executive " ability. " As for
the rest, sir, knocking out the peasants' teeth—I
understand that to perfection,"—he was wont to
say, almost gnashing his own teeth:—" because I
got used to it,"—he explained,—" in my former
vocation, you know." Had Zhitkóff been less
stupid, he would have understood, that the post
of manager to my mother was precisely the one
which he had no chance whatever of obtaining,
since to that end it would be necessary to super-
sede our actual manager, a certain Kvitzínsky, a
Pole of strong and active character, in whom my
mother had entire confidence. Zhitkóff had a

long, horse face, all overgrown with dusty-blond hair—even his cheeks up to his eyes were covered; even in the most severe cold weather, it was bedewed with copious perspiration, like dewdrops. At the sight of my mother, he immediately drew himself up in military style, his head began to tremble with zeal, his huge hands lightly tapped his hips, and his whole figure seemed to be crying aloud: "Command me! . . . . and I will fly headlong!" My mother was under no illusions as to his capacity, which, nevertheless, did not prevent her making efforts to marry him to Evlámpiya.

"Only, wilt thou be able to get along with her, my father?" she asked him one day.

Zhitkóff indulged in a self-satisfied smile.

"Goodness me, Natálya Nikoláevna! I have kept a whole company in order, they toed the mark, and what's this, ma'am? An insignificant affair, I spit upon it."

"A company of soldiers is one thing, my good man, and a well-born young girl, a wife, is quite another," remarked my mother, with displeasure.

"Good heavens, ma'am! Natálya Nikoláevna!" cried Zhitkóff again. "I can understand all that very well. In short: a young lady is a tender creature!"

"Well!"—my mother decided at last,—"Evlámpiya will not let herself be affronted."

X

ONE day—this took place in the month of June, and evening was drawing on—a footman announced the arrival of Martýn Petróvitch. My mother was astonished: We had not seen him for more than a week, but he had never called on us so late.

" Something has happened!" she exclaimed in an undertone. Martýn Petróvitch's face, when he presented himself in the room, and immediately dropped into a chair beside the door, wore such an unusual expression, it was so pensive and even pale, that my mother involuntarily repeated her exclamation aloud. Martýn Petróvitch fixed his little eyes upon her, remained silent, sighed heavily, again relapsed into silence, and announced, at last, that he had come about a matter of business . . . which . . . was of a nature, that in consequence . . . . .

Having muttered these incoherent words, he suddenly rose and left the room.

My mother rang the bell, ordered the lackey who entered to bring Martýn Petróvitch back immediately, but the latter had already succeeded in mounting his drozhky and driving off.

On the following morning, my mother, who

had been equally amazed and alarmed by Martýn Petróvitch's strange behaviour, and the expression of his face, was on the point of sending a messenger for him, when he himself again appeared before her. This time, he seemed to be more composed.

" Tell me, bátiushka,[1] tell me,"—exclaimed my mother, as soon as she caught sight of him,— " what has happened to you? I really thought yesterday: ' O Lord!' I thought,—' has n't our old neighbour gone out of his mind?' "

" I have not gone crazy, madam," replied Martýn Petróvitch:—" I 'm not that sort of a man. But I must take counsel with you."

" What about? "

" Only, I 'm in doubt, whether the same will be agreeable to you. . . . ."

" Speak, speak, father, and as simply as possible. Don't agitate me! why this *the same?* Speak simply. Have you got another fit of melancholy? "

Kharlóff contracted his brows. " No, not of melancholy—I have that at the time of the new moon; but permit me to ask you, madam, what you think about death? "

My mother was alarmed. " About what? "

" About death. Can death spare any one whomsoever in this world? "

---

[1] The genuine Russian form of address, literally, "dear little father."—TRANSLATOR.

" What other queer thing is this, that thou hast taken into thy head, my father? Thou, for instance, although thou wert born a giant—there will be an end to thee also."

" There will! okh, there will!" chimed in Kharlóff, and cast down his eyes. " There has happened to me a vision in my sleep . . . . ." he said slowly, at last. . .

" What art thou saying?"—my mother interrupted him.

" A vision in my sleep," he repeated. " I 'm a seer of visions, you know."

" Thou?"

" Yes. I! But did n't you know that?"— Kharlóff heaved a sigh. " Well, then . . . . I lay down a bit, madam, more than a week ago, just before the beginning of the Peter fast![1] I lay down after dinner, to rest a bit,—well,—and I fell asleep! and I saw something, as though it were a black colt, come running into the room, and up to me. And that colt began to prance about, and show its teeth. The colt was as black as a beetle."

Kharlóff ceased speaking.

" Well?"—said my mother.

" And that same colt suddenly wheels round, kicks me on the left elbow, right on the very

---

[1] The fast which precedes the day of St. Peter and St. Paul, June 29 (N. S. July 13): it varies in length, according to the date of Easter. — TRANSLATOR.

crazy-bone! . . . . I awoke! and lo and behold, that arm would n't work, neither would the left leg. Well, thinks I, 't is paralysis; but I kneaded it well, and it got into action again: only, the creeps kept coursing through my limbs for a long time, and are still doing so. Whenever I open my palm, they just begin to run up and down."

" Why, Martýn Petróvitch, thou must have been lying on thine arm, I 'm sure."

" No, madam, please not to say that! 'T is a forewarning to me . . . . . of my death, that is to say."

" Well, there he goes again! "—began my mother.

" 'T is a forewarning! As much as to say: ' Prepare thyself, man! ' And therefore, madam, this is what I have to announce to you, without the slightest delay. Not wishing,"—said Kharlóff, with a sudden shout,—" that that same death, should catch me, the servant of God, unawares, this is what I have decided upon in my own mind: that I must divide up my property now, during my lifetime, between my two daughters, Anna and Evlámpiya, as the Lord God shall put in my soul to do." Martýn Petróvitch paused, groaned, and added:—" Without the least delay."

" Well, what then? That is a good act,"—remarked my mother:—" only, I think that thou art making haste without a cause."

" And, as I desire, in this matter,"—went on

Kharlóff, elevating his voice to a still louder pitch,—" to observe the proper order and legality, I most respectfully request your young son, Dmítry Semyónovitch, and impose it upon my relative Bytchkóff as a direct duty—to be present at the consummation of the formal deed, and induction into possession of my two daughters, Anna, married, and Evlámpiya, spinster; which is to be put in effect the day after to-morrow, at twelve o'clock, noon, at my own estate of És'kovo, also known as Koziúlkino, assisted by the constituted authorities and officials, who have already been invited."

Martýn Petróvitch barely managed to finish this speech, which he had, obviously, committed to memory, and which was broken by numerous gasps. . . . It seemed as though there were a lack of air in his chest: his face, which had grown pallid, crimsoned once more, and he wiped the perspiration from it several times.

"And hast thou had the deed of partition drawn up already?" asked my mother. "When didst thou find the time for that?"

"I did . . . . . okh! Without a bite or a sup. . . . ."

"Didst thou write it thyself?"

"Volódka . . . . okh! helped me."

"And hast thou presented thy petition?"

"Yes, and the court has confirmed it, and the district judge has received his instructions, and

a special commission of the county court . . . .
okh! . . . has been designated to be present."

My mother laughed. "I perceive, Martýn
Petróvitch, that thou hast already taken all the
proper measures,—and how promptly! That
means, that thou hast not spared money?"

"No, I have not, madam."

"Indeed thou hast not! But thou sayest that
thou desirest to take counsel with me. Very well,
Mítenka may go, and I will let Souvenir go with
him, and I will tell Kvitzinsky. . . But hast thou
not invited Gavrílo Fedúlitch?"

"Gavrílo Fedúlitch . . . . Mr. Zhitkóff . . . .
has also been . . . . notified . . . . by me. In
his quality of betrothed it is proper that he should
be."

It was evident that Martýn Petróvitch had exhausted his entire store of eloquence. Moreover,
it had always seemed to me, that, somehow or
other, he was not quite well-disposed toward the
bridegroom whom my mother had picked out;
perhaps he had expected a more advantageous
match for his Evlámpiya.

He rose from his chair, and made a bow and
a scrape.—"Thanks for your consent!"

"Where art thou going?"—asked my mother.
"Sit down; I will order refreshments to be
served."

"Much obliged," replied Kharlóff. "But I
cannot. . . . . Okh! I must go home."

He retreated, and was on the point of sliding sideways through the door, according to his wont. . .

"Stop, stop,"—went on my mother,—"is it possible that thou art surrendering thy whole property, without reserve, to thy daughters?"

"Of course, without reserve."

"Well, and thou thyself . . . . where wilt thou live?"

Kharlóff even flourished his hands at this. "What do you mean by asking where? In my own house, as I have lived hitherto . . . . so I shall henceforth. What change can there be?"

"And hast thou so much confidence in thy daughters and in thy son-in-law?"

"Is it about Volódka that you are pleased to speak? About that rag? Why, I can shove him about anywhere, hither and yon. . . What power has he? And they, my daughters, that is to say, will furnish me with food, drink, shoes and clothing until I die. . . . . Good gracious! that's their first obligation! But I shall not long offend their eyes. Death is not far off, behind the mountains—but close, behind my shoulders."

"Death is in the power of the Lord God,"—remarked my mother,—"but that is their duty, it is true. Only, thou must pardon me, Martýn Petróvitch; thy eldest daughter, Anna, is well known to be a haughty chit,—well,—and thy second has the look of a wolf. . . . ."

" Natálya Nikoláevna! "—broke in Kharlóff, " what are you saying?—that they . . . . My daughters . . . . That I . . . . Are they going to renounce obedience? Why, they never would dream of such a thing! . . . . Offer resistance? To whom? To their parent?—Dare they? And would it take long to curse them? They have passed their life in trembling, and in submission,—and all of a sudden! . . . . . O Lord! "

Kharlóff cleared his throat: he had grown hoarse.

" Well, very good, very good,"—my mother hastened to soothe him:—" Only, I do not understand, nevertheless, why thou hast taken it into thy head to share the property between them *now*. In any case, it would have come to them after thy death. I suppose thy fit of melancholy is the cause of all this."

"Eh, mátushka,"[1] returned Kharlóff, not without irritation,—" you 're just wound up to say melancholy! Possibly, a higher power is acting in this matter, but you call it melancholy! And so, madam, I have taken it into my head, that I want to settle this personally, while I am in the land of the living,—who is to possess what,—and let the one whom I shall reward with anything hold possession of the same, and feel gratitude, and fulfil it, and regard that which her father and

---

[1] Literally, " dear little mother:" the genuine Russian address for women of all ranks.—TRANSLATOR.

benefactor has imposed upon her as a great mercy. . . . ."

Again Kharlóff's voice broke.

" Come, enough, my father, enough of that,"—my mother interrupted him; " or the black colt will straightway make his appearance."

" Okh, Natálya Nikoláevna, don't talk to me about him : "—groaned Kharlóff. " It was my death that came for me. I beg your forgiveness. And I shall have the honour to expect you, my little gentleman, the day after to-morrow! "

Martýn Petróvitch left the room; my mother looked after him, and shook her head significantly. " No good will come of this,"—she whispered;—" no good will come of it. Hast thou noticed," she said, turning to me:—" while he talked, he kept screwing up his eyes, as though to avoid the sun; thou must know that is a bad sign. When such a man feels heavy at heart, a calamity is threatening him. Go the day after to-morrow with Vikénty Osípovitch and Souvenir."

XI

On the appointed day, our big, four-seated, family carriage, drawn by six dark bay horses, with the chief "royal coachman," fat, grey-bearded Alexyéitch, on the box, rolled smoothly up to the porch of our house. The importance of the deed which Kharlóff was about to undertake, the solemnity with which he had invited us, had had their effect upon my mother. She herself had given orders to have precisely this extraordinary equipage harnessed up, and had commanded Souvenir and me to array ourselves in festive attire: evidently, she wished to show respect for her "protégé." As for Kvitzínsky,—he always went about in a dress-suit and a white neckcloth. Souvenir chattered like a magpie the whole way, giggled, discussed the question as to whether his dear brother would offer him anything, and then and there dubbed him an idol and a spectre. At last, Kvitzínsky, a morose, bilious man, could endure it no longer. "What possesses you,"—he said, with his clear-cut, Polish accent,—" to jabber such nonsense constantly? And is n't it possible to sit still, without any of that balderdash,—' which is of no use to any-

body ' ? (his favourite expression). " Well, immejutly,"—muttered Souvenir, with displeasure,
and riveted his squint-eyes on the window. A
quarter of an hour had not elapsed, the smoothly-
trotting horses had hardly begun to perspire
under the slender straps of the new harness, when
Kharlóff's manor-house came in sight. Through
the gates, which stood open, our carriage rolled
up to the courtyard; the tiny jockey, whose legs
hardly reached half-way down the horse's body,
bounded for the last time in his soft saddle with
a youthful yell, old Alexyéitch's elbows simultaneously spread out and rose, a faint " tprrrrr "
(whoa!) was audible, and we came to a halt. The
dogs did not greet us with barks, the little brats
of the house-serfs, in long shirts slightly open
over their big bellies, had also disappeared
somewhere. Kharlóff's son-in-law was waiting
for us on the threshold. I remember, that I was
particularly struck with the small birch-trees
which were stuck up on each side of the porch,
as on Trinity day.[1] " The Solemnity of Solem-
nities! "[2] sang Souvenir through his nose, as he
alighted first from the carriage. And, in fact,
solemnity was discernible in everything. Kharlóff's son-in-law wore a plush neckcloth, with a

---

[1] It is customary to decorate churches and houses with birch-trees
on that Sunday, which corresponds, in a way, to Whit-Sunday: the
following day, "the Day of the Spirit," being the actual Pentecost
festival, though the celebration is on "Trinity day."—TRANSLATOR.
[2] A quotation from the Easter hymns.—TRANSLATOR.

satin bow, and a remarkably tight-fitting dress-suit; and the hair of Maxím, who was popping up from behind his back, was drenched with home-made beer to such a degree, that it was even dripping with it. We entered the drawing-room, and beheld Martýn Petróvitch, towering up immovably,—precisely that, towering up,—in the middle of the room. I do not know what were the feelings of Souvenir and Kvitzínsky at the sight of his colossal figure, but I experienced something akin to reverence. Martýn Petróvitch had garbed himself in a grey jacket, with a black standing collar, which must have been his militia uniform in the year '12; the bronze medal was visible on his breast, the sword hung by his side; he had laid his left hand on the hilt, his right hand rested on a table covered with red cloth. Two sheets of paper covered with writing lay on that same table. Kharlóff did not move, did not even pant; and what dignity was expressed in his mien, what confidence in himself, in his unbounded and indubitable power! He barely greeted us with a nod, and saying hoarsely: " Pray be seated! " he pointed the index-finger of his left hand in the direction of a row of chairs. Against the right wall of the drawing-room stood both of Kharlóff's daughters, in their Sunday attire: Anna in a changeable gown of green and lilac, with a girdle of yellow silk; Evlámpiya in a pink gown, with flame-coloured ribbons. Beside them

stood Zhitkóff, in a new uniform, with his customary expression of stupid, greedy expectation in
his eyes, and with an unusually large amount of
perspiration on his hairy face. Against the left
wall of the drawing-room sat the priest, in a
threadbare snuff-coloured cassock—an old man,
with stiff, dark-brown hair. This hair, his dull
eyes, and his large, shrivelled hands, which
seemed to be a burden to himself, and lay, like
heaps, on his knees, and his oiled boots, which
peeped forth from beneath his cassock,—all
bore witness to his toilsome, cheerless life: his
parish was very poor. By his side sat the chief
of the rural police, a fat, pale, dirty little gentleman, with plump, short hands and feet, black
eyes, black, clipped moustache, and a constant,
pitiful though cheery smile on his face: he had
the reputation of being a great bribe-taker, and
even tyrant, as the expression ran in those days:
but not only the landed proprietors, but the peasants also had got used to him, and were fond of
him. He was gazing about in a very free-and-
easy and somewhat mocking manner: it was
plain, that this whole " procedure " amused him.
In reality, he was interested only in the impend-
ing luncheon with vodka. On the other hand, the
pettifogging lawyer who sat beside him, a gaunt
man with a long face, and narrow side-whiskers
running from his ear to his nose, as they were worn
under Alexander I, took a soul-felt interest in

274

Martýn Petróvitch's arrangements, and never removed from him his large, serious eyes; extremely strained attention and sympathy made him keep constantly moving and twisting his lips, but he did not open them. Souvenir took a seat by him, and entered into a whispered conversation with him, having preliminarily informed me, that he was the leading Freemason of the district. A special commission of the county court consists, as every one knows, of the chief of rural police, a lawyer and the commissary of police; but either there was no commissary, or else he kept himself in the background to such a degree that I did not observe him; however, he went in our district by the nickname of " the non-existent," just as there are some called " the non-rememberers." I sat down next to Souvenir, Kvitzínsky next to me. On the face of the practical Pole there was depicted manifest vexation at the " useless to anybody " trip, at the vain loss of time. . . . . . " Just like a fine lady! the freaks of these Russian gentry! " he seemed to be whispering to himself . . . . " These Russians are altogether too much for me! "

XII

WHEN we were all seated, Martýn Petróvitch elevated his shoulders, grunted, looked at us one after the other with his little bear-like eyes, and, sighing noisily, began thus:

"Dear sirs! I have invited you hither for the following cause. I am getting old, dear sirs, infirmities are beginning to overcome me. . . . I have already had a forewarning, the hour of death, like a thief in the night, is approaching. . . . Is n't that right, bátiushka," [1] he said, addressing the priest.

The priest was startled. "Yes, yes," he mumbled, wagging his little chin.

"And therefore,"—pursued Martýn Petróvitch, suddenly raising his voice,—"not wishing that that same death should overtake me unawares, I have settled in my own mind . . . ." Martýn Petróvitch repeated, word for word, the phrases which he had uttered at my mother's house, two days before. "In virtue of this my decision," he vociferated still more loudly, "this deed" (he smote the documents which were lying on the table) "has been drawn up by me, and

[1] Bátiushka, the general address to a man in any station of life, is specifically the title of the clergy.—TRANSLATOR.

the powers that be have been invited hither. As
to what my said will consists of, the points follow.
I have finished my reign, let there be an end of
me!"

Martýn Petróvitch placed his round iron spectacles on his nose, took from the table one of the
sheets of writing, and began:

"A deed of partition of the property of
retired bayonet-yunker[1] and hereditary noble,
Martýn Kharlóff, drawn up by himself in full
and sound mind, and according to his own good
judgment, and wherein are accurately specified
what usufructs are placed at the disposal of his
two daughters, Anna and Evlámpiya—make a
reverence!" (they made a reverence)—"are
placed at their disposal, and in what manner the
house-serfs and the other property and the poul-
try are to be divided between the said daughters.
And thereto I set my hand in confirmation!"

"He wants to read that document of his"—
whispered the chief of police, with his perpetual
smile, to Kvitzínsky,—"because of the beauty of
its style, but the legal document is drawn up in
proper form, without all those flourishes."

Souvenir began to giggle. . . . .

"In consonance with my will!"—put in Kharlóff; the chief of police's comment had not escaped his attention.

---

[1] An old-fashioned rank in the artillery, between sergeant
and lieutenant.—TRANSLATOR.

"It does agree in all points,"—replied the latter, hastily and cheerily;—"only, the form, you know, Martýn Petróvitch, cannot possibly be dispensed with. And superfluous details are eliminated. For the court cannot possibly enter into particulars as to piebald cows and Turkish drakes."

"Come hither, thou!"—yelled Kharlóff to his son-in-law, who had followed us into the room, and had stopped near the door, with an obsequious air. He immediately ran to his father-in-law.

"Here, take, read! It's difficult for me! Only, look out, don't gabble! Read so that all the gentlemen present may penetrate the meaning."

Slétkin took the sheet of paper with both hands, and began to read the deed of partition tremblingly, but intelligibly, with taste and feeling. Therein was defined, with the greatest accuracy, precisely what was allotted to Anna, and what to Evlámpiya, and in what manner they were to share. Kharlóff, from time to time, broke in on the reading with the words:—"Hearest thou, Anna, that is for thee, for thy zeal!"—or: "I present that to thee, Evlámpiushka!"—and both sisters bowed, Anna with her whole body to the waist, Evlámpiya with her head only. Kharlóff surveyed them with sombre pomposity. "The manor-house"—the new wing, he assigned to Evlámpiya, " as being the youngest daughter, according to custom from time immemorial "; the voice of the reader cracked and quivered as he articulated these words so unpleasant for himself : but Zhitkóff licked his lips. Evlámpiya cast a sidelong glance at him : had I been in Zhitkóff's place, I should not have liked that glance. Martýn Petróvitch reserved to himself the right to live in the chambers at present occupied by him, and stipulated for himself, under the appellation of " privy purse," full support " with natural provisions " and ten rubles in cash per month for shoes and clothing. Kharlóff insisted on reading the concluding clause in the deed of partition himself.

" And this my parental will,"—it ran,—" my daughters are to hold sacred and inviolate, as though it were my last will and testament; for, after God, I am their father and their head, and am not bound to render account to any one, neither have I rendered it; and if they shall fulfil my will, then shall my parental blessing be with them, but if they shall not fulfil my will, which God forbid, then shall my parental and irrevocable curse overtake them, now and unto ages of ages, amen! " Kharlóff elevated the sheet of paper high above his head. Anna instantly dropped briskly on her knees, and thumped the floor with her brow; her husband followed her with a similar somersault. " Well, and what art thou about?"—Kharlóff said to Evlámpiya. She flushed crimson all over, and also made a reverence to the earth: Zhitkóff bent his whole body forward.

"Sign!"—exclaimed Kharlóff, pointing his finger at the end of the deed. "Here: ⸜ I thank and accept, Anna! I thank and accept, Evlámpiya!'"

Both daughters rose to their feet, and signed, one after the other. Slétkin rose also, and made a motion to take the pen, but Kharlóff brushed him aside, thrusting his middle finger in his neckcloth so that he staggered back. The silence lasted for about a minute. All at once, Martýn Petróvitch gave a sort of gulp, and muttering, "Well, everything is yours now!" moved aside. His daughters and son-in-law exchanged glances, went to him, and began to kiss his arm, above the elbow. They could not reach his shoulder.[1]

[1] An ancient Russian custom, from inferiors to their superiors.—TRANSLATOR.

XIII

THE chief of police read the real, formal act, the deed of gift, drawn up by Martýn Petróvitch. Then he and the lawyer went out on the porch, and announced to the neighbours, who had assembled about the gate,—namely, the local inhabitants, summoned by the police as witnesses, the serfs on the Kharlóff estate, and several house-serfs,—the transaction which had been completed. Then began the induction into possession of the two new landed proprietresses, who also made their appearance on the porch, and at whom the chief of police pointed with his hand, when, slightly frowning and for the moment imparting to his care-free countenance a menacing aspect, he exhorted the peasants to " obedience."

He might have dispensed with this exhortation: I do not believe that more peaceable physiognomies than those of the Kharlóff peasants exist in nature. Clad in miserable cloth long coats and tattered sheepskin short coats, but very tightly girt, as is always proper on solemn occasions, they stood motionless as men of stone, and whenever the chief of police emitted interjections, in the nature of: " Listen, you fiends! under-

281

stand, you devils!" they made an abrupt inclination, all in unison, as though at the word of
command; each one of these "fiends and devils"
held his cap tightly clutched with both hands,
and never took his eyes from the window, through
which was visible the figure of Martýn Petróvitch. And the inhabitants of the locality offi-
cially bidden as witnesses were not much less
daunted.

"Do you know of any impediments whatsoever,"—shouted the chief at them,—"to the
induction into possession of these only and legiti-
mate heiresses and daughters of Martýn Petróvitch Kharlóff?"

All the official witnesses immediately seemed
to shrivel up.

"Do you know any, you devils?"—shouted
the chief of police again.

"We know of none, Your Well-born,"—man-
fully replied one small, pock-marked old fellow,
a retired soldier, with a close-clipped beard and
moustache.

"Well, now, Eremyéitch is a bold fellow!"—
the witnesses said of him, as they went their several ways.

Notwithstanding the chief's request, Kharlóff
would not go out on the porch with his daughters.
"My subjects will submit to my will without
that!"—he replied. A sort of depression had descended upon him after the consummation of the

deed. His face again had become pallid. This new, unprecedented expression of dejection so ill suited the expansive and kindly features of Martýn Petróvitch, that I decidedly did not know what to make of it. Could it be that a fit of melancholy was coming on?—the peasants, evidently, on their side, were puzzled also. And, in fact: " The master is as lively as ever—yonder he stands, and what a Master! Martýn Petró-vitch! And all of a sudden, he is not going to own them. . . . Astounding!" I know not whether Kharlóff divined the thoughts which were fermenting in the heads of his " subjects," whether he wanted to bluster for the last time, but suddenly he opened the hinged pane, put his head in the opening, and shouted in a voice of thunder: " Obey!" Then he slammed to the pane. The bewilderment of the peasants was not dispelled by this, of course, and neither was it diminished. They became more petrified than ever, and even, as it were, ceased to look. The group of house-serfs (among their number were two buxom girls, in short calico gowns, with such calves as are, probably, to be seen nowhere else except in Michael Angelo's " Last Judgment," and one other, very aged, half-blind old man, who was even covered with rime, so antique was he, in a rough frieze great-coat,—according to report, he had been a " horn-player " under Potémkin,[1]—

2 Pronounced *Patyómkin.*—Translator.

Kharlóff had retained the page Maxím for his own service),—this group evinced more animation than the peasants: at all events, it shifted from foot to foot. The new proprietresses bore themselves with much dignity, especially Anna. Compressing her thin lips, she kept her eyes persistently downcast . . . . her stern face did not augur much good. Neither did Evlámpiya raise her eyes; only once she turned round, and, as though with surprise, with a glance measured from head to foot her betrothed, Zhitkóff, who had considered it necessary that he should follow Slétkin out, and show himself on the porch. "By what right art thou here?" those beautiful, prominent eyes seemed to say. Slétkin had undergone a greater change than any of the rest. A hurried energy had made its appearance in his whole being, as though ravenous appetite had permeated him; the movements of his head, of his feet, had remained as obsequious as ever; but how gaily did he rub his hands, how eagerly did he twitch his elbows! As much as to say: "At last, I have reached my goal!"

Having accomplished the " procedure " of installing in possession, the chief of police, whose mouth was fairly watering with the near approach of luncheon, rubbed his hands in that peculiar manner which usually precedes the " plunging into one's self of the first glass of liquor " ; but it appeared, that Martýn Petró-

vitch wished to have a service of prayer with
blessing of water celebrated first. The priest
donned an old chasuble, which was almost falling to pieces: a barely-alive chanter emerged
from the kitchen, with difficulty blowing alight
the incense in an old brass censer. The prayer-
service began. Kharlóff sighed incessantly; he
could not make reverences to the ground, owing
to his obesity, but crossing himself with his right
hand, and bowing his head, he pointed at the
floor with the finger of his left hand. . Slétkin
was fairly beaming, and even shed tears; Zhitkóff, in a well-bred way, military fashion, crossed
himself by barely twitching his fingers between
the third and fourth buttons of his uniform;
Kvitzínsky, being a Roman Catholic, remained
in the adjoining room; on the other hand, the
lawyer prayed so fervently, sighed so sympa-
thetically in imitation of Martýn Petróvitch, and
whispered and moved his lips so violently, rolling his eyes heavenward the while, that as I
watched him I was much affected, and began to
pray also. At the conclusion of the prayer-ser-
vice and blessing of the water, when all present,
even Potémkin's blind " hornist," even Kvitzínsky, wet their eyes with the holy water, Anna
and Evlámpiya once more, at the command of
Martýn Petróvitch, returned thanks to him with
a ground-reverence: and then, at last, the moment for breakfast arrived. There were a great

many viands, and all were very savoury; we all over-ate ourselves dreadfully. The inevitable bottle of Don wine made its appearance. The chief of police, in his quality of a man who was more familiar than all the rest of us with the customs of society,—well, and also as a representative of the ruling powers,—was the first to propose a toast to the health of " the beautiful proprietresses!" Then he proposed that we should drink also to the health of the most highly respected and most magnanimous Martýn Petróvitch. At the words, "most magnanimous," Slétkin squealed aloud, and rushed to kiss his benefactor. . . . . " Come, all right, all right, there 's no necessity for that,"—muttered Kharlóff, thrusting him aside with his elbow, as though vexed. . . . . But at this point a not entirely pleasant episode, as the saying is, took place.

XIV

To wit: Souvenir, who had been drinking uninterruptedly ever since the beginning of the breakfast, suddenly rose from his chair, as crimson as a beet, and pointing his finger at Martýn Petróvitch, burst out with his quavering, pitiful laugh.

" Magnanimous! Magnanimous! " he shrilled, " well, let us just see whether this magnanimity will suit his taste, when he, the servant of God, is turned out, barebacked, ... and into the snow! "

" What nonsense art thou chattering? fool! " articulated Kharlóff, scornfully.

" Fool! fool! "—repeated Souvenir. " The Most High God alone knows which of us two is the real fool. See here, brother! you killed my sister, your spouse, and, to make it even, you have now wiped yourself out . . . . ha-ha-ha! "

" How dare you insult our respected benefactor? "—Slétkin flew to his defence, and wrenching free his shoulder, which Martýn Petróvitch had grasped, he rushed at Souvenir. " Don't you know, that if our benefactor wishes it, we can cancel that deed this very minute? " . . .

" Nevertheless, you will turn him out, stark-naked—into the snow . . ." interjected Souvenir, darting behind Kvitzínsky.

"Hold thy tongue!"—thundered Kharlóff.— "I'll give thee such a slap, that there will be nothing left but a wet spot where thou hast been. And do thou hold thy tongue, also, pup!"—he addressed Slétkin;—"don't thrust thyself in where thou art not asked! If I, Martýn Petróvitch Kharlóff, have made up my mind to draw up the said deed, then who can cancel it? who can oppose my will? Why, there is no power on earth . . . . . ."

"Martýn Petróvitch!"—suddenly remarked the lawyer, in a somnolent bass voice; he, also, had been drinking a great deal, but the only effect it had on him was to augment his pomposity. "Well, and what if the gentleman-proprietor has been pleased to speak the truth? You have done a great deed; well, and God forbid, that, as a matter of fact . . . . instead of the gratitude which is due, some affront should be the outcome."

I cast a stealthy glance at Martýn Petróvitch's two daughters. Anna was fairly boring her eyes into the speaker, and, positively, I had never yet beheld her handsome face more evil and snaky, and more beautiful even in its malice! Evlámpiya turned away, and folded her arms; a scornful smile made her full, rosy lips curl more than ever.

Kharlóff rose from his chair, opened his mouth, but evidently his tongue refused to move. . . . . He suddenly smote the table with his fist, so that everything in the room danced and clattered.

" Dear father," said Anna hastily; " they do not know us, and therefore have that opinion of us; but please do not do yourself an injury. There is no necessity for your being angry; why, your dear little face is positively distorted."

Kharlóff glanced at Evlámpiya; she did not move, although Zhitkóff, who sat beside her, nudged her in the side.

" I thank thee, my daughter Anna,"—said Kharlóff, in a dull voice;—" thou art my clever girl; I trust thee, and thy husband also." Again Slétkin squealed; Zhitkóff protruded his chest, and stamped his foot lightly; but Kharlóff did not notice his effort. " That blockhead," he went on, indicating Souvenir with his chin,—" is glad to tease me; but you, my dear sir,"—and he turned to the lawyer,—"have no right to judge of Martýn Kharlóff: you know nothing about him yet. And you are an official man, but your words are absurd. However, the matter is settled, there will be no change in my decision. . . Well, and good luck to me! I shall go away. I am no longer the host here, but a guest. Anna, manage affairs as thou wilt; but I 'm going off to my study. I 've had enough!"

Martýn Petróvitch wheeled round with his

back to us, and without adding another word, slowly left the room.

The sudden withdrawal of the master of the house could not but throw our company into confusion, the more so as both of the hostesses speedily disappeared also. In vain did Slétkin try to detain us. The chief of police did not fail to reprove the lawyer for his unseasonable frankness. " I could n't help it! "—replied the latter. " It was my conscience speaking! "

" There, 't is evident that he is a Freemason," —whispered Souvenir to me.

" Conscience! " retorted the chief of police. " We know all about your conscience! It 's located in your pocket, I think, as is the case with all of us sinners! "

The priest, in the meanwhile, still standing, but foreseeing a speedy end to the feast, was uninterruptedly sending one morsel after another into his mouth.

" You have a hearty appetite, I observe," Slétkin said to him sharply.

" I 'm laying in a supply,"—replied the priest, with a peaceable grimace; chronic hunger was audible in this reply.

The equipages rumbled up . . . and we dispersed.

On the way home, no one interfered with Souvenir's writhing and chattering, as Kvitzínsky had announced that he was tired of all these horrors, " of no use to any one," and had set out homeward in advance, on foot. Zhitkóff took his place in our carriage; the retired Major wore an extremely dissatisfied aspect, and kept continually waggling his moustache about, like a beetle.

" Well, your High-Well-Born," — lisped Souvenir:—" subordination is broken, I suppose? Wait a bit, this is only the beginning! You 'll catch it too. Akh, you poor bridegroom, poor miserable bridegroom, poor miserable little bridegroom! "

Souvenir was fairly intoxicated, and poor Zhitkóff merely waggled his moustache!

On reaching home, I narrated all that had occurred to my mother. She heard me to the end, and shook her head several times. " No good will come of it,"—she said:—" I don't like all these innovations! "

XV

On the following day, Martýn Petróvitch came
to dinner. My mother congratulated him on the
successful completion of the matter he had undertaken. "Now thou art a free man,"—she
said,—" and must feel relieved."

"I'm relieved, right enough, madam," replied
Martýn Petróvitch, but without showing in the
slightest degree by the expression of his countenance that he really was relieved. "Perhaps I
shall have a chance now to think of my soul, and
prepare myself for the hour of death, in the
proper manner."

"Well, how now?"—inquired my mother:—
"do you still have those convulsive twitches in
your palms?"

Kharlóff clenched and relaxed the palm of his
left hand a couple of times.

"Yes, madam;—and here's something I want
to tell you: when I am on the point of falling
asleep, some one shouts in my head: 'Beware!
Beware!'"

"It's . . . . nerves,"—remarked my mother,
and began to talk about the preceding day, al-
luding to several circumstances which had accompanied the consummation of the deed of partition.

"Well, yes, yes,"—Kharlóff interrupted her:
"there was something of that sort . . . . nothing of any importance. Only, see here, I must
inform you,"—he added, falteringly,—"Souvenir's empty words did not trouble me yesterday,—even the lawyer,—and he is an exact
man,—did not disconcert me; but the person who
did trouble me was . . . ." Here Kharlóff
hesitated.

"Who was it?"—asked my mother.

Kharlóff turned his eyes on her:—"Evlámpiya!"

"Evlámpiya! Thy daughter? In what way?"

"Good gracious, madam,—she was just like a
stone! a regular statue! Can it be that she has no
feeling? Her sister Anna,—well, she did everything that was fitting. She's an artful one!
But Evlámpiya—why, I 've shown her,—what 's
the use of hiding my sin!—I 've shown her
a great deal of partiality! Can it be that she
is not sorry for me? So I shall fare badly,—
so there is no longer any place for me on earth,
I foresee, if I surrender everything to them;
and she was like a stone! she might at least
have grunted! As for making me a reverence,
she did that—but there was no gratitude
visible."

"Wait,"—remarked my mother,—"we will
marry her to Gavrílo Fedúlitch . . . . she will
get tamed down in his hands."

Again Martýn Petróvitch cast a sidelong look at my mother. " Well, it is n't likely that Gavrílo Fedúlitch will do anything of that sort! You are placing your hopes on him, I suppose, madam? "

" Yes."

" Just so, ma'am; well, you might as well know it. Evlámpiya is just like me, I must inform you: we have the same disposition. Kazák blood—and hearts like coals of fire! "

" Have you really that sort of heart, my father? "

Kharlóff made no answer. A brief silence ensued.

" And as for thee, Martýn Petróvitch,"—began my mother,—" in what manner dost thou intend to save thy soul now? Shalt thou go to Mitrofány, or to Kíeff? or, perchance, thou wilt betake thyself to the Óptin desert hermitage, as it is in the neighbourhood? They say that such a holy monk has made his appearance there, ... his name is Father Makáry, and no one can recall such another! He sees straight through all sins."

" If she should really turn out to be an ungrateful daughter,"—said Kharlóff, in a hoarse voice,—" I think it will be easier for me to kill her with my own hands! "

" What ails thee! What ails thee! The Lord

be with thee! Come to thy senses!"—exclaimed my mother. "What speeches are these that thou art making! There now, that's exactly what the trouble is! thou shouldst have listened to me, the other day, when thou camest for advice! But now, thou wilt torture thyself—and nevertheless, thou canst not remedy the matter! Yes! Here thou art complaining now, growing timid. . . . . . ."

This reproach seemed to stab Kharlóff in the very heart. All his former pride rose up within him like a flood.

"I'm not the sort of man, madam, Natálya Nikoláevna, to complain or turn cowardly,"—he said grimly. "I merely wished to set forth my feelings to you, as my benefactress, and a person whom I respect. But the Lord God knows" (here he raised his hand above his head) "that this earthly sphere shall go to smash before I go back on my word, or . . . ." (here he even snorted) "or grow cowardly, or repent of anything I have done. There was cause, you know. But my daughters will not fail in obedience, unto ages of ages, amen!"

My mother stopped her ears. "Why dost thou blare like a trumpet, my father! If thou really hast confidence in the members of thy household, well, then thanks be to thee, O Lord! Thou hast completely shattered my head."

A KING LEAR OF THE STEPPES

Martýn Petróvitch made his excuses, heaved a couple of sighs, and fell silent. My mother again mentioned Kíeff, the Óptin hermitage, Father Makáry . . . Khárloff assented, saying: " It is necessary, necessary . . . . I must . . . . my soul . . . . ." and nothing more. Until the very moment of his departure, he did not cheer up; from time to time, he closed and opened his hand, stared at his palm, said that the most terrible thing of all to him would be to die without proper preparation, from apoplexy, and that he had sworn an oath to himself not to lose his temper, because the blood is spoiled from the heart and floods the head. . . . . Moreover, he had now set himself apart from everything; what cause would there be for him to lose his temper? Let others toil now and corrupt their blood!

As he took leave of my mother, he looked at her in a strange way, thoughtfully and interrogatively. . . And all at once, pulling the volume of " The Labourer at Rest " from his pocket with a swift movement, he thrust it into my mother's hand.

" What is this? " she asked.

" Read it . . . . here, in this place,"—he said hurriedly,—" where the corner of the page is turned down, about death. It strikes me, that it is very well said, but I can't possibly understand it. Will not you expound it to me, my benefactress? See here, I 'll come back, and you shall expound it to me."

With these words, Martýn Petróvitch left the room.

" There 's something wrong! ekh, there 's something wrong! "—remarked my mother, as soon as he had disappeared through the door—and she set to work on " The Labourer at Rest." On the page indicated by Kharlóff stood the following words:

" Death is a great and important work of nature. It consists in nothing else than this,—that inasmuch as the spirit is lighter, more delicate, and much more penetrating than those elements to whose power it has been given over, and also even than electric force, so it purifies itself chemically, and yearns until it feels a spiritual environment like itself . . . . ." and so forth.[1]

My mother perused this passage twice, exclaimed, " Pshaw! "—and flung the book aside.

Two days later she received word, that her sister's husband had died, and taking me with her, she set off for her country house. My mother had made arrangements to spend a month with her, but remained until late in the autumn—and we did not return to our country house until the end of September.

[1] See "The Labourer at Rest," 1785, Part II. Moscow.

XVI

THE first bit of news with which my valet, Prokófy (he regarded himself as the seigniorial
huntsman), greeted me on my arrival, was, that
an immense number of woodcock had alighted,
and that particularly in the birch grove near
És'kovo (the Kharlóff estate) they were fairly
swarming. It was still three hours to dinner-
time. I immediately seized my gun and game-
pouch, and, accompanied by Prokófy and a setter
dog, I ran to the És'kovo grove. We really did
find a great many woodcock there—and after
firing about thirty shots, we killed five birds. As
I was hastening homeward with my booty, I saw
a peasant ploughing by the roadside. His horse
had come to a standstill, and he, swearing tearfully and viciously, was tugging its head merci-
lessly on one side with the rope reins. I glanced
at the unhappy nag, whose ribs had almost broken
through the skin, and whose sides, drenched in
sweat, were heaving convulsively and unevenly,
like a blacksmith's bellows,—and instantly recognised it as the aged, emaciated mare with the scar
on her neck, which had served Martýn Petróvitch for so many years.

"Is Mr. Kharlóff alive?" I asked Prokófy. The hunt had so completely absorbed us, that up to that moment we had not discussed anything else.

"Yes, sir. Why do you ask, sir?"

"But, surely, this is his horse? Is it possible that he has sold her?"

"Just so, sir, it is his horse; only, as for selling her, he has n't; but they have taken her away from him—and given her to this peasant."

"What dost thou mean by saying that they have taken her away? And did he consent?"

"They did n't ask any consent of him, sir. There 's a new order of things been set up during your absence," replied Prokófy, with a faint grin, in reply to my glance of surprise,—"alas! O my God! Mr. Slétkin manages everything for them now."

"And Martýn Petróvitch?"

"And Martýn Petróvitch has become the very lowest person on the place, so he has. He has been put on a diet of dry food. They 've done him up completely. The first any one knows, they 'll drive him out of doors."

The idea that such a giant could be driven out absolutely refused to get itself into my head. "But why does n't Zhitkóff look after him?"— I inquired at last. "He married the second daughter, did n't he?"

"Married?" repeated Prokófy, and this time

299

grinned from ear to ear. " They won't let him enter the house. ' You 're not wanted,' say they; ' turn your shafts the other way,' say they. I 've told you how it is: Slétkin manages them all."

" But what does the bride say to that? "

" Evlámpiya Martýnovna, you mean? Ekh, master, I 'd like to tell you . . . . . but you 're young—that 's what it is. There have been such goings-on, that i . . . . i . . . . i! Eh! but I think Diánka is making a point."

In fact, my dog had halted, as though rooted to the spot, in front of a spreading oak bush in which terminated a narrow ravine that came out on the road. Prokófy and I ran to the dog; a woodcock rose from the bush. We both fired at it, and missed it; the woodcock changed its place; we followed it.

The soup was already on the table when I got home. My mother reprimanded me:

" What 's this? "—she said with displeasure,— " thou hast made us wait dinner for thee on the very first day." I presented her with the wood-cock which I had shot; she did not even look at them. In addition to her, Souvenir, Kvitzínsky, and Zhitkóff were in the room. The retired Major had hidden himself in a corner,—precisely like a naughty school-boy; the expression of his face revealed a mixture of perturbation and vexa-tion; his eyes were red. . . . . One might even have supposed that he had been weeping recently. My mother continued to be out of temper; it cost me no great effort to divine that my late arrival had nothing to do with the matter. During dinner, she spoke hardly at all; from time to time, the Major cast pitiful glances at her, but he ate heartily, nevertheless; Souvenir trembled; Kvitzínsky preserved his customary intrepidity of demeanour.

" Vikénty Osípitch," said my mother, addressing him;—" I request that to-morrow you will send the equipage for Martýn Petróvitch, as I have learned that he has no longer one of his own; and give orders that he is to be told, that he is to come without fail, that I wish to see him."

Kvitzínsky wanted to make some reply, but refrained.

" And give Slétkin to understand,"—went on my mother,—" that I command him to come to me. . . . . Do you hear? I com . . . . mand!"

" There, that's precisely . . . . what that scoundrel needs . . . . . ." began Zhitkóff in an undertone; but my mother cast such a scornful look at him, that he immediately turned away, and fell silent.

" Do you hear? I command!"—repeated my mother.

" I obey, ma'am,"—said Kvitzínsky, submissively, but with dignity.

" Martýn Petróvitch won't come!"—whis-

pered Souvenir to me, as we left the dining-room
together after dinner. "Just see, what he has
become! It's incredible!—I think—that no matter what is said to him,—he does n't understand
a single thing. Yes! They 've squeezed the ad-
der with pitchforks!"

And Souvenir broke into his quavering laugh.

XVII

Souvenir's prediction proved correct. Martýn
Petróvitch would not come to my mother. She
was displeased at this, and sent him a note; he
sent back to her a quarter of a sheet of paper, on
which, in big letters, the following words were
written: " Indeed, by heaven, I cannot. Shame
would kill me. Let me perish. Thanks. Don't
worry. Kharlóff Martýnko." Slétkin came,
but not on the day on which my mother had
" commanded " him to present himself, but a
whole day later. My mother gave orders that he
should be conducted to her boudoir. . . . . God
knows what their conversation was about, but it
lasted a very short time only: not more than a
quarter of an hour. Slétkin came out of my mother's room, all red in the face, and with such a
viciously-evil and impudent expression of countenance, that on encountering him in the drawing-
room, I was dumfounded, and Souvenir, who
was skipping about there, did not finish the laugh
which he had begun. My mother also emerged
from her boudoir all red in the face, and announced, in the hearing of all, that Mr. Slétkin,

henceforth, would not be admitted to her house on any pretext whatsoever; and that if Martýn Petróvitch's daughters should take it into their heads to present themselves—they were quite brazen-faced enough for that,—they, also, were to be sent about their business. At dinner, she suddenly exclaimed:—" What a wretched little Jew! And it was I who dragged him out of the gutter by his ears, it was I who made somebody of him, he is indebted to me for everything, everything—and he dares to tell me, that I have no right to intermeddle with their affairs!—that Martýn Petróvitch is a fool—and it is impossible to indulge him in his caprices! Indulge! Did you ever hear the like? Akh, he's an ungrateful young cub! A dirty little Jew!"—Major Zhitkóff, who was also among the diners, imagined that now God himself had bidden him take advantage of the opportunity, and put in his word . . . but my mother immediately snubbed him. " Well, and thou art a nice person, also, my father!"—said she. " Thou wert not able to get along with the girl, and yet thou art an officer! Thou hast commanded a company! I can imagine how it obeyed thee! And thou hadst aspirations to become my agent! A pretty agent thou wouldst have made!"

Kvitzínsky, who sat at the end of the table, smiled to himself, not without malevolent delight, while poor Zhitkóff merely wagged his moustache, and elevated his eyebrows, and buried the whole of his hairy face in his napkin.

After dinner, he went out on the porch to smoke his pipe, according to his habit,—and he seemed to me so pitiful and forlorn an object, that although I did not like him, I joined him.

" How did it come about, Gavrílo Fedúlitch," I began, without any circumlocution—" that your affair with Evlámpiya Martýnovna suffered shipwreck? I had supposed that you were married long ago."

The retired Major cast a dejected glance at me.

" The sly snake,"—he began, with mournful care pronouncing every letter of every word,— " has poisoned me with her sting, and has turned all my hopes in life to dust! And I would like to tell you, Dmítry Semyónovitch, all her viperous deeds, but I 'm afraid of angering your mother!" (" You 're still very young "—Prokófy's expression flashed through my mind.) " So be it. . . ."—Zhitkóff quacked.

" Endure it . . . . endure it . . . . nothing else remains to be done!" (He smote himself on the chest with his clenched fist.) " Be patient, faithful old soldier, endure! I have served the Tzar with fidelity and truth . . . uncomplainingly . . . . . yes! I have not spared my sweat and blood, but now what have I come to! Had this thing happened in the regiment—and had the matter depended upon me,"—he went on after a brief pause, pulling away convulsively at his cherry-wood tchibouk,—" I 'd have given it to him. . . . . I 'd have had him flogged with the flat of the sword, in three relays . . . that is, until he tumbled over. . . . ."

Zhitkóff took the pipe from his mouth, and riveted his gaze on space, as though inwardly admiring the picture which he had conjured up.

Souvenir ran up, and began to jeer at the Major. I stepped aside from them—and made up my mind that I would see Martýn Petróvitch, at whatever cost. . . . . My childish curiosity was strongly piqued.

XVIII

On the following day, I again set out with my
gun and dog, but without Prokófy, for the És'-
kovo grove. The day turned out to be magnificent. I think there are no such days anywhere
in September, except in Russia. Such silence
reigned, that one could hear a rabbit leaping
over the dry leaves a hundred paces off, and a
broken twig first faintly catching on other twigs,
and at last falling on the soft grass—falling for
good and all: never to stir again all the while it is
rotting. The air, neither warm nor cool, but only
fragrant, rather acrid, just pinched the eyes and
cheeks agreeably; slender as a thread of silk, with
a white little ball in the centre, a long spider's-
web floated along and caught on the barrel of my
gun, stretching straight upward in the air—an
infallible sign of warm weather. The sun shone,
but as mildly as though it were the moon. Woodcock turned up quite frequently; but I paid no
particular attention to them: I knew that the
grove extended almost to the very manor-house of
Kharlóff, to the very wattled fence of his garden
—and wended my steps in that direction—although I could not imagine how I was going to

make my way into the house itself, and even felt
doubtful as to whether I ought so much as to try
to enter there, as my mother was wroth with the
new owners.

Living human sounds surprised me in the far
distance. I began to listen. . . . Some one was
walking through the copse . . . . straight toward
me.

"But thou mightest have said so . . . ."—a
feminine voice became audible.

"Oh, you may talk!" interrupted another
voice,—a man's. "Dost thou suppose everything
can be done at once?"

I knew the voices. Glimpses of a woman's
sky-blue gown were visible through the thinning
nut-bushes; alongside it, a dark kaftán showed
itself. Another moment—and Slétkin and Evlámpiya emerged into the glade five paces from
me.

They suddenly became confused. Evlámpiya
instantly retreated into the bushes. Slétkin reflected—and advanced to meet me. On his face
there was no longer visible even a trace of that
servile submissiveness with which, four months
previously, he had walked up and down the yard
of the Kharlóff house, polishing the chain of my
horse's bridle; but neither could I read in it that
impudent defiance,—the defiance wherewith that
face had so astounded me on the preceding day,
on the threshold of my mother's boudoir. As of

yore, it was white and comely, but appeared to be
more solid and broader.

"Well, have you shot many woodcock?"—he
asked me, raising his cap, smirking, and passing
his hand over his black curls. "You are hunting
in our grove. . . . . You are welcome! We do
not hinder. . . On the contrary!"

"I have killed nothing to-day,"—said I, reply-
ing to his first question: "and I shall leave your
grove immediately."

Slétkin hastily replaced his cap. "Good gracious! why? We are not driving you out—and
we are even very glad. . . . Here's Evlámpiya
Martýnovna, who will say the same. Evlámpiya
Martýnovna, please come hither! Where have
you hidden yourself?"

Evlámpiya's head made its appearance from
behind the bushes; but she did not come to us.
She had become still handsomer of late—and
seemed to have grown taller and stouter.

"I must confess,"—went on Slétkin,—"that
it is even very agreeable for me to have 'met'
you. Although you are still young—yet you already possess genuine good sense. Your mother
was pleased to be angry with me yesterday—she
wouldn't listen to any reasons from me, but I
say to you, as I would say it in the presence of
God: I am not in the slightest degree to blame.
It is impossible to treat Martýn Petróvitch otherwise: he has fallen into utter childishness. It is

309

impossible for us to comply with all his caprices,
—good gracious! And we show him all due respect! Ask Evlámpiya Martýnovna here if we
don't!"

Evlámpiya did not stir; her habitual scornful
smile hovered over her lips—and her beautiful
eyes had an unfriendly gaze.

"But, Vladímir Vasílitch, why did you sell
Martýn Petróvitch's horse?" (That horse troubled me particularly by being in a peasant's possession.)

"Why did we sell his horse? But, mercy on me,
what was it good for? It merely devoured hay,
without earning it. But with the peasant, it can
still till the earth. But all Martýn Petróvitch has
to do, if he takes it into his head to go anywhere,
is to ask us. We don't refuse him an equipage.
On days when no work is going on, with the
greatest pleasure!"

"Vladímir Vasílievitch!"—said Evlámpiya,
in a low tone, as though calling him away, and
still not quitting her place. She was twisting
several stalks of plantain in her fingers, and had
cut off their heads by beating them against each
other.

"And here's another thing, about the page
Maxímka,"—went on Slétkin:—"Martýn Petróvitch complains, and wants to know why we
have taken him away from him and apprenticed
him. But, please judge for yourself: what would

he have done with Martýn Petróvitch? Spent his time in idleness; that's all. And serve properly he cannot, because of his stupidity and his youth. But now we have apprenticed him to the saddler. He'll come out a good workman—and will bring profit to himself, and will pay us quit-rent. And in our little household, that is an important point, sir! In our little household, nothing must be neglected!"

"And this is the man whom Martýn Petróvitch called a rag!"—I thought. "But who reads to Martýn Petróvitch now?"—I inquired.

"But what is there to read? There was one book,—but, luckily, it has disappeared somewhere or other. . . And what does he want of reading at his age!"

"But who shaves him?"—I asked another question.

Slétkin smiled approvingly, as though in response to an amusing jest. "Why, no one. At first, he used to singe it off with a candle, but now he lets it grow. And that's fine!"

"Vladímir Vasílievitch!"—repeated Evlámpiya, importunately. "Hey—Vladímir Vasílievitch!"

Slétkin made a sign to her with his hand.

"Martýn Petróvitch is shod, clothed, and fed, just as we are ourselves; what more does he want? He himself has declared, that he desires nothing more in the world, except to care for his soul. He

might take into consideration the fact, that—anyway—everything is ours now, not his. He says,
also, that we do not pay him his allowance; but
we don't always have money ourselves; and what
does he need it for, when he has everything provided for him? But we treat him as a relative
should be treated: I'm speaking the truth to
you. The rooms, for instance, in which he resides,—how much we need them! Without them,
we simply haven't space enough to turn round
in; but we don't mind—we endure it. We are
even thinking of how we may afford him diversion. For instance, I bought him some fish-hooks
as a present on St. Peter's day, sple-endid hooks,
real English: expensive hooks! so that he might
catch fish. There are carp in our pond. He
might sit and fish! If he were to sit there for an
hour or two, there'd be material for supper ready
to hand. It's a most dignified occupation for
old men!"

"Vladímir Vasílievitch!"—said Evlámpiya
for the third time, in a decisive tone, and flung
away the plantain-stalks which she had been
twirling in her fingers. "I'm going!" Her
eyes met mine. "I'm going away, Vladímir
Vasílievitch!" she repeated, and disappeared behind the bushes.

"I'll be there directly, Evlámpiya Martýnovna, I'll come directly!"—shouted Slétkin.
"Martýn Petróvitch himself now approves of

us,"—he continued, again addressing me. "At first, he really did take offence; and he even grumbled, until he came to understand, you know: he was, if you will please to remember, a hot-tempered, stubborn man—awfully so! Well, and now he has become perfectly quiet. Because, he has perceived that it is for his advantage. Your mamma—and oh, my God! how she did fall foul of me. . . . Of course, a lady prizes her power just as much as Martýn Petróvitch used to prize his; well now, come in and see for yourself—and seize the opportunity to say a word. I am very sensible of Natálya Niko-láevna's benefits; but we must live also, nevertheless!"

"But why was Zhitkóff dismissed?"—I asked.

"Fedúlitch, you mean? That big lubber?" Slétkin shrugged his shoulders. "Why, mercy on us, of what use could he be? He had spent all his life as a soldier, and then took it into his head to busy himself with farming. 'I can administer chastisement to the peasants,' says he. 'Because I'm accustomed to strike men in the face.' He can't do anything, sir. One must understand the proper way even to strike a man in the face. But Evlámpiya Martýnovna herself dismissed him. He's a wholly unsuitable man. Our whole prop-erty would have vanished with him around!"

"A-oo!"—rang out Evlámpiya's resonant voice.

"Immediately! immediately!" — responded Slétkin. He offered me his hand. I shook it, though unwillingly.

"Good-bye, Dmítry Semyónitch,"—said Slétkin, displaying all his white teeth. "Shoot as many woodcock as you please; they are birds of passage, they belong to no one in particular; but if you should come upon a hare,—you will be so good as to spare it; that's our property. Yes, and one thing more! do you happen to have a female pup from your bitch? We should be very glad if you would give it to us!"

"A-oo!"—rang out Evlámpiya's voice again.

"A-oo! a-oo!" — responded Slétkin, and rushed into the bushes.

XIX

I REMEMBER, that when I was left alone, I was occupied with the thought: how came it, that Kharlóff had not struck Slétkin in such a way "that only a wet blot would remain on the spot where he had been?"—and how came it, that Slétkin had not been afraid of such a fate? Evidently, Martýn Petróvitch really had become "quiet," I said to myself—and my desire to betake myself to És'kovo, and get at least a peep with one eye at that colossus, whom I could not possibly picture to myself as intimidated and submissive, grew stronger than ever. I had already reached the edge of the woods, when suddenly, from beneath my very feet, a large woodcock darted forth, with a vehement whirring of its wings, and flew headlong into the recesses of the grove. I took aim; my gun missed fire. I was very much vexed: the bird was a fine one, and I made up my mind to try and see whether I could not raise it again. I walked in the direction of its flight—and after proceeding for a couple of hundred paces, I espied on a small grass-plot, beneath a spreading birch-tree—not the woodcock,—but that same Mr. Slétkin. He was

315

lying on his back, with both hands clasped under his head,—and was staring up at the sky with a contented smile, as he dangled his left leg, which was thrown over his right knee. He did not perceive my advance. Evlámpiya was strolling about the glade, with downcast eyes, a few paces from him; she seemed to be hunting for something in the grass—mushrooms, perhaps,—now and then bending down, stretching out her hand,— and was singing in a low voice. I came to an instantaneous standstill, and began to listen. At first, I could not understand what it was that she was singing, but afterward I distinctly recognised the following familiar lines of an ancient ballad:

> " Come thou, storm-cloud, come,
> Kill, kill bátiushka-father-in-law.
> Strike thou, lightning, strike mátushka-mother-in-law,
> But I myself will slay the youthful wife."[1]

Evlámpiya sang louder and louder: she prolonged the concluding words with particular force. Slétkin continued to lie on his back and laugh, and she seemed to be constantly circling round him.

" What a girl thou art! "—he said at last. " And what queer ideas thou dost get into thy head! "

[1] Only the second and third lines rhyme in the original.—TRANSLATOR.

"What dost thou mean by that?"—asked Evlámpiya.

Slétkin raised his head a little. "What do I mean? What remarks are those that thou art making?"

"Thou knowest well enough, Volódya, that one can't omit words from a song," replied Evlámpiya, as she turned round, and caught sight of me. We both uttered an exclamation simultaneously, and both fled in opposite directions.

I hastily made my way out of the grove, and traversing a narrow glade, found myself in front of the Kharlóff garden.

XX

I HAD had no time to reflect on what I had seen,—
neither was there any reason why I should do
so. I remembered only the expression, "love-
spell," which I had been recently made acquainted
with, and whose significance had greatly amazed
me. I walked along the wattled fence of the garden, and a few moments later, from behind the
silver-poplars (they had not lost a single leaf, as
yet, and spread luxuriantly), I saw Martýn Petróvitch's yard and house. The whole garden
appeared to me to have been cleaned and spruced
up: everywhere traces of constant and strict su-
pervision were visible. Anna Martýnovna made
her appearance on the porch, and screwing up
her pale-blue eyes, she gazed long in the direction
of the grove.

"Hast thou seen thy master?"—she asked of
a peasant who was passing through the yard.

"Vladímir Vasílitch?"—replied the man,
plucking his cap from his head. "I think he
went to the grove."

"I know that he was in the grove. Has n't he
returned? Hast not thou seen him?"

"I have n't seen him . . . no."

The peasant continued to stand capless in front
of Anna Martýnovna.

318

"Well, go along,"—said she. "Or, no . . . stay . . . Where is Martýn Petróvitch? Dost thou know?"

"Why, Martýn Petróvitch,"—replied the peasant in a singsong tone, raising his right and his left hand alternately, as though pointing at something,—"is sitting yonder, by the pond, with a fishing-rod. He's catching fish, I suppose. God knows!"

"Good! . . . Go thy way,"—repeated Anna Martýnovna,—"and pick up that wheel; thou seest it is lying around."

The peasant flew to execute her command, and she stood for a few moments longer on the porch, and still kept gazing in the direction of the grove. Then she silently shook her fist, and slowly went into the house. "Aksiútka!"—rang out her imperious voice indoors.

Anna Martýnovna wore a wrathful aspect, and seemed to compress in a peculiarly firm manner her lips, which were thin enough already. She was carelessly dressed, and a lock of dishevelled hair fell on her shoulder. But notwithstanding the slatternliness of her attire, notwithstanding her ire, she seemed to me as attractive as ever, and it would have afforded me great pleasure to kiss the slender hand, that also seemed somehow malicious, with which, a couple of times, she swept back that dishevelled lock in anger.

XXI

" CAN it be possible that Martýn Petróvitch has
actually turned fisherman? " I asked myself, as
I wended my way to the pond, which lay on the
further side of the garden. I stepped upon the
dam, and glanced here and there. . . . Martýn
Petróvitch was nowhere to be seen. I strolled
along one of the shores of the pond,—and, at last,
almost at the very end of it, in a tiny bay, among
the flat, broken stalks of the rusty weeds, I espied
a vast, grayish crag. . . . . I took a closer look:
it was Kharlóff. Hatless, dishevelled, in a crash
kaftán split at the seams, with his legs tucked up
under him, he was sitting motionless on the bare
earth; so motionless did he sit, that a sandpiper,
at my approach, broke from the dried mud a
couple of paces from him, and flew away, flap-
ping its little wings and whistling, across the wa-
tery expanse. It must have been, that no one had
stirred in its vicinity for a long time, or frightened it. Kharlóff's whole figure was unusual to
such a degree, that no sooner did my dog catch
sight of him, than it stopped abruptly, planted
its legs, dropped its tail between its legs, and set
up a howl. He barely turned his head, and fixed

his wild eyes on my dog. His beard had changed him greatly, although short, but it was thick, and curled in white whorls, like Persian lambskin. In his right hand lay the end of a fishing-rod; the other end rocked feebly on the water. My heart involuntarily contracted with pain; but I plucked up my courage, went to him, and bade him good-morning. He winked slowly, as though he had just waked up.

" What are you doing here, Martýn Petró-vitch,"—I began,—" are you catching fish? "

" Yes . . . . . fish,"—he replied, in a hoarse voice, and jerked his rod upward; from its end dangled a fragment of line, about two feet in length, devoid of a hook.

" Your line is broken,"—I remarked, and then I perceived, that Martýn Petróvitch had neither bait-can nor worms beside him. . . . . And what fishing could there be in September, anyway?

" Is it broken? "—he said, and passed his hand over his face. " But it makes no difference."

Again he flung out his line.

" Are you Natálya Nikoláevna's son? "—he asked, after a couple of minutes, during which I had been scrutinising him, not without secret amazement. Although he had grown very thin, he still seemed a giant; but in what rags he was clad, and how neglected he was!

" Yes,"—I replied,—" I am the son of Na-tálya Nikoláevna B * * * "

" Is she well? "

" My mother is well. She was very much pained by your refusal," I added; " she did not in the least expect that you would not wish to go to her."

Martýn Petróvitch dropped his head. "And hast thou been there? " he asked, nodding his head to one side.

" Where? "

" Yonder, at the manor-house. Hast thou been? Go away. What hast thou to do here? Go away. There 's no use in talking to me. I don't like it."

He stopped.

" Thou wouldst like to play all the time with thy gun. When I was of thy age, I used to run that same road. Only, I had a father . . . . but I revered him, so I did!—not like the folks of the present day. My father used to thrash me with a long whip—and that settled it! I stopped playing! Therefore, I respected him . . . Phew! . . . Yes . . . . ."

Again Kharlóff ceased speaking.

" And thou must not stay here,"—he began again. " Go to the manor-house. The housekeeping is splendidly run there now. Volódka . . . ." He hesitated for a moment. " That Volódka of mine is a great hand at all sorts of things. A fine fellow! but what a beast he is, too! "

A KING LEAR OF THE STEPPES

I did not know what to say; Martýn Petróvitch spoke very calmly.

"And just look at my daughters! You remember that I had daughters, I suppose. They
are also . . . . . clever managers. But I am
getting old, brother; I have stepped aside. To
rest, thou knowest . . . . ."

"A pretty sort of rest!"—I said to myself,
casting a glance around me. "Martýn Petróvitch!"—I said aloud. "You must, positively,
come to us."

Kharlóff glanced at me. "Go away, brother;
that's my answer."

"Do not grieve my mother; do come."

"Go thy way, brother; go thy way,"—reit-
erated Kharlóff. "Why dost thou care to talk
to me?"

"If you have no equipage, mamma will send
you hers."

"Go away!"

"But really now, Martýn Petróvitch!"

Again Kharlóff hung his head—and it seemed
to me, that his cheeks, which had grown dark as
though covered with earth, flushed slightly.

"I mean it; do come,"—I went on. "Why
do you sit here? Why do you torture yourself?"

"What dost thou mean by torturing myself?"
he faltered.

"Precisely that—torturing thyself!"—I repeated.

323

Kharlóff maintained silence, and seemed to be absorbed in thought.

Encouraged by his silence, I decided to be frank, to act in a straightforward, open manner. (Do not forget, that I was only fifteen years old.)

"Martýn Petróvitch"—I began, seating my-self by his side:—"you see, I know everything, absolutely everything! I know how your son-in-law treats you—with the consent of your daughters, of course. And now you are in such a position . . . But why get low-spirited?"

Kharlóff persisted in his silence, and merely dropped his rod; and I—what a wise fellow, what a philosopher I felt myself to be!

"Of course,"—I began again,—"you acted incautiously, in surrendering everything to your daughters. That was very magnanimous on your part . . . and I shall not reproach you for it. It is far too rare a trait in our days! But if your daughters are so ungrateful—then you ought to display scorn . . . precisely that—scorn . . . but not get cast down . . . . ."

"Let me alone!"—whispered Kharlóff, sud-denly gnashing his teeth, and his eyes, which were riveted on the pond, sparkled wrathfully. . . . . "Go away!"

"But, Martýn Petróvitch . . . ."

"Go away, I tell thee . . . if thou dost not, I 'll kill thee!"

I had moved up quite close to him; but at his last words, I involuntarily sprang to my feet. " What was that you said, Martýn Petróvitch? "

" I 'll kill thee, I tell thee: begone! "—With a fierce groan and roar, his voice forced itself from Kharlóff's breast, but he did not turn his head, and went on wrathfully staring straight in front of him. " I 'll take and fling thee and all thy foolish advice into the water. That will teach thee not to bother old folks, thou green stripling! "

" He has gone mad! " flashed through my mind.

I looked at him more intently, and was completely dumfounded. Martýn Petróvitch was weeping! Tear after tear trickled from his eyelashes upon his cheeks . . . . and his face had assumed a thoroughly savage expression. . . . . .

" Begone! "—he shouted once more,—" or I 'll kill thee, by God! so that it won't become a habit with others! "

His whole body twitched to one side, as it were, and showed his teeth in a snarl, like a wild boar; I seized my gun, and set off on a run. My dog followed me, barking. It was frightened also.

On reaching home, I did not, of course, hint to my mother, by so much as a word, what I had seen; but when I met Souvenir, I—the devil knows why—told him all. That repulsive man was so delighted at my narrative, and burst into such a squealing laugh, and even leaped up and down, that I came near giving him a thrashing.

"Ekh! Would n't I have liked to see"—he kept repeating, choking with laughter,—"how that idol, the 'Vshede' Kharlus, has crawled into the mud, and sits there . . ."

"Go to him at the pond, if you are so curious."

"Yes; but what if he should kill me?"

I was very tired of Souvenir, and repented of my ill-judged loquacity. . . . Zhitkóff, to whom he communicated my story, looked at the matter in a somewhat different light.

"We shall have to appeal to the police,"—he said decisively,—"and, possibly, it will be necessary to send for a detachment of soldiers."

His presentiment as to the military detachment did not come to pass,—but something remarkable really did happen.

XXII

In the middle of October, three weeks after my meeting with Martýn Petróvitch, I was standing at the window of my chamber, in the second storey of our house, and, thinking of nothing at all, was staring dejectedly into the yard, and at the highway which ran on the other side of it. This was the fifth day that the weather had been disgusting: one could not even think of such a thing as hunting. Every living thing had taken to cover; even the sparrows had become mute, and the daws had long since disappeared. The wind was alternately howling dully and whistling in gusts: the low-hanging sky, without a chink of light, had passed over from a disagreeable white colour to a leaden and still more ominous hue,— and the rain, which had been pouring, pouring down pitilessly and incessantly, suddenly became heavier, more slanting,—and dashed against the window-panes with a shriek. The trees were all storm-tossed, and had turned a sort of grey: it seemed as though everything had been stripped from them,—and then, all of a sudden, the wind would begin to harry them again. Everywhere stood puddles choked with dead leaves; large bubbles, constantly breaking and forming again,

327

skipped and glided across them. The mire in
the road was too deep to wade through; the cold
penetrated my chamber, beneath my clothing,
into my very bones; an involuntary shiver coursed
over my body—and into what an evil plight did
my soul fall! Precisely that—evil, not melancholy. It seemed as though there would never
be any more sun, or brightness, or beauty in the
world; only that mire and slime, and grey moisture, and acrid wetness—and the wind would
shriek and howl forever! So, then, I was standing, in a thoughtful sort of way, at the window
—and I remember: a sudden darkness descended,
a blue gloom,—although by the clock it was only
twelve. All at once, it seemed to me that a bear
was dashing across our yard,—from the gate to
the porch! Not on all fours, it is true, but such
as they are depicted when they rear up on their
hind paws. I did not believe my eyes. And even
if I had not beheld a bear, at any rate it was something huge, black, shaggy. . . . Before I had
time to consider what it might be, a wild shriek
suddenly rang out down-stairs. It seemed as
though something unexpected, something dreadful had forced itself into our house. A bustle
arose, a running to and fro. . . . . .

I briskly descended the stairs, and ran into the
dining-room. . . .

In the door of the drawing-room, with her
face toward me, stood my mother, as though

rooted to the spot; behind her several frightened
women's faces were visible; the butler, two foot-
men, and a page, with mouths wide open from
amazement, had crammed themselves into the
door leading into the anteroom; and in the middle of the dining-room, covered with mud, dishevelled, tattered, wet,—so wet that steam rose
around him, and the water ran in streams across
the floor,—knelt, swaying heavily to and fro, and
apparently swooning, that same monster who
had dashed across the yard in my sight! But who
was that monster? Kharlóff! I approached from
one side, and beheld—not his face,—but his head,
which he had clasped in his hands, all plastered
with mud as it was. He was breathing heavily,
convulsively: there was even a gurgling in his
chest—and the only point which could be clearly
discerned in all that dark, bespattered mass was
the tiny, wildly roving whites of his eyes. He
was frightful! I called to mind the dignitary
whom he had once taken up short for comparing
him to a mastodon. As a matter of fact, precisely such must have been the aspect of an antediluvian animal which had just escaped from
another and more powerful wild beast that had
attacked him in the midst of the everlasting and
primeval marshes.

"Martýn Petróvitch!"—exclaimed my mother
at last, and wrung her hands. "Is it thou! Oh,
merciful Lord God!"

A KING LEAR OF THE STEPPES

" 'T is I . . . . I . . ." a broken voice made
itself heard, apparently expelling every sound
with an effort and pain. " Okh! 'T is I!"

" But what ails thee, good Lord!"

" Natálya Nikoláv . . . . . na . . . . I have
fled to you . . . . straight from home, on
foo . . . ot."

" In this mud! But thou hast not the sem-
blance of a man. Rise, sit down at least . . . . .
And you,"—she said, addressing the maids,—
" run for towels, as quickly as you can. And
is n't there some dry clothing? "—she asked the
butler.

The butler signalled with his hands, as much
as to say,—where is anything to be found of that
size?—" However, I can bring a coverlet,"—he
said:—" or there is a new horse-cloth."

" Come, get up, get up, Martýn Petróvitch;
sit down,"—repeated my mother.

" They have driven me out, madam,"—moaned
Kharlóff, suddenly—and he threw back his head,
and thrust his hands out in front of him.
" They have turned me out, Natálya Nikoláevna! My own daughters, from my own
home . . . ."

My mother cried out:

" What sayest thou? They have turned thee
out! What a sin! what a sin!"—(She crossed
herself)—" Only rise, Martýn Petróvitch, for
pity's sake."

A KING LEAR OF THE STEPPES

Two maids entered with towels, and stood in front of Kharlóff. It was evident that they could not even imagine where they were to begin on such a mass of mud. " They have turned me out, madam; they have turned me out! "—Kharlóff kept repeating the while. The butler returned with a large woollen coverlet, and also halted in perplexity. Souvenir's head was thrust through the door, then vanished.

" Martýn Petróvitch, rise! rise! sit down! and tell me all about it, in its proper order,"—commanded my mother, in a tone of decision.

Kharlóff half rose to his feet. . . . The butler attempted to aid him, but merely soiled his hands, and shaking his fingers, he retreated to the door. Waddling and reeling, Kharlóff made his way to a chair, and sat down. The maids again approached him with the towels, but he waved them aside with a gesture, and refused the coverlet also. And my mother also ceased to insist: evidently, to dry Kharlóff was an impossibility; only his tracks on the floor were hastily wiped up. . . . .

331

XXIII

" How did they come to turn thee out? "—my
mother asked Kharlóff, as soon as he had somewhat recovered his breath.

" Madam! Natálya Nikoláevna! "—he began,
in a constrained voice,—and again I was struck
by the uneasy roving of his eyes,—" I will tell
you the truth: I myself am to blame most of all."

" Precisely so; thou wouldst not listen to
me,"—said my mother, sinking into an arm-chair,
and lightly waving in front of her nose her perfumed handkerchief: the stench from Kharlóff
was excessive . . . . the odour is not so strong in
a forest swamp.

" Okh, not therein lay my error, madam, but
in pride. Pride has ruined me, just as it did
King Nebuchadnezzar. I thought: the Lord
God has not been unkind to me in the matter of
brains; if I have made up my mind about a thing,
that means that it must be right. . . . But in
that case the terror of death seized upon me. . . .
I went astray completely! Says I to myself, I 'll
show my power and my will for the last time!
I 'll reward them—and they must feel sensible of
it to the grave. . . . ." (Suddenly Kharlóff

quivered all over. . . .)   "They've driven me
out of the house, like a cur! That's their gratitude for you!"

"But how did it come about,"—my mother
was beginning again . . . . .

"They took my page Maxím away from me,"
—Kharlóff interrupted her (his eyes continued
to rove, he held both hands under his chin, with
locked fingers)—" they took away my equipage,
they cut off my monthly allowance, they did not
pay me the stipulated stipend,—they docked me
all round,—still I held my peace, still I bore it
patiently! And the reason I bore it patiently
. . . . okh! . . . was again that pride of mine!
So that my enemies might not be able to say:
See, now, the old fool repents! And you, also,
madam, forewarned me: 'Don't bite your own
nose off,' you said,—so I bore it patiently. . . .
Only, to-day I go to my room—and it is already
occupied—and they had flung my bed out into the
store-room! 'Thou mayest sleep there,' said
they: 'we endure thee out of charity, anyway: we
need thy rooms for the housekeeping,' they said.
And who is it that says that to me! Volódka Slétkin, that scoundrel, that dir . . . . . ."

Kharlóff's voice broke.

"But thy daughters? What about them?"—
asked my mother.

"But I continued to be patient,"—Kharlóff
pursued his narrative:—" it was bitter, bitter to

me, so it was, and mortifying to me. . . . I did not feel like looking at God's world! That is why I would not come to you, mátushka—because of that same mortification, of shame! For you see, my mátushka, I tried everything: wheedling and threatening; and I exhorted them, and what not all besides! I bowed down before them . . . . so " (Kharlóff showed how he had bowed.) "And all in vain! And still I bore it patiently! At the start, in the early days of it, I did not have such thoughts. I said to myself, I 'll give them a sound thrashing, I 'll pitch them all out, so that not a seed of them shall remain. . . . I 'll teach them! Well, but, later on, I—I submitted! This cross has been sent to me, I thought; it signifies that I must prepare myself for death. And all of a sudden, to-day, I 'm treated like a dog! And who did it? Volódka! And as you were good enough to inquire about my daughters,—why, have they any will of their own? They are Volódka's slaves! Yes!"

My mother was amazed. "I can understand that as regards Anna; she is his wife. But why does thy second . . . ."

"Evlámpiya, you mean? She 's worse than Anna! She has surrendered herself utterly into Volódka's hands. And that 's the reason, too, why she refused your soldier. At his, Volódka's command. Anna—evidently—ought to feel injured, and, in fact, she cannot bear her sister—but

she submits! He has bewitched her, the accursed
fellow! And then, you see, it must be pleasant
for her, for Anna, to think, ' Here art thou, Evlámpiya, who wert always such a proud creature,
and now just see what thou hast come to!' . . . .
O . . . . okh, okh! My God, my God!"

My mother cast a perturbed glance at me. I
withdrew a little to one side, by way of precaution, lest I should be sent out of the room.

" I am very sorry, Martýn Petróvitch,"—she
began;—" that my former nursling should have
caused you pain, and should have turned out to
be so bad a man; but I was deceived in him, you
see. . . . Who could have expected that from
him!"

" Madam,"—groaned Kharlóff, and smote his
breast,—" I cannot endure the ingratitude of my
daughters. I cannot, madam! You see, I gave
up everything to them, everything! And moreover, my conscience has tormented me. Many
things . . . okh! . . . many things have I pon-
ered, as I sat by the pond, and fished! ' If thou
hadst but done any good to any one in thy life!'
I meditated:—' given to the poor, set the serfs at
liberty, perhaps, because they had been eternally
preyed upon! Surely, thou art responsible for
them in the sight of God! Then their tears would
be poured out for thee! But what is their lot
now: the pit was deep under my rule—why
should I conceal my sin—but now its bottom

cannot be seen!' All these sins have I taken upon my soul, I have sacrificed my conscience for my children, and by way of reward they scorn me! They have kicked me out of the house, like a dog!"

"Stop thinking about it, Martýn Petróvitch," remarked my mother.

"And when he said to me, that Volódka of yours,"—resumed Kharlóff, with fresh vigour, —"when he said to me, that I could no longer dwell in my chamber,—and I had set every beam of that chamber in place with my own hands,— when he told me that,—God knows what came over me then! My head got confused, a knife seemed to cut my heart. . . . Well! It was a choice between cutting his throat and rushing out of the house! . . . . . And so I fled to you, my benefactress, Natálya Nikoláevna . . . . And where was I to lay my head? And it was raining, and muddy . . . . I think I must have fallen down a score of times! And now . . . . in this horrible condition . . . . ."

Kharlóff surveyed himself with a glance, and fidgeted about on his chair, as though he were preparing to rise.

"Enough, enough, Martýn Petróvitch," said my mother, hastily, "where is the harm in that? Thou hast soiled the floor? That is of no consequence whatever! But this is the proposition which I have to make to thee. Listen! Thou shalt

now be conducted to a private room, thou shalt
have a clean bed—thou art to undress and wash
thyself, then lie down and sleep. . . . ."

" Mátushka, Natálya Nikoláevna! I can't
sleep! "—said Kharlóff, mournfully. " It seems
as though hammers were beating in my brain!
For, like a useless weed, I . . . ."

" Lie down, sleep,"—repeated my mother, insistently. " And then we will give thee tea—well,
and we will discuss matters with thee. Be not
cast down, my old friend! If thou hast been
turned out of thy house, thou wilt always find a
refuge in *mine*. . . . For, seest thou, I have not
forgotten that thou savedst my life."

" My benefactress! " moaned Kharlóff, and
covered his face with his hands. " Do *you* save
me now! "

This appeal moved my mother almost to tears.
" I am ready and glad to aid thee, Martýn Petróvitch, in every way that is within my power; but
thou must promise me, that thou wilt obey me
in future, and banish from thy mind all unkind
thoughts."

Kharlóff removed his hands from his face.
" If necessary," he said, " I can even forgive! "

My mother nodded approvingly. " I am delighted to see that thou art in such a truly Chris-
tian frame of mind, Martýn Petróvitch; but we
will talk of that hereafter. In the meanwhile,
put thyself in order,—and, chief of all, sleep.

Conduct Martýn Petróvitch to the green study of thy deceased master,"—said my mother, addressing the butler,—" and whatever he asks for, give it to him on the instant! Give orders that his clothing shall be dried and cleaned—and ask the housekeeper for whatever linen is required—dost hear? "

" I obey,"—replied the butler.

" And when he wakes up, order the tailor to take his measure; and his beard must be shaved. Not immediately, but later on."

" I obey,"—repeated the butler. " Martýn Petróvitch,—be so good . . ." Kharlóff rose, looked at my mother, started to approach her, but halted, made her a bow to the girdle, crossed himself thrice before the holy image,[1] and followed the butler. I slipped out of the room in his wake.

[1] It is customary to have an ikóna, or holy image (picture), in dining-rooms and bedrooms. — TRANSLATOR.

XXIV

THE butler conducted Kharlóff to the green study, and immediately ran for the housekeeper, as there turned out to be no linen on the bed. Souvenir, who met us in the anteroom, and skipped into the study with us, instantly began, with writhing and laughter, to hover around Kharlóff, who had halted in a brown study, in the middle of the room, with his arms and legs somewhat extended. The water still continued to trickle from him.

"The Vshede! The Vshede Kharlus!"—squeaked Souvenir, bending double, and holding on to his sides. "Great founder of the famous race of the Kharlóffs, look upon thy descendant. Isn't he a sight? Canst recognise him? Ha, ha, ha! Your illustrious highness, allow me to kiss your hand! why do you wear black gloves?"

I tried to stop Souvenir, but it was of no use.

"He called me a parasite, a sluggard! 'Thou hast no roof of thine own,' says he. But now, I rather think, he has become just such another parasite as sinful I! Martýn Petróvitch is just as much of a homeless tramp now as Souvenir!

339

He, also, will be supported by gifts! They will take the crust of discarded bread, which the dog sniffed at and then went his way . . . . as much as to say—come now, eat it! Ha-ha-ha!"

Kharlóff still stood motionless, with drooping head, and arms and legs outstretched.

"Martýn Kharlóff, hereditary noble!" pursued Souvenir, shrilly. "What importance he has assumed, oh my, phew! 'Don't come near me,' says he; 'I'll do you an injury!' And when he, out of his great wisdom, began to give away and portion out his property—how he did crow! 'Gratitude!' he yells, 'gratitude!' But why did he insult me? Why did n't he give me something? Possibly, I might have shown more feeling! And the best of it is, that I told the truth, that they would turn him out, naked. . . . ."

"Souvenir!" I shouted; but Souvenir did not stop. Still Kharlóff did not move: it seemed as though he had only just begun to realise how wet everything on him was, and was waiting to have everything taken off him. But the butler did not return.

"And a warrior, to boot!"—began Souvenir again. "In the year '12 he saved his fatherland! he displayed his bravery! That's precisely the point: to strip the measly marauders of their breeches—that's quite in our line; but when a hussy stamps her foot at us, our own soul drops into our breeches. . . . . ."

"Souvenir!"—I cried a second time.

Kharlóff shot a sidelong glance at Souvenir; up to that moment, he had not even noticed his presence, to all appearances, and only my exclamation had aroused his attention.

"Look out, brother!"—he bellowed sullenly, —"don't go skipping into a catastrophe!"

Souvenir fairly rolled with laughter. "Okh, how you frightened me, most respected brother! how terrible you are, really now! You had better comb your hair; otherwise,—which God forbid,—it will dry, and it can't be washed out afterward; it will have to be mowed with a scythe." All at once, Souvenir waxed angry. "You're looking consequential again! A naked beggar, yet he puts on big airs! Where's your roof now? You'd better tell me; you were always bragging of it. 'I've got a roof,' says he; but now thou art roofless! 'My roof is hereditary,' says he." (This expression had struck Souvenir's fancy.)

"Mr. Bytchkóff," said I. "What are you doing! Come to your senses!"

But he continued to rattle on, and kept skipping and darting about close round Kharlóff. . . . . And still the butler and the housekeeper did not come! I became alarmed. I began to observe that Kharlóff, who, in the course of the conversation with my mother, had gradually calmed down, and even, toward the end, had, apparently, become reconciled to his fate, had again begun to grow excited; he was breathing more rapidly, he seemed suddenly to swell up under the ears, his fingers began to twitch, again his eyes began to roll about in the midst of the dark mask of his mud-begrimed face. . . . .

" Souvenir! Souvenir! " I cried. " Stop! I shall tell mamma."

But Souvenir seemed possessed of a devil.

" Yes, yes, my most respected! "—he snarled again,—" just see in what subtle circumstances you and I now find ourselves! And your daughters, with your son-in-law, Vladímir Vasílievitch, are laughing their fill at you under your *roof!* And you might, at least, have cursed them, according to your promise! But you were n't equal even to that much! And you 're no match for Vladímir Vasílievitch, anyway! And you have called him Volódka, into the bargain! How is he Volódka [1] to you? He is Vladímir Vasílievitch, Mr. Slétkin, landed proprietor, a gentleman,— and as for thee—what art thou? "

A fierce roar drowned Souvenir's speech. . . Kharlóff had exploded. His fists clenched themselves and rose aloft, his face turned blue, foam made its appearance on his chapped lips, he quivered with rage. " Roof, sayest thou! " he thundered with his iron voice,—" a curse! sayest

---

[1] Meaning, "dirty, miserable little Vladímir." The diminutive in *ka* almost always expresses contempt: hence the two forms used in this story at different points—*Volodya* and *Volodka.*—TRANSLATOR.

thou. . . . . No! I will not curse them. . . . .
Much they care for that! But the roof . . . .
I 'll destroy their roof, and they shall have no
roof, any more than I have! They shall learn
to know Martýn Kharlóff! My strength has not
vanished yet! I 'll teach them to jeer at me! . . .
They shall have no roof! "

I was dumfounded; never in my life had I
been witness to such boundless wrath. It was
not a human being—but a fierce wild beast which
was ramping about in front of me! I was
stunned . . . . but Souvenir,—crawled under
the table in affright.

" They shall have none! "—shouted Kharlóff
for the last time, and almost upsetting the housekeeper and butler, who entered at that moment,
he rushed out of the house. . . . . He dashed
headlong through the yard, and disappeared beyond the gate.

XXV

My mother was frightfully angry when the butler came, with troubled countenance, to announce Martýn Petróvitch's new and sudden departure. He dared not conceal from her the cause of that departure: I was compelled to confirm his statements. " So it is all thy fault! " —shrieked my mother at Souvenir, who started to run forward like a hare, and even kissed her hand:—" thine abominable tongue is to blame for it all! "—" Good gracious! I 'll immejutly, immejutly . . . ." lisped Souvenir, stammering and jerking his elbows behind his back. . . . . .

" ' Immejutly . . . . . immejutly . . . .'—I know all about thy ' immejutly ' ! " repeated my mother, reproachfully, and sent him out of the room. Then she rang the bell, commanded that Kvitzínsky should be summoned, and gave him her orders: to set out without delay for És'kovo in her equipage, hunt up Martýn Petróvitch, at any cost, and bring him back. " Don't present yourself before me without him! "—she said in conclusion. The grim-visaged Pole bowed silently, and withdrew.

I returned to my own room, seated myself by

the window again, and meditated long on what had taken place before my eyes. I was bewildered; I could not possibly understand why Kharlóff, who had endured, almost without remonstrance, the insult dealt him by the members of his household, had not been able to control himself, and had failed to endure the jeers and taunts of such an insignificant creature as Souvenir. I did not then know what intolerable bitterness may be contained, sometimes, in an empty reproach, even when it proceeds from contemptible lips. . . . . . . The hated name of Slétkin, uttered by Souvenir, had fallen like a spark in powder; the sore spot had not been able to bear this last sting.

About an hour elapsed. Our calash drove into the yard; but in it sat our steward alone. Yet my mother had said to him: " Do not present yourself without *him!* " Kvitzínsky sprang hastily from the carriage, and ran up the steps. His face wore a perturbed aspect,—a thing which hardly ever happened with him. I immediately went down-stairs, and followed on his heels into the drawing-room.

" Well? have you brought him? "—asked my mother.

" No,"—replied Kvitzínsky,—" and I could not bring him."

" Why so? did you see him? "

" Yes."

"What has happened to him? A stroke of apoplexy?"

"Not at all; nothing has happened to him."

"Then why have not you brought him?"

"He is destroying his house."

"What?"

"He is standing on the roof of the new wing —and destroying it. Forty or more of the planks, I should say, have already flown off." ("They shall have no roof!" Kharlóff's words recurred to my mind.)

My mother stared at Kvitzínsky. "He is standing . . . . alone . . . on the roof, and tearing it to pieces?"

"Precisely so, madam. He is walking along the planking on the roof-tree, and breaking down on the right and the left. His strength is supernatural, as you know! Well, and the roof, to tell the truth, is a miserable one: it is laid with gaps,[1] it is nailed on with the thinnest sort of upper boards, two-and-a-quarter-inch nails."

My mother glanced at me, as though to assure herself whether she had not, in some way, heard wrongly. "Thin boards with spaces,"—she repeated, evidently not understanding the meaning of a single one of these words. . . . .

---

[1] That is, when between every pair of planks an open space is left, covered over on top with another plank: such a roof is cheaper, but less durable. The thinnest upper boards are half a vershók in thickness, the ordinary board being three-quarters of a vershók. (The vershók is one and three-quarter inches.)—AUTHOR'S NOTE.

"Well, and what do you want?"—she said at last.

"I am come for instructions. Without men to help, nothing can be done. The peasants there have all hidden themselves with fright."

"And his daughters—what of them?"

"His daughters are all right. They are rushing about at random .... shrieking ... But what good does that do?"

"And is Slétkin there?"

"Yes, he's there also. He's yelling the worst of all—but he can do nothing."

"And Martýn Petróvitch is standing on the roof?"

"Yes—on the roof ... that is to say, in the garret, and is destroying the roof."

"Yes, yes,"—said my mother,—"the thin boards. ..."

Evidently, an unusual case had presented itself.

What was to be done? Send to town for the chief of the rural police—assemble the peasants? My mother was utterly at a loss.

Zhitkóff, who had come to dinner, was equally at a loss. Truth to tell, he again made mention of his military command, but he offered no advice, and only wore a submissive and devoted air. Kvitzínsky, perceiving that he would get no instructions, announced to my mother, with the scornful respect peculiar to him, that if she would permit him to take several of the stable-men, gardeners, and other house-serfs, he would make an effort . . . . .

"Yes, yes,"—my mother interrupted him,— "do make an effort, my dear Vikénty Osípitch! Only, be quick about it, pray, and I will assume all the responsibility!"

Kvitzínsky smiled frigidly. "Allow me to explain one thing to you in advance, madam: it is impossible to answer for the results, for Mr. Kharlóff's strength is great, and so is his despair: he considers himself greatly wronged!"

"Yes, yes,"—assented my mother:—"and that abominable Souvenir is to blame for all! I shall never forgive him for this. Go, take men with you, proceed, Vikénty Osipitch!"

"Take as many ropes as possible, Mr. Man-ager,—and fire-hooks,"—said Zhitkóff in his bass voice,—"and if you have a net,—it would n't be a bad thing to take that also. Now once upon a time, in our regiment . . . . ."

"Be so good as not to instruct me, my dear sir,"—interrupted Kvitzínsky, with vexation: "I know what is required, without any sugges-tions from you."

Zhitkóff took offence, and remarked that as he assumed that he also was bidden . . .

"No, no,"—interposed my mother. "Thou hadst better stay here. . . Vikénty Osípitch will act alone. . . . Go, Vikénty Osípitch!"

A KING LEAR OF THE STEPPES

Zhitkóff was more angry than before, but Kvitzínsky bowed and left the room.

I flew to the stable, hastily saddled my horse with my own hands, and set off at a gallop on the road to És'kovo.

XXVI

THE rain had ceased; but the wind was blowing with redoubled violence—straight in my face. Half way on my road, my saddle came near turning with me: the girth had loosened: I alighted, and set to dragging at the strap with my teeth. . . . . All at once, I heard some one calling me by name. . . Souvenir was running toward me over the grass. . "Well, little father,"—he shouted at me, while still afar off,— "has curiosity conquered you? Well, you couldn't help yourself. . . And I'm going thither also, straight, on Kharlóff's tracks. . . . . Why, you'll never see such a sight again in all your life!"

"You want to admire the work of your hands,"—I said indignantly, sprang on my horse, and set off again at a gallop; but the indefatigable Souvenir did not leave me, and even shouted with laughter and writhed as he ran. And here, at last, was És'kovo, here was the dam,—and yonder were the long wattled fence and the willows of the manor. . . I rode up to the gate, alighted, and tied my horse; and stood stock-still in amazement.

A KING LEAR OF THE STEPPES

Of the front third of the roof, on the new wing of the mezzanine, only the skeleton remained, the shingles and sheathing-boards lay in formless heaps upon the ground, on both sides of the wing. Admitting that the roof had been, according to Kvitzínsky's expression, a paltry one; nevertheless, the thing was incredible. On the planking of the loft, stirring up dust and rubbish, a blackish-grey mass was moving about with clumsy agility, and now shaking loose the remaining chimney, built of bricks (the other had already fallen), now ripping off a board, and hurling it down, now clutching at the very rafters themselves. It was Kharlóff. He seemed to me then a perfect bear: his head, and his back, and his shoulders were those of a bear, and he planted his legs wide apart, without bending the bottom of his feet, just as a bear does. The keen wind was blowing a gale around him on every side, lifting his matted hair; it was terrible to see, his naked body gleaming red through the rents in his tattered raiment: it was terrible to hear his fierce, hoarse muttering. The yard was filled with people: peasant women, dirty little boys, housemaids were ranged along the fence; a few peasant men had clustered together in a separate group at a distance. The old priest, whom I knew, was standing hatless on the steps of the other wing, and clasping a brass cross in both hands, silently and hopelessly raised it

351

aloft, from time to time, and seemed to be showing it to Kharlóff. By the priest's side stood Evlámpiya, and with her back propped against the
wall, she gazed immovably at her father; Anna
now thrust her head out of the little window,
again she vanished, now she ran out into the
yard, again she went back into the house; Slétkin, all pale, sallow, in an old dressing-gown and
a skull-cap, with a single-barrelled gun in his
hands, was running back and forth, with short
steps. He had become a thorough-going Jew,
as the expression is: he panted, and threatened,
shook himself, took aim at Kharlóff, then flung
his gun on his shoulder, again took aim, shouted,
wept. . . . On catching sight of me and Souvenir, he fairly hurled himself at us.

"Look, look, what is going on yonder!"—he
squeaked,—"look! He has gone crazy, he has
got into a fury . . . . and see what he is doing!
I have sent for the police,—but no one comes!
No one comes! If I were to shoot him, the law
could not call me to account, because every man
has a right to defend his property! And I will
shoot! . . . By God, I 'll shoot!"

He ran toward the house.

"Martýn Petróvitch, beware! If you don't
come down, I 'll shoot!"

"Shoot away!"—rang out a hoarse voice from
the roof. "Shoot away! And meanwhile, here 's
a gift for thee!"

A KING LEAR OF THE STEPPES

A long board flew down from above—and turning a couple of times in the air, crashed to the ground directly at Slétkin's feet. The latter fairly leaped into the air, and Kharlóff burst into a loud laugh.

"Oh, Lord Jesus!"—faltered some one behind my back.

I glanced round: it was Souvenir. "Ah!" I thought; "he has stopped laughing now!"

Slétkin seized by the collar a peasant who stood near.

"Come, climb up, climb up, climb up, you devils!" he yelled, shaking him with all his might —"save my property!"

The peasant took a couple of steps, flung back his head, waved his hands, shouted: "Hey! you! sir!"—stamped up and down a bit where he stood, and round about face.

"A ladder! fetch a ladder!"—Slétkin shouted at the remaining peasants.

"And where are we to get it?"—resounded in reply.

"And even if there were a ladder,"—remarked one voice, in a leisurely way,—"who wants to climb up there? You must think we are fools! He'd wring thy neck—in the twinkling of an eye!"

"He'd kill him d'rectly"—said one young, fair-haired fellow with a very evil face.

"And why shouldn't he?"—chimed in the

353

rest. It seemed to me, that even had there been
no self-evident danger, still the peasants would
not willingly have obeyed the orders of their new
master. They all but encouraged Kharlóff—
although he had surprised them.

"Akh, you bandits!" groaned Slétkin, "I'll
give it to you all. . . ."

But at this point the last chimney came down
with a crash, and in the midst of clouds of yellow
dust which arose for a moment, Kharlóff, emit-
ting a piercing yell, and raising his blood-stained
hands aloft, turned his face toward us. Again
Slétkin took aim at him.

Evlámpiya pulled him back by the elbow.

"Don't meddle!" he vented his wrath fiercely
on her.

"And as for thee—don't dare!"—said she;
—and her blue eyes flashed menacingly from
beneath her knitted brows. "My father is destroying his own house. It's his property."

"Thou liest: it is ours!"

"Thou sayest: 'it is ours:'—but I say 't is
his."

Slétkin hissed with rage; Evlámpiya fairly
bored her eyes into his face.

"Ah, how d' ye do! how d' ye do! my amiable
daughter!"—thundered Kharlóff from on high.
"Good-morning, Evlámpiya Martýnovna! How
dost thou get along with thy friend?—Do you
kiss and fondle each other nicely?"

" Father!"—rang out Evlámpiya's resonant
voice.

" What, dear daughter?"—replied Kharlóff,
and moved forward to the very brink of the wall.
So far as could be seen, a strange grin had made
its appearance on his face—a bright, cheery,
and, precisely for that reason, peculiarly dreadful grin. . . . . Many years afterward, I saw
exactly that same sort of grin on the face of a
man condemned to death.

" Stop, father; come down!" (Evlámpiya did
not call him " bátiushka "—dear little father.)
" We are guilty; we will give thee back everything. Come down."

" And why art thou making arrangements
for us?"—put in Slétkin. Evlámpiya merely
contracted her brows still more.

" I will restore to thee my portion—I will give
thee everything. Stop; come down, father!
Forgive us; forgive me! "

Still Kharlóff went on grinning. " Too late,
my dear little dove,"—said he, and every word
of his had the ring of brass. " Thy stony soul
has stirred too late! The ball has started to roll
down hill—thou canst not stop it now! And thou
needst not look at me! I 'm a doomed man!
Look rather at thy Volódka: see what a beauty
thou hast sought out for thyself! And look at
thy viper of a sister: yonder she is sticking her
foxy nose out of the window, yonder she is egg-

ing her nice little husband on! No, my dear young madams! You have wanted to deprive me of a roof—therefore I will not leave you one beam upon another! With my own hands I placed them, with my own hands I will destroy —just as I am, with my hands alone! See, I have not taken an axe! "

He spat on both his palms, and again grasped the rafters.

"Enough, father,"—Evlámpiya was saying in the meanwhile, and her voice, somehow, grew wonderfully caressing,—" forget the past. Come, believe me; thou hast always trusted me. Do come down; come to my chamber, to my soft bed. I will dry thee, and warm thee; I will bind up thy wounds, for thou hast flayed thy hands. Thou shalt live with me as though thou wert in Christ's bosom, eat sweetly, and sleep still more sweetly. Come, we have been to blame, well, and we have grown arrogant, we have sinned; come, forgive! "

Kharlóff shook his head. "Jabber away! As though I would believe you! You have killed belief within me! You have killed everything! I was an eagle—and made myself a worm for you . . . . . and you—mean to crush the worm? Enough of that! I loved thee, thou knowest it,— but now thou art not my daughter—and I am not thy father . . . I'm a doomed man! Don't interfere! And as for thee, fire away, thou coward, woe-hero!" bellowed Kharlóff suddenly at Slétkin. "Why dost thou keep taking aim? Hast thou called to mind the law: if he that has received a gift shall be guilty of an attempt on the life of the giver,"—said Kharlóff, pausing between the words,—"then the giver has a right to demand the return of everything? Ha, ha,— have no fear, thou man versed in law! I shall not demand it—I shall finish it all myself. . . Here goes!"

"Father!" implored Evlámpiya, for the last time.

"Hold thy tongue!"

"Martýn Petróvitch, brother, be magnanimous, forgive!"—faltered Souvenir.

"Father, darling!"

"Silence, bitch!"—yelled Kharlóff. He did not even look at Souvenir—but merely spat in his direction.

XXVII

At that moment, Kvitzínsky with his whole squad—in three peasant carts—made his appearance at the gate. The weary horses snorted, the men, one after another, sprang out into the mud.

"Ehe!" shouted Kharlóff, at the top of his voice. "An army, there it is, an army! They are setting in array a whole army against me. Very good! Only, I give you warning, that if any one comes hither to me on the roof—I'll pitch him down head over heels! I'm a surly host, I don't like untimely guests! So there, now!"

He clutched the front pair of rafters in both hands, the so-called "legs" of the pediment,— and began to rock them to and fro violently. Hanging from the edge of the planking, he drew them after him, as it were, chanting in measured rhythm, stevedore fashion: "Heave-ho! heave-ho! ukh!"

Slétkin ran to Kvitzínsky, and began to complain and to whimper. . . . The latter requested him "not to meddle," and proceeded to put in execution the plan which he had formed. He himself took up his stand in front of the house, and began by way of creating a diversion, to explain to Kharlóff that what he was about was not a deed worthy of a nobleman. . . . .

" Heave-ho! heave-ho! "—chanted Kharlóff.

. . . . That Natálya Nikoláevna was very much displeased with him, and had not expected this of him. . . . .

" Heave-ho! heave-ho! ukh! "—chanted Kharlóff;—and, in the meantime, Kvitzínsky had detailed four of the most robust and daring of the stablemen to the opposite side of the house, with the object of having them mount to the roof from behind. But the plan of attack did not escape Kharlóff's notice; he suddenly abandoned the rafters, and ran nimbly to the rear part of the mezzanine. His aspect was so terrifying, that two stablemen, who had already succeeded in ascending to the garret, instantly slid back to the ground by the water-spout, to the no small satisfaction and even laughter of the little boys of the house-servants. Kharlóff shook his fist after them, and returning to the front portion of the house, he again seized hold of the rafters, and again began to rock them, again chanting, in stevedore style.

Suddenly he stopped, and looked about him. . .

" Maxímushka, friend! comrade! " he cried: " do I behold thee? "

I glanced round. . . . . In fact, Maxímka, the page, had detached himself from the throng of peasants, and smirking and displaying his teeth in a grin, had stepped forward. His master, the saddler, had probably allowed him to return home for a brief visit.

" Climb up here to me, Maxímushka, my faithful servant,"—went on Kharlóff;—" we will together ward off the savage Tatár folk, the Lithuanian thieves! "

Maxímka, still grinning, instantly climbed to the roof. . But he was seized and dragged back —God knows why—perhaps by way of example for the rest; he could not have rendered much aid to Martýn Petróvitch.

" Well, very good! All right! "—articulated Kharlóff in a menacing voice, and again set to work at the rafters.

" Vikénty Osípovitch! with your permission, I will shoot! "—said Slétkin to Kvitzínsky; —" you see, my gun is loaded with bird-shot, chiefly by way of frightening him." But before Kvitzínsky could answer him, the foremost pair of rafters, vigorously shaken by the iron hands of Kharlóff, heeled over, cracked, and fell into the yard—and with them, being unable to hold himself back, fell Kharlóff himself, and crashed heavily on the ground. All shuddered, cried out. . . Kharlóff lay motionless, and against his back rested lengthwise the upper beam of the roof, the roof-tree, which had followed the falling pediment.

XXVIII

THE people rushed to Kharlóff, dragged the
beam away from him, turned him over on his
back; his face was lifeless, there was blood about
his mouth; he was not breathing. " The spirit
is knocked out of him,"—muttered the peasants
who had stepped forward. They ran to the well
for water, they brought a whole bucketful, and
drenched Kharlóff's head: the mud and dust left
his face, but its lifeless aspect remained as before. They dragged up a bench, placed it close
against the wing, and with difficulty lifting Martýn Petróvitch's huge body, they placed it upon
the bench, with his head leaning against the wall.
The page Maxímka approached, knelt down on
one knee, and thrusting the other leg far out,
supported the arm of his former master in a the-
atrical sort of way. Evlámpiya, pale as death
itself, stood directly in front of her father, with
her huge eyes riveted immovably on him. Anna
and Slétkin did not come near. All maintained
silence, all waited for something or other. At
last, broken, throbbing sounds became audible in
Kharlóff's throat—as though he were choking.
. . . Then he feebly moved one hand—the
right one (Maxímka was holding the left),
opened one eye,—the right,—and slowly gazing

around him, as though drunk with some terrible
sort of intoxication, he groaned,—articulated, in-
distinctly:—" I am in . . . . jured . . . . ."
And then he added, as though after a brief reflection:—" this is it . . . . the bla . . . ack
co . . . . olt! "

The blood suddenly welled in a thick torrent
from his mouth—his whole body quivered . . . . .

" It is the end! " I thought. . . . . But again
Kharlóff opened one eye,—it was still the right
one (the left eyelid did not move, any more than
that of a corpse),—and fixing it on Evlámpiya,
he articulated, in a barely audible tone:

" Well, daugh . . . . ter, I do not for . . . . . . "
Kvitzínsky, with a sharp gesture, called up the
priest, who was still standing on the steps of the
wing. . . . The old man drew near, entangling
his weak knees in his narrow cassock. But all
at once, Kharlóff's legs twitched in a horrible
manner, and so did his trunk; athwart his face,
from below upward, coursed a nervous convul-
sion—and Evlámpiya's face was distorted in
precisely the same manner. Maxímka began to
cross himself. . . . I was horrified, I ran to the
gate, and leaned my breast against it, without
glancing round. A minute later, a soft murmur
broke from all the mouths behind me—and I
understood that Martýn Petróvitch was dead.

The roof-tree had broken the nape of his neck,
and he had smashed in his breast himself, as was
proved at the autopsy.

XXIX

" WHAT was it that he tried to say to her, as he
was dying? " I asked myself, as I rode homeward
on my trotter; " ' I do not curse thee? ' or ' I do
not for . . . . give thee?' " [1]   The rain was
again pouring down, but I rode at a foot-pace,
I wished to remain alone as long as possible,—I
wished to give myself up to my meditations.
Souvenir set off in one of the carts, which had
arrived with Kvitzínsky.   Young and giddy as
I was at that period, yet the sudden, general
change (not in minor details alone) which is always evoked in all hearts by the unexpected or
the expected (it makes no difference!) appearance of death, its solemnity, importance and
righteousness—could not but impress me.   And
impressed I was . . . . but nevertheless, my
perturbed, childish gaze immediately took note of
many things: it noted how Slétkin flung his gun
on one side, promptly and timidly, just as though
it were a stolen article, how he and his wife both
instantaneously became the object of a silent but
universal avoidance, how a vacant space was

[1] The point here cannot be made apparent in English.   The half-
uttered word in Russian might be either: *pro . . klinyáiu* (curse) or
pro . . shtcháiu (forgive). —TRANSLATOR.

363

formed around them. . . . This avoidance was
not extended to Evlámpiya, although, in all
probability, her fault was no less grave than that
of her sister. She even aroused a certain amount
of compassion for herself, when she flung herself down in a heap at the feet of her dead father.
But that she was guilty was felt by all, notwithstanding. "You wronged the old man,"—
said one greyish-haired, big-headed peasant,
propping both hands and his beard on a long
staff, like some judge of ancient times. "The
sin is on your souls! You wronged him!" That
word, "wronged," was immediately accepted by
every one as a verdict from which there could be
no appeal. The popular judgment had been
pronounced,—I instantly comprehended that
fact. I also noticed that Slétkin did not, at first,
dare to take charge of affairs. Without any action on his part, the people lifted the body and
bore it into the house; without consulting him,
the priest wended his way to the church for the
requisite articles, while the village elder ran to
the village, to despatch a vehicle to town; even
Anna Martýnovna could not bring herself to
give orders, in her usual commanding tone, that
the samovár should be prepared,—"in order that
there may be warm water wherewith to wash the
deceased." Her order resembled an entreaty—
and she received a rude reply. . . . . .

But I was still engrossed with the question:

What had he really meant to say to his daughter? Had he meant to forgive her, or to curse her? I finally decided, that he intended to—forgive her.

Three days later, Martýn Petróvitch's funeral took place, at the cost of my mother, who was greatly grieved by his death, and gave orders that no expense was to be spared. She herself did not go to the church—because she did not wish, as she expressed it, to see those two hussies and that abominable . . . little Jew; but she sent Kvitzínsky, me, and Zhitkóff, whom, by the way, from that time forth, she never alluded to otherwise than as an old woman. She would not permit Souvenir in her sight, and for a long time afterward she was angry with him, calling him the murderer of her friend. He felt this exile profoundly: he was constantly stealing about on tiptoe in the room adjoining that in which my mother was, and gave himself up to a sort of perturbed and dastardly melancholy, shuddering and whispering: "Immejutly!"

In the church, and during the funeral procession, Slétkin seemed to me to have completely recovered his spirits. He issued orders and bustled about as of yore, and watched greedily, that not a single superfluous kopék should be squandered, although, as a matter of fact, the affair did not concern his own pocket. Maxímka, in a new short jacket, also provided by my mother, emitted in the choir such tenor notes, that no one could, of course, cherish any doubt as to the sincerity of his attachment to the deceased! Both sisters were in mourning, as was proper,—but appeared to be more abashed than afflicted,—especially Evlámpiya. Anna assumed a subdued and wan aspect, but did not force herself to shed tears, and merely kept passing her thin, handsome hand over her hair and cheeks. Evlámpiya was absorbed in thought. The general, irrevocable avoidance and condemnation which I had observed on the day of Kharlóff's death, I thought I now descried in the countenances of all who were present in the church, in all their movements, in their glances,—but still more in a staid and unsympathetic manner. It seemed as though all these people knew that the sin into which the Kharlóff family had fallen—that great sin—had now come under the jurisdiction of the one Righteous Judge, and that, consequently, there was no longer anything for them to worry about or feel indignant over. They prayed assiduously for the soul of the deceased, whom they had not particularly loved, and had even feared, during his lifetime. Death had come so very suddenly.

" He might at least have had the comfort of dying from drink," said one peasant to another, on the church porch.

"A man can get drunk without drinking,"—replied the latter. "What things do happen!"

"They wronged him,"—the first peasant repeated the decisive word.

"They wronged him,"—others said after him.

"But surely, the deceased used to oppress you himself, didn't he?"—I asked of a peasant whom I recognised as one of Kharlóff's.

"He was the master, of course,"—replied the peasant:—"nevertheless . . . . they wronged him!"

At the grave, Evlámpiya stood as though bewildered. Musing, ... painful musing, tormented her. I noticed that she treated Slétkin, who spoke to her several times, as she had treated Zhitkóff—and much worse.

A few days later, a rumour became current in our neighbourhood, that Evlámpiya Martýnovna Kharlóff had left the paternal home forever, abandoning to her sister and her brother-in-law all the property which had fallen to her, and taking with her only a few hundred rubles. . . . . "That Anna has, evidently, bought her freedom!"—remarked my mother:—"only, thou and I have unskilful hands!"—she added, addressing Zhitkóff, with whom she was playing piquet—he had superseded Souvenir with her. Zhitkóff cast a dejected glance at his hairy paws. . . . " They certainly are unskilful! " he seemed to be saying to himself. . . . .

Soon after this, my mother and I removed our residence to Moscow,—and many years elapsed before I chanced to see the two daughters of Martýn Petróvitch again.

XXX

BUT see them I did. I encountered Anna Martýnovna in the most commonplace fashion. While
visiting our country-place, where I had not been
for fifteen years, after the death of my mother,
I received an invitation from the arbitrator—(at
that time, all over Russia, the delimitation of the
alternating strips of land belonging to proprietors and peasants was proceeding with a slow-
ness which has not been forgotten to this day)
—an invitation to come for consultation with
the other owners of our country-side, to the
estate of widow Anna Slétkin. The information that my mother's " dirty little Jew," with
his little eyes like dried prunes, was no longer in
the land of the living, did not cause me the slightest grief, I admit; but I thought it would be interesting to have a look at his widow. She had
the reputation, in our parts, of being a capital
manager. And it was true: her estate and home-
farm, and even her house—(I cast an involuntary glance at the roof; it was of iron),—all
proved to be in superlative order, everything was
accurately, neatly kept, and where it was necessary, things were painted—as though they had

A KING LEAR OF THE STEPPES

belonged to a German woman. Anna Martýnovna herself had, of course, grown older; but
that peculiar gaunt and, as it were, malicious
charm, which had formerly excited me, had not
entirely left her. She was dressed in country
fashion, but elegantly. She received us—not
cordially,—that word did not suit her,—but courteously, and, on seeing me, the witness of that
dreadful episode, she did not move a muscle.
Not a syllable did she utter about my mother, nor
about her father or her sister, nor even her husband, any more than if they had never existed.[1]

She had two daughters, both very pretty, well-
built girls, with sweet little faces, and a merry,
caressing look in their black eyes; she had also
a son, who took somewhat after his father, but
he also was a very fine little boy. During the
progress of the discussion between the proprietors, Anna Martýnovna bore herself calmly, with
dignity, displaying neither special stubbornness
nor special covetousness. But no one understood
his advantages any better than she did hers, and
no one understood how to set forth more convincingly and to defend all her rights. All the
" laws which were applicable," even the minis-
terial circulars, were well known to her; she said
little, and that in a quiet voice, but every word
hit the mark. It ended by our expressing our

[1] Russian: "Exactly as though she had her mouth
full of water."—TRANSLATOR.

assent to all her demands, and making such concessions, that there was nothing left for us to do but wonder at them. On the way home, some of the well-born landed proprietors even cursed themselves roundly; all groaned and shook their heads.

" What a clever woman? "—said one.

" A crafty rogue! "—interposed a second and less delicate proprietor:—" The bed is soft in the making, but hard to sleep on! "

" Yes, and a miser, into the bargain! "—added a third:—" Would it have hurt her to give us a glass of vódka and a bit of caviár? "

" What do you expect from her? "—chimed in rashly a proprietor who had hitherto held his peace;—" who does not know that she poisoned her husband? "

To my amazement, no one considered it necessary to refute this frightful accusation, which, assuredly, had no foundation! This surprised me the more, because, despite the objurgatory expressions which I have quoted, all felt respect for Anna Martýnovna, not even excepting the indelicate proprietor. The arbitrator even waxed pathetic.

" Put her on a throne,"—he exclaimed,— " and she 'd be a regular Semiramis or Katherine II! The obedience of her peasants is exemplary. . . The way she has reared her children is exemplary! What a head! What a brain! "

A KING LEAR OF THE STEPPES

Leaving Semiramis and Katherine II out of the question,—there was no doubt that Anna Martýnovna led a very happy life. The woman herself, her family, her whole surroundings, fairly reeked with inward and outward contentment, with the agreeable tranquillity of spiritual well-being. To what degree she was deserving of that happiness . . . is another question. However, one puts such questions only in youth. Everything in the world, both good and bad, is bestowed upon a man, not in accordance with his merits, but as the result of some unknown but logical laws, which I will not even take it upon myself to indicate, although it sometimes seems to me that I dimly discern them.

XXXI

I INQUIRED of the arbitrator concerning Evlámpiya Martýnovna—and learned that as soon as
she had left her home she had vanished without a
trace—and probably had long since "flown up
on high."

That was the way our arbitrator put it . . . .
but I am convinced that I have *seen* Evlámpiya,
that I have met her. And this is how it came
about.

About four years after my meeting with Anna
Martýnovna, I settled down for the summer at
Múrino, a small village near Petersburg, well
known to summer-villa residents of moderate
means. The hunting was not bad around Múrino, at that epoch,—and I went out with my
gun nearly every day. I had a comrade, a certain Vikúloff, a member of the petty burgher
class—a good-natured and far from stupid
young fellow,—but, as he was wont to say of
himself, a man of completely "lost" conduct.

Where and what had not that man been! Nothing could astonish him, he knew everything,
—but he loved nothing except hunting—and
liquor. Well, one day he and I were return-

ing to Múrino, and we had to pass a certain
house, which stood at the intersection of two
roads, and was enclosed in a tall, close paling-
fence. It was not the first time I had seen this
house, and on every occasion it had aroused my
curiosity; there was something mysterious, fast-
locked, grimly-dumb, something which reminded
the beholder of a prison or a hospital, about it.
All that could be seen from the road was a steep
roof, painted in a dark hue. In all the fence
there was but one gate, and that appeared to be
hermetically fastened; no sound was ever audible
behind it. Nevertheless, you felt that some one
certainly dwelt in that house; it did not, in the
least, present the aspect of an abandoned dwelling. On the contrary, everything about it was
so durable, and firm, and stout, that it could have
stood a siege.

"What sort of a fortress is this?"—I asked
my companion. "Do you know?"

Vikúloff gave a sly wink. "A remarkable
edifice, is n't it? The local chief of police gets
a large income from it!"

"How so?"

"Why, because he does. You have heard, I
suppose, about the dissenters called the Scourgers—those who live without priests?"

"Yes, I have heard of them."

"Well, this is where their head-mother lives."

"A woman?"

A KING LEAR OF THE STEPPES

"Yes—the mother; the Birthgiver of God, according to them." [1]

"What do you mean?"

"Just what I'm telling you. Such a stern woman she is, they say. . . . A regular female commander-in-chief! She rules over thousands! I'd just like to take all those Birthgivers of God, and give it to them. . . . But what's the use of saying anything!"

He called up his Pegáshka, a remarkable dog, with a splendid scent, but without the slightest comprehension of pointing. Vikúloff was obliged to tie up its hind leg, to keep it from running about wildly.

His words sank into my memory. I used to go out of my way purposely, in order that I might pass the mysterious house. And lo, one day, suddenly, as I came opposite it,—wonderful to relate! the bolt thundered in the gate, the key squeaked in the lock,—then the gate itself opened gently—a powerful horse's head, with braided forelock, under a pattern-painted shaft-arch, made its appearance, and out on the road, at a leisurely pace, rolled a small waggon of the sort in which drive little ladies of the fast set and the mistresses of merchants. On the leathern cushion of the waggon, nearest to me, sat a man

---

[1] The Russian title of the Virgin is correctly translated thus, and all the peculiar Russian sects (almost without exception) have Madonnas—some even Christs. — TRANSLATOR.

of about thirty years of age, of remarkably handsome and benevolent appearance, in a neat black
long-coat, and with a black cap of military shape
pulled low down upon his brow; he was driving,
in a sedate way, the broad-backed horse, full-
fed to bursting; and by the side of the man, on
the other side of the waggon, sat a woman of
lofty stature, straight as an arrow. A costly
black shawl covered her head; she was dressed in
a short velvet sacque, olive in hue, and a dark-
blue merino petticoat; her white hands, staidly
folded on her lap, supported each other. The
waggon turned into the road to the left,—and
the woman was brought within two paces of me;
she turned her head slightly,—and I recognised
Evlámpiya Kharlóff. I recognised her instantly,
—I did not hesitate for a single moment,—
and, indeed, hesitation was impossible: such eyes
as she had,—and especially such a curve of the
lips, arrogant and sensual,—I have never beheld
in any one else. Her face had grown longer and
thinner, her skin had darkened, here and there
wrinkles were visible; but the expression of that
face in particular had undergone a change! It
is difficult to convey in words to what a degree it
had become self-confident, stern, haughty! It
was not the simple composure of authority,—but
the utter permeation of authority, which every
feature breathed forth; the careless glance which
she dropped on me expressed a long-established,

ingrained habit of encountering only adoring, unquestioning submission. This woman—evidently—lived surrounded not by admirers,—but by slaves: obviously, she had even forgotten the time when any command or even wish of hers had not been instantly fulfilled! I called her loudly by name and patronymic; she gave a barely perceptible start, cast another glance at me—not of alarm,—but of scornful indignation: as much as to say: " Who dares to disturb me? " —and barely opening her lips, she uttered an imperious word. The man who sat beside her gave a start, dealt a flourishing blow with the reins to the horse,—which moved on with a brisk, large trot,—and the waggon disappeared.

I have never met Evlámpiya since. How the daughter of Martýn Petróvitch came to be the Birthgiver of God to the Scourgers—I cannot even imagine; but who knows—perhaps she was the founder of a sect, which will be called—or is even now called, by her name,—" the Evlámpi-yevshtchina " ? All sorts of things come to pass.

And this is what I had to tell you about my " King Lear of the Steppe," his family and his doings.

The narrator ceased speaking—and we chatted a while, then went our ways.

CPSIA information can be obtained
at www.ICGtesting.com
Printed in the USA
FSOW01n1915031115

9 781434 496355